MISS LESLIE'S
Secret

MISS
LESLIE'S
Secret

A Regency Romance by

JENNIFER MOORE

Covenant Communications, Inc.

*To Carla Kelly, for being an inspiration,
mentor, and most of all, a friend.
And for teaching me that "research" can
have a variety of meanings. (wink)*

Acknowledgments

WHEN I SIT DOWN TO write the acknowledgments, without fail, my heart grows warm thinking of all the people that help me along the way as I try to turn an idea into a book.

First of all, so many thanks go to my family. It's not always easy to have a wife or a mom who hides away for hours in her office or to step in and run kids around when she leaves for weekend writing retreats. Thank you for understanding and eating cereal for dinner, and for listening to plot ideas and my attempt at a Scottish accent. Frank, James, Ben, Andrew, and Joey, you all deserve a medal.

I have two wonderful writing partners, Josi Kilpack and Nancy Allen, who are willing to answer panicked texts late at night when I feel like my plot went off the rails. Their inspiration and encouragement means more to me than I can even put into words.

A historical novel requires so much research, and I am so lucky to meet wonderful people as I look for information and sources. Karen Pierotti, thank you for reading my rough draft, for helping with this dialog and the nuances only a Scottish lass would know. I can't wait to see your books on the shelf some day. Debbie Peterson, I so enjoy reading your *Spirit of the Knight* book, and thank you for taking the time to answer questions and give me great resources. And of course, Carla Kelly, whose book *Doing No Harm* introduced me to the Highland Clearances and made me want to know more. Thank you to the Beekeepers of Scotland Facebook group for letting me join your online community and for answering my questions. You are all a lovely group of people, and I hope this year brings to you healthy hives and lots of honey.

Thanks to the team at Covenant for turning this manuscript into a book. Stacey Turner, your edits shine it up and make it sparkle. Editors do so much more than make red marks on paper, and I'm so grateful you're there all along the way to help me when I feel insecure or crazy. Christina Marcano, thank you for your fantastic artwork and for making the cover and the inside pages look beautiful.

And last of all, thank you to my grandma, Marmé, for taking me to Scotland when I was eleven and instilling in me such a love for the country, the customs, and shortbread.

Chapter 1

A COLOR SERGEANT OF HIS Majesty's Royal Marines, decorated as a war hero and discharged with honor, does not weep, Conall Stewart reminded himself as he swallowed against the burning in his throat. He swept his gaze over the glen he'd dreamed of since he'd taken the king's shilling and run off to adventure and glory ten years earlier. His eyes stung when they lit on the blackened stone and burnt timbers, and he blinked rapidly, turning his back, lest his companion see the swell of emotion.

Walking a few paces, Conall rolled back his shoulders and took a deep breath, letting it out slowly. The smell of pine and soil and the soft noise of the brook were so familiar he nearly expected to see his da emerge from the trees leading a string of shaggy cattle or hear his ma call for him to wash for supper.

Over the years, he'd worried that his memories of the Scottish Highlands had become warped, crossing from reality into the realm of fantasy. Surely no place could be as beautiful as the Glengarry of his dreams. But as he'd neared his childhood home, traveling over heather-covered moorlands, crossing smooth blue lochs, and climbing craggy mountains, he found that his remembrances of the land's splendor hadn't been exaggerated in the least. He felt his lips tremble and pressed them together tightly.

"Difficult tae see wi' yer own eyes, 'tis, surely?"

Conall glanced at Davy MacKay. When he had inquired after a horse in Dunaid, Davy had offered to accompany him to the tract of land on the slopes of Loch Nevis that Conall's family had farmed for generations. He didn't know whether he was glad of the company or resentful that the man should be present as Conall fought with his emotions.

"The sheriff and his officers burnt yon houses to keep the tenants from returnin'." Davy sat on a flat rock, stretching out his wooden leg before him. "And ye'll see more o' the same in every glen from here to Strathnaver." He swept his arm in a wide gesture. "Naught but ghosts left behind."

Conall nodded, not trusting his voice. He'd heard the rumors over the course of the war, both from other soldiers and convict prisoners, but hearing was one thing. While he considered himself a realist, his mind had not allowed him to accept the possibility that the farm wouldn't be there when he returned. His home had seemed so strong and permanent. "I'd not imagined it could be true," he finally said. "Not here in County Ross. Alexander Randalson MacDonell is a friend to the Highlanders." He heard the pleading tone in his voice and stopped it immediately, tamping down his emotions by focusing on the facts. "What changed?"

Davy blew out a puff of air, squinting with an expression that seemed a blend of disgust and tired acceptance. "The lairds are no longer protectors of their clans, ye see, Sergeant Stewart." He poked his toe into a clump of buttercups, watching the yellow blossoms bounce as he talked. "Educated abroad, livin' in Town, sons ha' forgotten the ways of their fathers and loosed the ties that bound them to the clan. They marry Sassenach women, attend fancy parties in Edinburgh and London, and seldom journey to their Highland holdings, save for a hunting trip or land inspection."

Years earlier, Conall's da had observed much the same thing. In order to remain in the king's good graces after Bonnie Prince

Charlie's failed rebellion, clans broke apart. The surviving chieftains attempted to appear as English as possible, forgetting Gaelic and turning their backs on their Highland roots lest they be mistaken for Jacobite sympathizers. With the exception of their last names, the succeeding generations of lairds were as Sassenach—or English—as a powdered wig.

"But Glengarry," Conall said, using the laird's nickname. "I thought he was different. He understood *duthchas*." The sound of the old word brought a new swell of emotions as Conall thought of his clansmen's deep connection to their lands and to each other.

"Och, aye." Davy smirked and swept his boot over the flowers, crushing down the stems and breaking off their tops. "Garbed himself in plaids and blew the pipes, carryin' a fancy decorative dirk in his belt. He enjoyed the romance of the auld ways, but in the end, I suppose stone walls and homespuns lost their charm for a man who'd been raised wi' the finer things."

Conall crossed the space between them and sat on a rock of his own. He rubbed his forehead, knowing the rest of the story without Davy needing to tell it. Property was more profitable to the laird as pastureland. As a young child, he'd heard of complaints and disputes in surrounding areas. Landowners increased rent, refused to grant new leases when old ones expired, and drove families from their farms with a combination of law, violence, and intimidation.

He remembered the sky darkened with smoke as dead heath on the moors was burned so cotton grass could grow more richly. *Bliadhna nan Caorach*, his da had called it, the year of the sheep. Glens were emptied by commissions, law agents, and soldiers to make room for the wool producing beasts. But in Glengarry, the people had been spared.

Conall stared down the green slope to the glassy surface of the loch and beyond to the other side, where white specks indicated one of the laird's flocks.

"The MacDonells' four-footed clansmen." Davy's voice was bitter as he lifted his chin toward the sheep.

As if in response, the sound of a bleat carried across the water.

Conall looked back at the burned shell of his childhood home with an ache as if something had been torn from him. "And how long ago?"

"A year a' least." Davy squinted. "Ye never received word?"

He shook his head. "My parents don't read or write. My sister, Elspeth, occasionally sent a letter, but I've been travelin' the better part of a year."

"Someone in the village will ken where yer family's gone to. And set yerself at ease. 'Twasn't a violent business here in Glengarry. Not like the evictions in Sutherland." He twisted to face east, as if he could see over the miles of mountains. "Aye, but 'twas brutal. We've a few in Dunaid with tragic tales: Sleepin' in the snow-covered kirkyard with family members too ill to travel, auld women burned alive in their homes. Ye see, most o' the men were away, fightin' with the Highland regiment at Waterloo." He sighed, glancing down at his wooden leg and leaving no question as to why he'd not been with them. "The duchess's factor, Patrick Sellar, cared naught a whit for those he expelled. He seized furniture and cattle, leaving women and children with no shelter in the cold winter."

Conall had seen his share of human suffering in ten years of military service. He thought of the convicts wallowing on prison hulks to Australia, of war-ravaged Spain and France. Widows, starving children, wounded and dying soldiers. The horrors humankind was capable of . . . but how could such things happen here? The peace and beauty of his home had been a tether, something to cling to when depravity and violence seemed to have no end. Even now, the place looked so peaceful.

"Come, Sergeant. We'll ask aboot in the village. Perhaps the minister, Mr. Graham, kens where ye might be findin' yer kin. I'd reckon they've gone to Canada or America."

The ache inside grew as Conall imagined his parents, now ten years older than when he'd last seen them, trying to forge a new life in a faraway land. He attempted to picture his mother in an American frontier cabin and found he couldn't do it.

The motion of Davy rising to his feet shook Conall from his contemplations. He'd remained rudely silent for the majority of the day and felt as if he should say something. "And what of yerself then?" He folded his arms, studying the young man. "Why've ye remained?"

"A fair question," Davy said, shifting around to balance on the slope. "Between my leg and my sick auld gran, I was in no shape to board a ship. Instead, I made a home on a croft farm in Dunaid. Most o' the folks in the village are those wi'out the means or strength to leave the Highlands. Women and children, mainly. And plenty o' gray-hairs." He smirked, jabbing Conall with his elbow. "But 'tisn't as bad as all tha'. You'll like Dunaid. A fine place indeed. You'll find your answers there."

Conall thought the man's description far from convincing. A village of displaced orphans and elderly exiles was hardly what he'd had in mind when he'd returned to his homeland.

Davy elbowed him again. "Come. I'll buy ye a drink."

Conall followed the man to where they'd tethered their horses. Once he'd received word that the war had ended, it had taken him more than a year to return home. A long year of sailing, riding, and walking from the other side of the world. The very thought of stepping foot on a ship to America so soon was more than he could bear. But Dunaid?

He knew the village, of course. 'Twas located less than twenty miles from his childhood home. He used to travel the distance a few times a year with his father, usually to see the blacksmith about a tool repair. From what he remembered and what he'd seen earlier today, Dunaid was hardly anything special. The main road ran along one edge of a deep inlet—a firth—giving Dunaid the feel of both a seaside fishing village and a farm town.

He'd returned to the Highlands to find his home and family gone. Now it seemed his only choices were to remain here alone or leave his beloved land all together. At the moment, neither option held the slightest appeal. A spring rain broke, soaking his woolen coat. The cold, heavy garment perfectly reflected his mood.

Chapter 2

AILEEN LESLIE DASHED ACROSS THE road, holding the bundle tightly against her chest to block it from the sudden rain. She ducked beneath the overhanging mossy roof of the cottage, knocking on the door. "I brought yer candles, Mrs. Campbell."

The door swung open, and Dores Campbell stepped through with a swiftness that defied her delicate appearance. She tugged on Aileen's arm, pulling her through the doorway. "Hurry yerself ben, lass."

Aileen smiled at the older woman. Dores was slender with a height shy of five feet. Her hair was pulled back tightly, and a snood wrapped around her silver bun, giving it the appearance of a herring caught in a net, but her plucky personality was far from that of an aging matron. She took a step back and surveyed her young neighbor from head to toe with a disapproving lift of her left eyebrow. While age had turned her hair a uniform gray, Dores's brows were dark as crow feathers and somehow managed to convey worlds of meaning with their slightest movements. "Well, yer *droukit*, are ye not?"

"I am a' that." Aileen glanced down at her wet dress. Droukit— soaked—was right. She held out the bundle of candles.

Dores didn't take them. She crossed her arms, the left brow raising higher. "Ye could have waited. 'Twasn't a matter o' life or death, now was it?"

"I was already halfway here when the clouds opened." Aileen set the candles on the scrubbed wooden table. "I don't think the wicks are wet."

Dores shrugged. "Och, well, there's naught to do but pour the tea. Come, sit ye there by the fire, or you'll catch yer death."

Aileen sat, grateful for a chance to rest her legs, though she would have rather remained a bit longer in the cool rain after an entire morning of dipping candles. She used a rag to lift the kettle from the hook above the fire and poured hot water into the teapot.

"Ye look to be tired." Dores leaned closer to peer at her. "Not working too hard, I hope?"

She shook her head. "Not too hard."

Dores reached forward to touch her forehead, muttering.

Aileen recognized the worry in her friend's face. Nearly a year had passed since she'd taken ill with fever and Dores had cared for her, nursing her back to health. Aileen truly believed Dores had saved her life, and for that she could put up with a bit of mollycoddling. She took the older woman's hand from her forehead, giving it a grateful squeeze and looking Dores directly in the eyes. "I feel fine." She poured the tea into two cups.

In truth, Aileen felt exhausted. 'Twasn't yet time for supper, and she'd already had a long day. Hive preparations in the spring were time consuming, and the majority of the work needed to be done before the sun had risen. She was pleased with how the colonies had wintered; their laying patterns looked healthy and the combs strong. The hives would be ready to take out to the heather and local farms after the first day of spring—Beltane. She'd spent the early-morning hours setting up bait skeps to entice new swarms, then melting down and straining some of the older combs into wax, making a fresh batch of candles.

Aileen sighed in pleasure as she took a sip of the warm tea.

"And where's Jamie got to this afternoon?" Dores sipped her own tea, settling back into the wooden chair for a visit.

"He's had lessons a' the kirk with Mr. Graham earlier, then I suppose he's off about the village wi' the other laddies." She smiled, thinking how grateful she was for the minister's lessons, although Jamie didn't appreciate sitting on the hard pews each weekday as well as on the Sabbath.

"And ye reckon he's stayin' out o' mischief then?" Dores spoke without meeting her eye, and Aileen's defenses rose into place.

"Why would ye be wonderin' such a thing? Jamie's a sweet lad. Perfectly behaved. No' like some o' the other troublemakers in the village."

"Ye ken I love the lad. I do. But a bit o' discipline now an' then wouldn't be misplaced is all I'm sayin'." Dores's telltale left brow ticked.

Aileen sighed. "Och, but yer an awful liar, Mrs. Campbell."

Dores set her teacup into the saucer with a clank that made Aileen jump. "Liar, am I? You'd question my devotion to that child? After our history?"

The reminder of their shared secret sent a shiver of dread through Aileen. "Of course I'd never question yer love o' Jamie." She spoke in a soft voice and glanced at the door, the familiar fear that someone might overhear made her muscles tighten.

"There's no mother loves her bairn as you love that lad." Dores's voice took on a soft tone. She reached for Aileen's hand. "But love doesna mean turnin' a blind eye to misbehavior."

Aileen allowed her hand to be held but did not relax. Dores was the only other person who knew the truth about Jamie. She'd been there on that cold night in the cemetery, one of three women huddled together in the snow as their township burned around them. Their pleas to Patrick Sellar and the Duchess of

Sutherland for assistance had fallen on deaf ears. Aileen's dearest friend, Sorcha, had birthed the lad, then, with no midwife to care for her, had died moments later. Sorcha's final words were a plea to keep the child hidden from his father.

With Dores's help, Aileen had taken Jamie as her own, concealing his identity by giving him her own last name. War and relocation had created enough young widows that none ever gave a second thought to Mrs. Aileen Leslie and her son, James. Especially here in Dunaid, so far away from Croick. Only the two women knew the truth, and neither had as much as whispered the lad's father's name in eight years.

Aileen glanced down at their joined hands, and her heart softened. The three of them, though unrelated by blood, were as close to a family as she had. "I ken ye only want the best for the lad," she said. "But Mr. McLeod's mistaken. Jamie assured me 'twas the Murray boys chased the goats from the pen. And Fiona Brodie's red bloomers must have blown off her clothesline. Jamie didn't hang them from the kirk steeple belfry. He wouldn't do such a thing. I'm sure of it." She rose, ignoring the tick of Dores's left brow and pushed aside a curtain, noting that the rain had slowed to a drizzle. "If you'll excuse me, I've supper to prepare. I thank ye for the tea. And the visit."

Dores stood and followed her to the door. "Until tomorrow then, dearie."

"Until tomorrow." Aileen kissed her friend on the cheek and hurried back across the muddy street to her own cottage. She stepped inside, and exhaustion settled into her shoulders. Candles in various stages of completion hung from strings crisscrossing the cottage. The table was covered with dried weeds being woven into skep beehives. Water had leaked through the rags she'd stuffed between loose stones in the walls, creating puddles on the muddy floor. And it looked like there was another hole in the roof. She moved the bucket beneath it to catch the dripping water. At least the spring weather was warm enough to keep the goat outside, she thought, glancing to the side of the cottage where the animal had been penned during the winter.

She put another hunk of peat onto the fire, realizing too late that it was wet and scowled at the smoke billowing from the hearth. It appeared the new hole in the roof would do some good after all. She pushed wet strands of hair from her face, scratched a drip of dried wax off her apron, and moved the unfinished hives to the floor; then she set about attempting to make yet another supper of bread and dried herring look appealing to an eight-year-old boy. With any luck, Jamie would return too tired to complain about the meal and they'd go to sleep early. She wondered if there was the slightest possibility that his clothes weren't covered in mud.

A pounding sounded on the door, giving her the usual burst of fear that Jamie's father had found them at last.

"Hello?" a man's voice called from outside. "Color Sergeant Conall Stewart. I'd like a word."

Aileen's worry dissipated. She, of course, knew of the man. In a village of this size, a new resident was a novelty. She'd seen Sergeant Stewart twice in kirk on Sunday. He seemed pleasant enough, tipping his hat to the women, speaking after the service with the minister. The women in the village were quite taken with him and understandably so. He was handsome indeed.

According to Dores, he'd returned from the war a hero and had taken the largest house in Dunaid, rejuvenating the neglected land and orchards surrounding it. Good news for Aileen. Orchards needed bees, and she was the only one in the village to supply them. Perhaps that was the reason for his call this evening?

Aileen opened the door and drew back with a gasp. Sergeant Stewart stood at the threshold, one large hand holding Jamie by the arm. The child twisted trying to escape his grip.

"Good evening. Mrs. Leslie, I presume?" His voice was polite in spite of his angry expression. He inclined his head but did not loose his hold. "May I speak to your husband?"

"No, you may not." Aileen's hands tightened into fists. "And I'll thank ye to release my son immediately, or I shall call for the constable. What is the meaning of this, sir?"

Sergeant Stewart's eyes widened for an instant, then his expression returned to a scowl. "Madam, perhaps 'tis *I* who should call the constable." He glared down at Jamie. "I discovered this lad sneaking aboot my library."

"Unhand him at once."

The sergeant released his hold, and Jamie ran toward her. She clasped him in her arms. He appeared unharmed, only frightened. "Jamie, *mo croí*. My love, did he hurt ye?"

Jamie shook his head and moved behind Aileen, burying his face against her skirts.

The sight of tears on his freckled cheeks made heat boil up inside her. She turned toward the man in the doorway. "Have ye no decency a'tall? Treatin' a wee child like a criminal." She jabbed a finger toward his face. "Yer library? And what would ye accuse him of then? Thievin' yer books?"

"*Éist!* Listen!" He held up a hand, stopping her rant.

Aileen hadn't realized that, in her anger, she'd switched to speaking Gaelic until he answered in the same. Just as well. She considered it a far more suitable language for an argument.

"'Tisn't only books in there. There are other things—dangerous things to be wary o'. Muskets, blades, a bayonet . . . I'd not want the lad to hurt himself."

"And I don' think his well-being was forefront in yer thoughts when ye dragged him home, frightened and weeping." She turned, bending down to Jamie's level, lowering her voice to a gentle tone. "My darlin', tell us. What were ye doin' in the sergeant's house then?"

Jamie shot a scared glance at the sergeant then looked up at her, his eyes still wet and his lip trembling. "The cat, Mam. He ran in through the open door, and I just thought tae chase him out again."

"O' course ye did, my dearest." She stroked his soft hair and kissed his cheek. The fact that he allowed it attested to his apprehension. She gave him a push toward the table. "Now eat yer supper there, and worry yerself no more."

She turned back to the sergeant and returned her fists to her hips. "Perhaps, Sergeant, ye should learn the facts before makin' accusations." If only Aileen possessed Mrs. Campbell's expressive brows, she would be able convey the depths of her indignation with only a slight lift.

The man's face reddened, and he stepped closer, lowering his voice to a harsh whisper. "Perhaps ye should open yer eyes instead of allowin' personal bias and female irrationality to blind ye to the truth." He glanced toward Jamie then slowly back to her, his gaze taking in the room.

Seeing the arrogant man survey the smoke, the tangles of dry weeds, the meager meal, the muddy floor, and the strings of candles in the leaky cottage, Aileen's chest heated in embarrassment, and that only caused her ire to rise further. "And exactly what *truth* is it that I'm blind to, Sergeant?"

He looked down at her, and she stood taller, not wishing to appear intimidated. "Madam, I've spent the past few years guarding prisoners in New South Wales. A child like yours needs discipline—thievery is only the beginning of a criminal career. Do you have any idea what life is like in a penal colony?"

That was the second time in just a few hours that her ability to raise her son had been called in to question. She glanced toward the table, where Jamie's hands were pressed together and his head bowed in prayer. How could a person believe the lad was any other than a perfect child? "I don't like what yer suggesting, sir. The lad already explained his actions." She stepped around him, holding on to the doorknob and fighting to keep her voice steady. "I thank ye for returning Jamie safely home, and for yer well-meant but poor child-rearing advice. I will instruct him in the future to stay far away from your verra dangerous library, and I'll pray my cat doesna make the mistake o' trespassin' again."

"Mrs. Leslie, the lad has you fooled. He—"

She raised her voice to cut off his words. "Yer an intolerant, cruel man, Sergeant, and I'd thank ye not to trouble me or my son again."

"Madam, that child—"

Even though he still stood in the way, she started closing the door. "Good evenin' to ye, sir."

He took a few surprised steps backward. "But . . ."

"I said, good evenin' to ye." Aileen shut the door with a bang. She imagined it closing just a few inches in front of the sergeant's nose, and the thought was satisfying indeed. She stood for a moment, fists clenched and shaking, breathing heavily as her wrath dispersed, leaving her feeling wrung out.

Small arms wrapped around her from behind. "Mam, I'm sorry. I didna mean to make the man angry."

She turned, crouching down and pulling him into an embrace. "Jamie, my precious, perfect lad, ye've done naught to apologize for. Now come. 'Twas a wearying day. Let's get ye out of those muddy clothes and ready for sleep."

Chapter 3

THE SOUND OF THE SLAMMING door still rang in his ears as Conall stormed up the path toward his house. Rain dripped into his collar, and he was glad for the cooling. How had he come away from the confrontation looking like 'twas *he* in the wrong? Mrs. Leslie's inability to see the truth was absurd. She was stubborn and sharp-tongued and unable to have a rational conversation when it came to her son. 'Twas a pity, really. The woman seemed intelligent and witty. The kind of person he'd have liked to have as a friend in this sparsely inhabited village.

Her words returned to him. *Cruel. Intolerant. No decency.* He picked up his pace, indignation flowing over him in hot waves. That woman had no idea what sort of man he was. She'd seen him at his worst, in a moment of anger. And anyway, why should he care what she or anyone else in Dunaid thought of him?

He turned at the fork in the road, heading up the hill away from the village.

For just an instant, he'd felt a burst of shame when she'd embraced the lad, soothing with a gentle touch and soft voice. At that moment, Mrs. Leslie's actions reminded Conall so much of his own mother that he'd actually opened his mouth to apologize and take his leave, but then the boy had peeked around his mother's skirts, giving a knowing smirk, and Conall's anger had surged.

Jamie Leslie had his mother completely hoodwinked. The lad was a delinquent in the making. His performance—the tears; the wide, innocent eyes; even the impromptu prayer—was a classic display of manipulation. Conall had seen criminals of the very worst kind in his assignments to the New South Wales penal colony. He had enough practice seeing through deception, and this lad . . . Conall tightened his jaw, wishing the child hadn't gotten the better of him.

And where was the boy's father? The beekeeper? Spending the evening in the tavern? The man was obviously not caring properly for his family. He was a poor role model to his son. The home was in need of repair. Based on the smoke, the chimney was likely plugged, and from what he'd seen, the family meal consisted of a wee fish and part of a loaf of dry bread. Without knowing him, Conall thought very poorly of Mr. Leslie.

A bead of guilt trickled through his anger, softening it to a mild frustration. It was difficult to remain angry with the boy when his father was negligent and his mother coddled him. He'd seen a number of soldiers from indulgent families, newly arrived to the battlefield. With no one to take care of them, they'd been unable to handle the simplest tasks, often turning to rebellion. And it had been Conall's duty to enforce the discipline, keep them from trouble, and turn them into soldiers.

He climbed the steps, opened the heavy oak door, and met his housekeeper in the entry hall. The stout woman took one look at him and pulled him forward to drip on the rug. "Och, ye knew 'twas *dreich* weather today, Sergeant." She pulled off his coat, wrinkling her nose at the wet wool. "Why did ye no' wear yer oilskin?"

"If you remember, Mrs. Ross, I left in a bit o' a rush."

"Aye, so ye did." She laid the offending garment over the stair railing. "And did ye return young Jamie to his ma then?"

He gave a nod.

"And I reckon Aileen Leslie wasna at all pleased wi' yer complaints aboot her lad." Mrs. Ross's mouth pulled to the side in the expression she made when she tried to subdue a smile.

Conall removed his hat, placing it atop the wet coat. "That's puttin' it mildly, Mrs. Ross."

"I ken. She'll not heed any ill words aboot him."

"Well, she should. Tha' boy's a nuisance an' his ma worsens the problem by refusin' to acknowledge it."

Mrs. Ross nodded. "I suppose when a person's lost everythin', she gives all her love to the one she has left—even if he is a wee menace." She gave a wink. "Come. I've yer supper waitin'."

Conall considered what she'd said. Though she'd spoken with a teasing tone, there was some truth to her words. What if his family lived here in Dunaid? He'd defend any of them to his dying breath. His ill feelings toward Mrs. Leslie softened a bit. She'd been through hard times, just like everyone else in Dunaid. If only the laird hadn't grown greedy, he thought. If only the war had ended a few years earlier. *If only* . . . A man could drive himself mad with those two words. He ran his fingers through his hair and followed Mrs. Ross into the dining room.

"Davy MacKay dropped by wi' yer mended plow harness." She took the cover from a warm plate of food. "Left it in the stables."

"Good. I'll turn under the north field tomorrow." Conall sat at the table. When he slid his chair forward, the movement made his chest muscles twinge. He grunted and rubbed his sternum. The old pruning shears he'd used on the fruit trees had left his arms, chest, and back sore.

Mrs. Ross shook her head. "You're workin' yerself too hard. Ye need some help, if ye don' mind my sayin' so. There's plenty o' young men in the village willin' to work. You've been away so long fightin' the French. Let yerself rest, Sergeant. Ye deserve a rest."

He gave her a nod and cut into the slice of lamb. "I'll consider it."

She curtseyed and left him to his meal.

Conall knew very well he'd not consider it. Luckily, he'd been stationed upon extremely successful ships, and his share of prize money was a tidy little sum building interest in a London Bank. He didn't need to work to support himself. When he'd taken the house, he'd intended to do just what Mrs. Ross suggested: read some books, take long leisurely walks through the heatherlands, and enjoy the gentle life of a man of adequate means. But within a few days, he'd come to find that the consequences of an idle mind and rested body were horrific dreams that haunted his nights. In the quiet hours, his memories surfaced, bringing with them the fear and horrors of war that he'd thought he'd left far behind.

Within a week, he'd cleared the overgrowth that had crept into the orchard and then started chopping off dead branches to prepare the fruit trees. He'd purchased horses and cattle and the equipment to plow and sow the fields. The labor left him exhausted each night and able to sleep without hearing the sounds of musket fire and the cries of the wounded and dying. And he was surprised to find that he enjoyed the work. The same dull farm labor he'd hated as a youth had become his salvation.

If only his da could see him now. If only Conall could tell him. *If only . . .*

***

Aileen helped Jamie remove his muddy clothes, noticing how short the sleeves were on his nearly threadbare shirt. She slipped an old nightshirt over his head and wiped the smudges from his face with a wet rag. "There ye are, my dearest. Handsome as ever a young man was."

He smiled with sleepy eyes and knelt on the pallet beside her, holding his palms together as he recited the Lord's Prayer.

These quiet moments before bed were Aileen's favorite part of the day. "Now, lay your head, mo croí." She covered him with the blanket. "And what story would ye be wantin' tonight?"

"Tell me aboot Fionn mac Cumhaill, Mam."

"Och, tha's one o' my favorites." She shifted around, tucking her legs beneath her.

Jamie's eyelids grew heavy as he listened to the story of the ancient warrior and his quest for the salmon of wisdom.

Aileen had hardly begun when she heard a snore. "Sleep now, lad." She brushed his hair from his forehead, smiling at the angelic face, so peaceful in sleep. She examined his dirty garments as she gathered them. Jamie had only two sets of clothes, and one was for Sunday. So unless she meant to send him out tomorrow wearing naught but his skin, she'd washing to do tonight.

She took down the hunk of lye soap and fetched the bucket of rain water from beneath the hole in the roof, moving as quietly as possible. Her head had started to ache an hour ago, and she desperately wished to go to sleep and put this day behind her.

For Jamie's sake, Aileen had kept a smile on her face through supper, but inside, she was fuming. How dare that man come here and accuse her boy of a crime? Now that the incident was over, she realized the true reason for her anger wasn't simply offense at his words, but the fear that he might truly call the constable. Thievery wasn't looked upon with the least bit of tolerance, and Sergeant Stewart was wealthy. He would have much more influence on a magistrate than would a poor widow.

Jamie muttered something in his sleep, and she smiled. Her boy was truly a dear, and if only the sergeant had met him under different circumstances, he would find Jamie to be a smart lad full of energy and curiosity. Not a criminal.

The harsh smell of the soap seemed to make her headache stronger. She brought the large pot from the hearth, pouring some of the hot water into the bucket.

Her mouth still tasted bitter from the confrontation. She wasn't one to cast insults at a stranger, but Sergeant Conall Stewart certainly earned them. His supposition was utterly without cause. Perhaps spending time around criminals caused a person to assume the worst about everyone he met.

She tossed the shirt in the water, using the soap on the muddy spots. Candlelight made discerning cleanliness difficult, but after a few moments, she was satisfied that she'd gotten the worst of it. She rinsed and wrung the shirt, hanging it to dry over the back of a chair near the fire.

Aileen sighed as she lifted the trousers. The knees were nearly worn through. She felt something heavy in a pocket, another rock no doubt. Why did lads collect—

Her thoughts froze as she withdrew the object. Gold-colored, it appeared to be a coin of some sort with a symbol in the center. A sick feeling rose from her stomach as she held the object near the candlelight and studied the engraving—an anchor resting on laurel branches beneath crown. Not a coin at all, but a medal. Her heartbeat sped up, and her mouth went dry. Circling the image were the words: *His Majesty's Royal Marines.*

Aileen pressed her eyes closed. *Oh, Jamie.*

Chapter 4

CONALL SPREAD BUTTER OVER ANOTHER of Mrs. Ross's excellent scones and took a bite, chewing slowly and washing it down with fresh coffee. He looked up when the housekeeper entered the dining room. "Another excellent breakfast, Mrs. Ross. Yer spoilin' me."

Her round cheeks turned pink, and her mouth tugged to the side. "Thank ye, Sergeant." She dipped in a small curtsey. "Now, if ye please, sir, ye've visitors."

He raised his brows, looking to Miss Ross for a clue as to the visitors' identities, but she gave none. "Verra well then. Show them in."

Callers at this early hour was surprising. He didn't imagine it was a social visit. Perhaps Davy had returned to tell him something more about the plow.

He took another bite of scone and was still chewing when Mrs. Aileen Leslie and Jamie entered.

The boy's eyes were red as if he'd been weeping, and his mother's face was pale. She clutched the boy's arm, much as Conall had done the day before. Conall felt instantly wary.

"Mrs. Leslie. Jamie." He wiped his mouth and stood, dropping his napkin onto the table. "To what do I owe the pleasure?"

She released Jamie's arm, giving him a small push forward. "Go on then."

Conall was surprised to hear her voice shake.

Jamie looked up at his mother, his eyes wide and pleading. "Mam, do I have to?"

She nodded, her brows drawn tightly together. "Aye, lad."

Conall looked between them. There was no trace of the coddling he'd seen last night. Mrs. Leslie's expression was firm, but her eyes seemed sad and anxious. His curiosity grew, as did his unease.

Jamie exhaled. He turned and took a step toward Conall. He glanced back once more at his mother then held forward his fist.

Conall glanced at Mrs. Leslie then reached out. Jamie placed his brass shako plate into his palm and stepped back, not lifting his eyes.

Aileen's hands were clenched together. She cleared her throat, speaking in a voice that managed to be gentle and firm at the same time. "Go on now, Jamie."

"I'm sorry, Sergeant Stewart," Jamie said, his voice nearly too soft to hear. "I'm sorry I took yer golden treasure charm."

Conall slipped the shako plate into his pocket. "Jamie, robbery is a serious crime." He looked up at the sound of Mrs. Leslie's gasp.

"Please don't call the constable, Sergeant." Her voice shook, and her eyes filled. "Jamie won't do it again. And he intends to pay for his mistake." The woman was nearly frantic.

Conall looked back at Jamie.

The boy raised his head, pushing back his shoulders, but his chin trembled. "I'll make it right. I can take care o' yer animals or dig rocks from the garden. Whatever ye need. I'm a strong worker, Sergeant Stewart."

Conall was tempted to tell the boy his offer wasn't necessary and send them home, but he knew from experience, if he let Jamie leave with no more than a warning, he'd not learn a lesson. "Nay, I won't call the constable." From the corner of his eye, he saw Mrs. Leslie's shoulders relax. "But if something like this happens again . . ."

"'Twon't, Sergeant," Jamie said. "You've my word."

"Verra well then." Conall considered for a moment what type of work he could have the lad do. He could send him into the kitchen with Mrs. Ross or to beat rugs with Brighid the maid, but he had a feeling Jamie should be treated like a man, and giving him adult responsibilities would grow the boy's confidence and hopefully keep him from more trouble.

Raising his gaze from the lad, he met Aileen's eyes and, for a moment, stared. He'd not noticed their light-blue color last night in the smoky cottage. When they weren't flashing with anger, her eyes were remarkably bright, even compressed with worry as they were now. "Come, Mrs. Leslie. I'll walk ye to the door."

As they left the room, Conall thought through the tasks still needing to be done on the farm and tried to determine something appropriate for a young lad—something that would challenge him yet leave him with a feeling of accomplishment. She tapped his arm and his mind registered the fact that she'd spoken. "I beg yer pardon. What did you say?"

"I said thank you, Sergeant Stewart."

"Yer welcome, Mrs. Leslie."

She looked as if she intended to say more, but she closed her mouth and glanced at the door.

Conall opened it.

"I'll call for him this evenin', then, shall I?" she said.

"No need. I'll see him home."

Aileen nodded and stepped over the threshold but then stopped. "Sergeant?"

It took only a glance at the apprehension in her face to know what she meant to say. "Don' fret yerself. No harm will come to the lad in my care."

"I ken he'll be safe here, but . . ."

"I consider corporeal punishment to be a duty for a father or a commanding officer, Mrs. Leslie."

The tension in her face relaxed into relief. She curtseyed and departed.

Conall returned to the dining room and found Jamie standing where he'd left him. The boy's gaze was fixed on a plate of sausage.

"Well, Jamie. The chore I've in mind requires a verra strong man. I'm tryin' to decide whether I think yer up to the task."

"I told you. I'm strong." Jamie looked up at him as he spoke then darted another glance at the sausage.

Conall clasped his hands behind his back. "Tell me, lad. Did ye have breakfast this mornin'?"

"Aye," Jamie said. "Porritch."

"And did it fill yer belly? Or would ye have a bit more?"

Jamie's eyes grew wide, and he looked to the table but just as quickly looked back. "I thank ye, sir, but me mam's porritch is all I need."

Conall knew firsthand the stubbornness of Highlanders and their unwillingness to accept any sort of charity. "Well, ye see," Conall rubbed his chin between his thumb and forefinger. "For farm work, a man needs his strength. I'll not have ye too weak to work because ye've not eaten enough meat."

Jamie chewed on his lip. Conall could just imagine the struggle going on in the boy's head: the worry that he'd already disappointed his mother battling with a growing boy's constantly empty belly.

"And ye see, ye'd be doin' me a favor," Conall said. "Mrs. Ross made far too much sausage this mornin'. How can I ever finish it all?"

Jamie finally gave a shy smile. "I'll help ye."

Ten minutes later, after Jamie had eaten every scrap of pork on the breakfast table, Conall led him out through the kitchen, across the back garden, past the byre and stable, and inside the storehouse. He watched the lad studying everything around him with a child's curiosity. In the storehouse, he handed the child buckets, chisels, and a trowel, indicating they should go into the hand wagon.

Conall hefted two sacks into the wagon and pulled it out of the building, heading toward the orchard. Jamie grabbed the handle and pulled beside him.

The pair followed the path around the edge of the orchard until they reached a spot where the stones of the wall had crumbled.

"Do ye ken how to repair a wall, Jamie?"

The lad hesitated then shook his head. "Nay, but Mr. Graham says I'm a quick learner."

Conall smiled at the boy's eagerness to please. "It's lucky that the sun's shinin' today." He lifted a sack from the cart. "The mortar, 'twon't set in the rain."

"And what are those?" Jamie pointed to the sacks.

"One's lime, and th' other's aggregate."

"Aggregate?" He pronounced the word slowly, as if testing the feel of it in his mouth.

"Aye. River sand. To bond the mortar."

Jamie pointed at the bucket. "We mix them together?"

"Right ye are, but first we'll need to remove the auld mortar from the stones." He handed Jamie a chisel and showed him how to chip and scrape away the crumbled grout.

The task was one Conall had hated as a boy. Cleaning old rocks was time consuming and dull. But each time he stopped to watch Jamie, the lad was focused, meticulously inspecting each stone then, when he was satisfied, moving it to the growing pile. He worked with an energy that Conall envied, doing a thorough job, which was commendable. As a lad, Conall had complained constantly and let himself become distracted. His da had again and again pulled his focus back to the task. But Jamie seemed intent on the chore, wanting to do his best work.

Eventually, when they'd cleared away all the loose rocks and mortar, Conall sent Jamie to the brook to fetch a bucketful of water.

As he waited, leaning back against the wall, he spied Mrs. Ross walking up the path. He strode toward her, sliding the basket from her arm.

She looked toward the broken wall, her lips tugging to the side. "I've brought yer luncheon. But it appears Jamie Leslie's escaped already."

"He's gone for water." Conall lifted the cloth from the basket, peeking beneath at the food. He raised his brows. "Buns, cheese, and . . . sausage?"

She shrugged, her mouth pulling to the side. "I thought ye needed a robust meal after all yer gruelin' labor."

Conall wasn't fooled in the least. So far, his days of "gruelin' labor" had been rewarded with a bun, cheese, and sometimes a bit o' broth.

Jamie's face lit up when he saw the food, his thanks making Mrs. Ross blush. Once she'd ensured they wanted for naught else, she returned to the house, and the pair of them sat on the wall to eat their luncheon.

"Do ye eat meat every day, Sergeant?"

Conall turned toward the lad, glad they wouldn't eat their meal in an unpleasant silence. The child watched him with an open expression, seeming to have completely forgiven their earlier conflict. "Aye, I suppose I do."

Jamie's mouth formed an *O*, and his eyes rounded. "Most days, we have fish for supper." He wrinkled his nose. "Herring or haddock." He licked a drip of grease off his bun. "But when the honey comes in, sometimes we get to eat lamb." He took another bite, speaking as he chewed. "Once, Mr. Ferguson paid for candles with a piece o' venison. Have ye eaten venison, Sergeant Stewart?"

Conall nodded, feeling something verra close to sympathy for the young burglar.

Jamie brushed crumbs from his legs and eyed another link of sausage. "Mam says ye fought in the war."

"Aye, she speaks true."

"And did ye fight Napoleon then?" Jamie's legs swung, not reaching the ground as he sat atop the low wall.

Conall grinned. "Not personally, but I did see him one time."

"An' what was he like? Mrs. Campbell showed me a drawing." Jamie wrinkled his nose. "He looked to be short and stout and sulky."

"Tha's just how he appeared," Conall said, chuckling. "But I didna see him close. A ship I was assigned to, *Undaunted,* was part o' the convoy, escortin' Napoleon to his exile in Elba. I saw him for just a moment as he went aboard the French ship. He was short and stout and sulky, just like ye said." He lifted the basket, offering Jamie the last piece of sausage. "But there was somethin' aboot the man. He radiated power. I could feel it clear across the water, though I wasn't near enough to even see his face clearly."

Jamie froze, staring at him with the sausage halfway to his mouth. "And did he see ye?"

Conall frowned and set down the basket. "Nay, I dinna think so."

"If he did, he'd have been frightened."

"Ye think I'm frightening, do ye?" he said, amused.

"Aye. When ye're angry, ye're verra frightening." Jamie blushed and took a bite of the sausage. "And I think ye'd have been angry at ol' Boney. I reckon if he had seen ye when ye were cross, he'd have run away cryin', '*Ooh la la!*'"

Conall burst into laughter. "Aye, I'd have liked to see it, Jamie lad."

Jamie grinned and, seeing Conall rise, hopped off the wall to join him.

Conall tore both bags, pouring aggregate and lime into the bucket. He handed a trowel to Jamie. "Stir it well. We want the consistency to be even. Now pour in the water slowly. That's it."

Jamie's tongue popped out of the corner of his mouth as he concentrated. "Like this?"

"Aye."

"And do we put it on the rocks now?"

"Not yet." Conall shook his head. "We'll be needin' to take our time. Mortar tha's not mixed well won' set right, and ye'll get spaces between the stones."

Jamie stopped stirring, his brows drawing together for an instant as he apparently thought about what Conall said. He blinked and continued moving the trowel through the thick mixture, a sheen appearing on his face from the effort.

Once it was mixed thoroughly, Conall stopped him, sticking the tool into the mortar. "There now. 'Tis finished when the trowel stands upright."

Jamie let out a breath and wiped his arm across his forehead. Conall showed the lad how to use the trowel to apply the mortar then set a stone, careful to ensure a tight bond.

"And spaces create gaps in the wall, right, Sergeant?"

"Aye." When the repair was nearly complete, Conall stepped back and watched the lad, who was intent in his task. Conall poured more of the mixture into the bucket and stirred, creating another batch of mortar.

"I dinna think we need so much now. 'Tis nearly finished," Jamie said.

Conall looked at the wall, complete save for a few more stones. "Och, lad, I overestimated. I suppose I'll have to throw out the rest." He glanced at Jamie.

The boy was watching the bucket, and Conall could practically hear his mind working. "If ye please, Sergeant. Perhaps I could take away the mortar. If ye mean to throw it out, that is."

Conall felt much like Mrs. Ross as he held back a smile. "Would ye, Jamie? I'd appreciate it verra much."

Once the wall was completed and they both agreed it would last as long as Hadrian's Wall, the pair started back. Conall had decided to walk the long way around the orchard to check if any other sections of wall needed repair.

They walked quietly, enjoying the companionable silence as they pulled along the wooden wagon. Despite years of neglect, the orchard seemed in good condition. Healthy buds covered the branches, ready to burst.

Jamie stopped suddenly. "Sergeant, 'tis yer apiary." He hurried from the path then slowed, walking in a circle around the structure.

Built of the same stone as the orchard wall, the apiary was about six feet tall, divided horizontally into two shelves with an overhanging sod roof. Conall didn't know when last it had been used, but he thought it would likely need some work before 'twas ready for hives.

"Look ye here, Sergeant." Jamie waved him over. "A bird nest. 'Twill need to be swept out. And here." He pointed to another section. "Some o' the stones are missin'. The bees won't like the draft nor the rain."

The boy must tend the bees with his father.

Jamie stepped back, folding his arms as he scrutinized the apiary with an expert eye. "Would ye like me to put it to rights? I can return tomorrow after my lessons wi' the minister."

Conall studied the lad. He saw no deceit in his face, just a desire to please. Was he truly willing to return and work? "Thank you, Jamie. I'd be verra grateful to ye."

Jamie gave a proud nod. "I ken all about bees. Did ye ken worker bees dance to tell the others where to go for pollen? And they don't like the smell o' horses. Sometimes I'm allowed to look inside the hive and find the queen. She's the longest bee. The drones are fat with large eyes. Would ye like to help harvest the honey, Sergeant? Mam might give ye a piece o' sweet comb to chew."

Conall shuddered. Bees were one thing he wasn't keen to learn more about. A boy who'd made the mistake of throwing a rock at a swarm had learned to keep his distance. "I'll leave that chore to the beekeeper."

They returned to the wagon and walked the remainder of the way to the storehouse, listening to the lowing of the cattle and the singing of the birds around them.

"Sergeant Stewart?"

After the boy's chatter throughout the day, the hesitant way he spoke told Conall he had something serious on his mind. "Aye, Jamie."

"I didn't mean to take it. Your golden treasure charm."

"And why did ye then?"

"Like I told ye, 'twas the cat ran in yer house, an' when I followed him inside, he ran into the bookroom and hopped out o' the window." He glanced up at Conall. "I should have left, but I saw yer treasures on the table. I only wanted to have a look. But when I heard ye comin', I hid away. I didn't mean ta put it in my pocket, ye ken. I was frightened." He looked down at his bare feet. "I'm not a thief," he said in a soft voice.

"I believe ye."

***

After seeing Jamie safely home to the cottage, Conall took the longer route out of the village toward his farm. Lifting stones and scraping mortar had left his lower back in need of a stretch. Jamie hadn't seemed to mind working through the day. He'd not run out of energy even after hours of lifting rocks—the blessing of a young body. Conall couldn't help his smile as he thought of the lad. Jamie Leslie was earnest, hardworking, and anxious to please, and Conall had found his conversation amusing. Something he'd have not imagined possible after the evening before.

The child's guileless questions, his honest curiosity—no wonder Mrs. Ross had cooked up an extra serving of sausage. Those red curls and his infectious laugh could enchant the fairy queen herself. Conall stopped, looking over the village and the harbor below as realization settled. He was actually fond of the boy. Well, tha' was unexpected.

He continued walking, chuckling to himself at the image of Napoleon fleeing from the English soldiers with the cry of "Ooh la la!" Aye, he was fond of the lad indeed.

Chapter 5

"Jamie's workin' for the sergeant today, is he?" Dores poured some cream into her tea. "Isna that a fine thing?"

Aileen watched the older woman for any movement of her brow. When it remained in its natural arc, she nodded. "Aye. A fine thing." She fought her urge to fidget, feeling restless as she worried about the lad spending the day with the stern marine.

"A blessed addition to the village, the sergeant." Her brows wiggled. "And he's handsome, to be sure. Broad shoulders 'neath his coat, caramel curls fallin' over his ears and forehead. And ye ken what they say about a man with a cleft in his chin . . ." She waggled her brows again.

Aileen rolled her eyes. "Mrs. Cambell, yer a hopeless case."

Dores grinned wickedly, her teeth shining in the firelight. "And a kind man he is, to take our Jamie and put him to work."

In spite of herself, Aileen smiled. She hadn't told Dores the circumstances leading up to Jamie's employment, not after the woman's criticism yesterday, and as a result, Sergeant Stewart appeared the hero, takin' the boy under his wing and keeping him from becoming a miscreant. That she could bear. But for Dores, or anyone for that matter, to think ill of her boy . . . 'twould break Aileen's heart.

"Some more tea then?" Mrs. Campbell asked.

Aileen looked down at her cup and realized she'd drained the entire thing without noticing. "Oh, aye. Thank you." Her foot tapped on the hard-packed floor as she worried how the man might be treating her darling. Was he critical? Insulting? Was her boy at this very moment crying for his mother? Jamie had been in the wrong, but he didn't deserve cruelty.

"Perhaps we should become better acquainted wi' Sergeant Conall Stewart." Dores's brow wiggled. "Livin' up on the hill in that grand house. It must get lonely. Mrs. Ross tells me he's fond of scones. Perhaps I'll invite him to supper. You and Jamie too, o' course."

Aileen set her teacup onto the table. "I dinna think the sergeant wants to spend th' evenin' with a group o' strangers."

"Strangers?" Dores looked appalled at the term. "He tipped his hat to me after Sunday service. Even said, 'Good mornin,' polite as could be."

"Perhaps he fancies you." Aileen waggled her own brows, earning a chuckle from the old woman. She brushed off her apron and stood. "I need to be goin' now, Mrs. Campbell. I thank ye for the tea."

Dores gasped, and Aileen whipped around. "What is it? Is somethin' wrong?"

The older woman stretched out her arm, pointing to the fire. "There. See that bit o' wood? It fell from the fire in yer direction."

"I hardly think that's cause for alarm." Aileen lifted the iron poker and pushed the branch back.

"No, my dearie. Fire bodes marriage."

Aileen gave her a flat look.

"We were jes' discussin' Sergeant Stewart." Dores tapped her finger against her chin, talking to herself. "And the fire pointed toward ye. I think 'tis a sign. One that shouldna be ignored."

Aileen rolled her eyes and kissed her friend's cheek. "I'm leavin' now."

"Wait, wait! Before ye go, I've somethin' for ye." Dores crossed the room and returned with a bundle of clothing. "For Jamie. Bless the lad, but he's growin' like Prinny's belt size."

Aileen unfolded the clothes, inspecting the homespun material. They looked as if they belonged to a man at least twice Jamie's size.

"They'll take some adjustin', but—"

"Mrs. Campbell, 'tisn't necessary. I—I can't accept these."

She crossed her arms. "Well, why ever not?"

"I'll find clothes for Jamie myself, once the honey's harvested."

"That's months away. The boy needs clothes now."

"Aye, but I should be the one to provide them. I'll not take yer charity, Mrs. Campbell." She held up another shirt. "And where did ye get these anyway?"

Dores became very interested with something on her sleeve. "Ye heard Hamish Lachlan's passed . . ."

"An' ye took a dead man's clothes?" Aileen couldn't keep her voice from growing louder.

"Well, he doesna need them anymore, does he?" Dores's tone rose to match hers.

Aileen didn't know whether to laugh or cry. She rubbed her eyes with her fingertips and blew out a breath. "Ye've taken leave o' your senses."

Dores grinned. "And jes' think how fine our Jamie will look on Beltane."

Aileen gathered the clothes, wondering what on earth the old woman was thinking and at the same time feeling overwhelmed with gratitude. Even if Dores showed her love in strange ways, 'twas love all the same. "Mrs. Campbell, yer always doin' kind things fer me an' Jamie. I can't pay ye in honey and candles forever."

"'Tis all I've need o', dearie. Besides yer visits every day."

"But 'tisn't enough."

Dores's mouth twisted in a mischevious smirk, and her brow lurched upward. "I'll think o' somethin' ye can do to pay me back."

Aileen didn't like the sound of that. "As long as it doesn't involve dinner with former marines."

"*Handsome* former marines," Dores corrected. "An' I'll be makin' no promises."

Aileen took her leave of Dores and crossed the street. When she entered the cottage, she found Jamie kneeling beside a wall, chipping off the plaster she'd used to fill a leaking gap.

When he saw her, he jumped up. "Mam! Sergeant Stewart learnt me how to use mortar. I'm repairin' the cottage." He pointed with the chisel in his hand toward a few other spots that had been patched.

She let out a breath of relief. Jamie didn't seem worse for his experience. If anything, he appeared happy. She joined him near the wall.

"Ye need to remove the ol' mortar. That's verra important, or th' new mortar won't bond tight to the stone," Jamie explained.

She cupped his freckled cheek in her hand. "And how was yer day, mo croí?"

Jamie kept scraping the stones as he talked. "Sergeant Stewart told me aboot the time he saw Napoleon. And he has two horses. One is gray and the other brown. I'm settin' his apiary in order tomorrow after my lessons."

Aileen started. "Ye're going back?"

"Aye. There's plenty o' work to do on th' farm and in th' orchard. But nay to worry. I'll not shirk my chores at home."

She stood, astonished at the transformation in the lad's attitude. This morning, she'd left behind a frightened boy. And now . . . How could a few hours with Sergeant Stewart have made such a change? She couldn't fault the lad for wanting to work, and it appeared as though the sergeant had been kind to him. How could she be angry about that? Jamie needed men in his life to show him things like how to mortar stones and to tell him about Napoleon. She set the clothes on the table beside a basket she didn't recognize. "What's this then, Jamie?"

"Mutton. Sergeant Stewart sent it for our supper."

She peeked beneath the cloth, and anger kindled in her chest, burning up her neck to her cheeks. Just because Jamie thought of the sergeant as a hero didn't mean she had to accept a handout from the man. "And what did he do that for?"

She must have been unable to hide the resentment in her tone because Jamie set down the trowel and joined her. "'Tis nay charity, Mam. Sergeant Stewart said Mrs. Ross prepared too much for him to eat alone." He lifted the cloth all the way off. "'Twas a favor I did for him, takin' the mutton away."

"I see." Aileen had half a mind to march up the hill, bang on the sergeant's door, plop down the basket in front of him, and give him a talkin' to. But of course, a woman couldn't call on a single gentleman unless she had business to discuss. Was this business? She couldn't bring herself to justify it as such. And besides, Jamie hadn't eaten meat in months. How could she take it away from him?

The heat continued to build. Why did everyone consider her incapable of caring for her son? A small part of her wondered if they were right. The anger swirled with no outlet, turning her stomach sick.

Jamie returned to the wall, using his trowel to spread the pasty substance. "There, that's seen it." He stood straight with a pride she'd seen but rarely. "I've just a bit o' the mortar left. I'll have a look at Mrs. Campbell's garden wall afore I wash oot the bucket."

Once Jamie left, Aileen sat staring at the freshly repaired spots in her cottage walls. Her unkind thoughts toward Sergeant Stewart made her feel petty. The man had done nothing but show a bit of attention to her son.

Jamie was growing up, and sooner than she'd like, he'd be a man. His time with Sergeant Stewart had only made that fact more apparent. After only a day with the sergeant, Jamie had brought home a finer meal than they'd seen in months. He spoke and worked with a man's confidence. A boy needs a hero. His love of stories, of Fionn mac Cumhaill, made that all too apparent. She should be happy, proud of what he was becoming, but instead she was filled with unease and even jealousy.

The anger turned into bitter guilt, and she wiped a tear from her cheek. Jamie was her world, and now his own world was expanding, leaving her feeling unneeded and alone.

Chapter 6

CONALL PULLED BACK ON THE leads, stopping the wagon at the end of the road. He climbed down and patted the workhorse, surveying the area. The plot of land sat high on a stony ridge above the harbor. Below, he could hear the water lapping against the rocks of the shore, though he couldn't see it through the morning fog. He moved to the back of the wagon and started hauling out branches.

'Twas easy to see exactly where he was meant to pile the wood. A flat, ash-stained spot on raised stones in the center of the field was obviously where the people of Dunaid had built their Beltane bonfire for generations. He glanced back along the road and saw the kirk steeple poking out of the fog. He estimated himself to be less than half a mile from the center of the village—a fine location for the celebration.

As he'd ridden through Dunaid, he'd seen decorated May bushes in front of houses and businesses, a sign that May had arrived. Not only was Dunaid busily planning for the festivities, but for the first time in years, arrangements were also taking place in his own house. Mrs. Ross and Brighid were busy at work, weaving yellow flowers into wreaths and garlands, decorating the

May bush in front of his door with ribbons and flowers, and cleaning the hearths in preparation for the sacred fire.

The day before, Conall had brought a sheep to the minister for his wife and the church ladies to prepare for the Beltane feast. Everyone in the village would contribute something, and he knew most had only a small bit to give. His stomach growled as he thought of the mutton roasted slowly on a spit, the boiled eel, and the Highlander haggis the British soldiers had teased him about. They had no idea what a true delicacy 'twas.

He whistled a tune as he worked, surprised at how much he looked forward to Beltane and its traditions. More than ten years had passed since he'd enjoyed the grand bonfire or eaten *bannoch Bealltainn*, the holiday's special oatcake. The last time he'd attended the festival was only a few months before he'd run away to become a soldier. He smiled as he remembered helping his ma gather flowers to adorn the farmhouse's door and windows. Elspeth, his sister, had decorated the family's May bush, and Conall had helped his father lead their cattle and goats and even a few chickens around the bonfire, making sure the smoke blew over them to protect the animals from disease. The memories brought an ache, and he wondered if the absence of his family and the worry about where they'd gone would cast a shadow over the festival.

Once the wagon was empty and the dead wood piled in a heap, he turned and started back along the main road toward the village. The fog had turned into a damp, misty spray which he wouldn't quite describe as rain but wouldn't describe as "not rain" either. *Smirr* was the word his ma had used to describe this type of damp. Conall smiled. As much as he loved this weather, it left him very evenly drenched.

Perhaps he'd stop at the Stag and Thistle and get something warm to drink. He left the wagon outside Davy's livery shop and walked toward the inn. Villagers were bustling about, preparing

May bushes in front of their shops and homes, adorning their doors and windows with yellow flowers, and calling well-wishes. The excitement of the holiday buzzed in the wet air.

From ahead, he heard children's voices. One he recognized, and it brought him up short. Jamie Leslie was hollerin', and he sounded angry. Conall hurried toward the dry goods store, finding Jamie, red cheeked and hands fisted, standing face-to-face with a girl a few years older than him.

"Yer a wee pest, Jamie!" the girl shouted.

"An' yer a rag-headed ninny!" The lad yelled the words in an indignant outburst.

So intent were they on their argument that they didn't notice Conall's approach until he spoke. "Good mornin' to ye, Jamie lad."

Jamie turned away from the girl, his angry expression falling away when he saw Conall. "Mornin', Sergeant." He smiled then shot a glare to the girl.

"And what's upset ye then?" Conall asked. "Surely nothin' tae do wi' this bonny lass."

"Robena." Jamie spoke the name with a scowl.

Robena scowled back.

"Tell me then. What's caused the two o' ye to cross swords?"

Jamie folded his arms. "Mr. Graham read to us about Judas Iscariot in lessons, and Robena said red hair's the mark o' the devil."

Conall glanced at Robena. The girl had pulled back, becoming shy when he'd approached.

Jamie's scowl relaxed, but his brows still pulled together tightly in worry. "'Tisn't so, is it, Sergeant? Jes 'cause I played a trick on cranky auld Mrs. Brodie, I'm not an evil lad."

Conall coughed to hide a smile. He'd heard of the infamous red-bloomers affair. But looking at the boy's earnest face, his amusement changed to sympathy. He felt the urge to put a reassuring arm around Jamie, take him away, and give the girl a scolding, but he thought such an action would just lead to more teasing in the future. He rubbed his chin. "Can't be true now, can it?" he mused in a conversational tone. "I ken Robert the Bruce and Mary, Queen o' Scots, had red hair. And, o' course, Cú Chulainn. Now, I'd no' consider any o' them to be evil, would ye?"

"Nay," said Jamie.

Robena remained silent, shifting her feet.

"An' my own ma, she's bonny red hair, much brighter than Jamie's. A sweeter soul you'd nay find anywhere. 'Twouldn't do for someone to call my ma evil."

"I'm sorry," Robena said.

Conall smiled. "O' course ye are, lass." He jerked his chin upward. "Now off ye go then."

The girl looked toward Jamie, but instead of speaking, she gave Conall a quick curtsey and made her escape, dashing off down the street.

Jamie watched her go then looked up. "Is it true, Sergeant? Yer mam's hair is red like mine?"

"Aye, although she'd a bit o' gray above her ears the last time I saw her. 'Twas over ten years ago."

"You must miss her."

Conall nodded, swallowing. "Robena shouldna have said those things to ye. But, lad, ye must always be a gentleman, no matter what a lass says." He held up his hand when Jamie opened his mouth to disagree. "*Always*. Think o' somethin' kind to say, bow when ye meet and when ye depart"—he demonstrated, bending his head forward, his hand on his heart—"and most of all, ye mustn't yell at a lady. Not ever."

"But Robena isn't a lady," Jamie said, his nose wrinkling. "She's naught but a lassie. And a bad-mannered one at that."

"Aye, lad." He tried to keep his face somber, though 'twas becomin' more difficult. "Ye can't change her. But *yer* duty is to be a gentleman. Ye ken?"

Jamie shrugged, looking reluctant. "Aye."

"That's a good lad." He patted the lad's shoulder. "An' what's brought ye to town today then, Jamie?"

He shrugged. "Lessons wi' the minister. We finished early because o' the holiday. My mam was to meet me after, but—" He looked past Conall and waved. "Och, there she is now."

Conall turned and saw Mrs. Leslie walking toward them, a covered basket over her arm. He tipped his hat when she neared and inclined his head. "A good day to ye, Mrs. Leslie."

Jamie laid his hand on his chest and inclined his head as well. "A good day to ye, Mam."

Mrs. Leslie looked back and forth between the two, raising her brows. "Good day, Sergeant. Jamie."

"Sergeant Stewart is learnin' me aboot bein' a gentleman," Jamie said.

"Is he now?" She glanced at Conall with a curious expression.

"Aye," Jamie said. "A gentleman should bow to a lady. And say somethin' nice. An' he should never yell at her. Even if she is a rag-headed ninny." He muttered the last sentence beneath his breath, and Conall pressed his finger to his lips, the urge to laugh nearly triumphing.

Mrs. Leslie's brows remained arched, but her lips twitched. "It sounds like a verra timely lesson. How nice of Sergeant Stewart." She turned toward Conall. "Sir, if you don't mind, I'll have a word wi' ye."

He dipped his head and turned to the side, indicating for her to lead the way.

Mrs. Leslie smiled at her son. "Run on home with ye, Jamie. I'll be along in a bit."

"Mam, must I?" His gaze moved to Conall, and Conall couldn't help but feel flattered that the lad wished to remain with him.

"Aye." She gave Jamie a smile that made her bright eyes twinkle, a welcome sight on such a bleak morning. "Mrs. Campbell told me she could use some help decoratin' her May bush." She winked. "An' ye ken, she's likely makin' bannock cakes already."

Jamie grinned, starting away and calling over his shoulder. "I'll save one for ye, Mam. And ye as well, Sergeant, if ye'd like."

Conall smiled at Mrs. Leslie's persuasion technique. When in doubt, mention food. "That would be fine, lad. I thank ye."

Jamie had only gone a few yards when he stopped and ran back to join them. He put his hand over his heart and dipped his head in a bow. "Goodbye, Mam." Then he turned and dashed up the street.

Conall grinned, a combination of amusement and affection, as he watched the lad go. He turned toward Mrs. Leslie and schooled his features when he saw that she wasn't smiling. He reached out his hand, offering to carry her basket, but she pulled it tighter into the bend of her arm and walked past.

Mrs. Leslie led him away from the front of the store to a space at the corner of the building where the two could speak without blocking any shoppers.

She set down the basket beneath the overhang of the roof and turned, her face serious and her eyes fiery. "Sergeant Stewart, I'll have ye know I'm a capable woman, able to feed and care for my own family. I'll not be beholden to anyone."

He studied her, trying to discern what had brought on her resentment. "Mrs. Leslie, any distress I've caused has been unintentional, I assure ye. And since I've no idea of what yer speakin', I'll ask ye to clarify if ye don't mind."

"The mutton, Sergeant." She folded her arms. "And the cheese and sausage ye've sent home with Jamie. Not to mention the milk, firewood, and mortar that ye were apparently just meaning to throw oot." She flipped her hand, and her cheeks reddened, but he thought she looked more ashamed than angry. She lifted her chin in a look of stubbornness. "I'll *not* accept yer charity."

Conall knew too well about the Highlanders' belief of giving assistance to those in need—and how very at odds it was with their stubborn natures. A paradoxical people that was both frustrating and wonderful. He'd seen people go without, both because they'd given their last to a person in need and because they'd refused to accept it when they were the ones wanting. He would wager if the tables were turned, Mrs. Leslie wouldn't hesitate to aid him, down to her last penny. But of course, he couldn't tell her that. She'd dig in her heels, and there was no budging a determined Scotswoman. Especially when 'twas her pride on the line.

He chose another tactic. "Mrs. Leslie, in the past five days since yer son's been workin' for me, he's repaired loose stones from every wall and buildin' on the property—most without me askin'. He's pulled weeds and underbrush from the orchard and paths, fed and cleaned up after the animals, and swept my storage barn. The lad works harder than some grown men I've known and always with a smile on his face." He saw her expression soften slightly. "I regard Jamie as a valuable employee, and I don't consider the payment unreasonable. But if you'd prefer me to settle upon a weekly sum, I'll discuss the particulars with the lad." He intended to do so anyway, but neither he nor Mrs. Ross could bear seeing the boy hungry, and convincing Jamie to take home food was no easy task. He was as stubborn as his mother.

Mrs. Leslie shifted, rubbing her arm. "I can take care of my son, sir."

"Aye, and ye're doin' a fine job. I can see he's been well raised."

She continued to look uncomfortable, her eyes turned away and her brows furrowed.

He touched her elbow to regain her attention. "Mrs. Leslie, I spent much o' the last ten years hungry: Marchin' through Spain in the winter, eatin' only what we could forage along the way; aboard a ship in the middle o' the South Sea, runnin' low on rations; then reachin' Sydneytowne and realizin' the convicts' supplies were scarce as well." He rubbed his cheek, noticing his skin was quite wet from standing in the drizzle so long. He hoped Mrs. Leslie's bonnet and thin coat were keeping her dry. "But I was an adult. 'Twas difficult, but I could manage." He blew out a breath. "I remember how 'twas bein' a young lad, always with an empty belly." He glanced in the direction Jamie had gone. "'Tis only a bit o' mutton or a chunk o' cheese, but the givin' of it is more for my own benefit, ye ken?"

She squinted, regarding him for a long moment, and he suddenly felt vulnerable at revealing so much to a person who was practically a stranger. Her bright-blue eyes held an intelligence that he found appealing. It might be very enjoyable to have a conversation with Mrs. Leslie if an opportunity ever arose when she wasn't angry with him.

She finally spoke. "As a mother, 'tis my worst fear, imaginin' my Jamie hungry. I thank ye for yer kindness to him." She spoke slowly as if thinking through the words. "I'm sorry for yer own sufferin', Sergeant. I'd not considered it."

His discomfort grew. What must this woman think of him? Sharing such personal stories, complainin' about his time at war when there were so many who suffered much worse and others who didna return at all. "I'm sorry. I should not have burdened ye wi' that."

She touched his arm, much as he'd done to her a moment earlier. "'Tis all right ye did."

Conall met her gaze, contemplating again how he enjoyed it, but just as quickly looked away, aware that his perceptions of Mrs. Leslie's bright eyes were approaching the realm of inappropriate, as they pertained to a married woman.

He cleared his throat and rocked back on his heels, changing the subject. "Jamie's finally deemed my apiary satisfactory. I suppose the next step is to fill it with bees. Is it yer husband I speak to about hirin' hives?"

Mrs. Leslie's brow wrinkled. "My husband?"

"Aye. He's the beekeeper, is he nay?"

"If 'tis bees yer wantin', ye speak to me." She folded her arms and raised her chin. "I have no husband."

Conall blinked. "Oh, I beg yer pardon. I thought . . . uh . . . yer the beekeeper?"

Her face tightened, and her stance became defensive. "Is it impossible to believe, Sergeant Stewart?"

His plan to have a conversation without angering her was already failing. He opened his mouth then closed it, unsure of what to say.

She continued to regard him, arms folded and one brow raised.

"Nay, 'tisn't impossible to believe. I apologize, I shouldna have assumed . . ."

"'Tis rather unconventional, I suppose, but there are few payin' positions in Dunaid for a woman." She pulled her coat tighter. "My father kept bees before he joined the Ninety-Second Regiment and sailed to France. When Jamie and I had to leave our home, 'twas all I knew to do." She paused as a pair of men approached leading horses toward the livery. She nodded a greeting.

The interruption seemed to shake Mrs. Leslie from her discomfort, and her attitude became more businesslike. "If you're worried about the bees, please inquire about my qualifications with the other farmers in the village. However, you'll nay find another beekeeper for miles."

She curtseyed and opened her mouth, he assumed to make a farewell, but Conall had one more matter to discuss with her, and in light of recent discoveries, the topic had become much more pleasant. He even felt a tingle of nervousness, which he took to be a good sign.

"Mrs. Leslie, I'll be needin' help gettin' my animals to the bonfire tonight. Would Jamie be available?"

She looked away but not before he saw hurt in her eyes. "I'll ask him, o' course, but I'm sure he'll not mind."

Conall wished he'd worded his request better. He'd intended to invite the both of them—he wouldn't separate a family on such a night—but he'd not had time to plan his words, not so soon after Mrs. Leslie's revelation about her marital status had left him reassessing his intentions. Her declaration had taken him aback, and he'd still not fully arranged his thoughts. He realized his hands were clenched and forced them to relax. "Mrs. Leslie . . ."

But she did not turn back to him. Instead, she waved at a pair walking toward them. Conall's housekeeper, Mrs. Ross, carried a sturdy-looking box on her hip. She was accompanied by a small woman with striking eyebrows. The two made a comical duo, one tall and stout and the other slender and short.

"I assume Mrs. Ross is preparin' yer house?" Mrs. Leslie asked. She lifted her basket and spoke without looking at him. Her voice sounded strained as if she were trying to find a comfortable topic.

"Aye, that she is. Flowers everywhere ye can imagine, and she and poor Brighid have been scrubbin' every inch o' the place since before dawn."

Mrs. Leslie gave a smart nod. "She'll do ye right."

The women joined them, and Mrs. Leslie turned to Conall to introduce her neighbor, a person Conall recognized from Sunday services as Mrs. Campbell. The older woman's brow rose as she looked him over, then she looked to Mrs. Leslie with a knowing expression and a small smirk.

"Nice to see the two o' ye this mornin'," Mrs. Leslie said, ignoring her neighbor's teasing with a slight shake of her head that conveyed a world of meaning and also suggested a close relationship. "I was just takin' the goat cheese to Mrs. Graham."

"I've some food for the feast as well." Mrs. Ross tipped her head toward the box she carried. "I'll deliver yer cheese if ye like. Then ye can hurry back to yer bairn."

"Thank you." Mrs. Leslie hooked the basket's handle over the housekeeper's ample arm.

"I left Jamie at home wi' the bannoch Bealltainn," Mrs. Campbell said. "I wonder if there will be any remainin' when I return?"

"I'm sure ye'll make up another batch before tonight, Dores." Mrs. Ross shifted the box on her hip, shaking her head. "Ye always make too much."

Mrs. Campbell waved her hands in the air dramatically. "I'll not have the village fallin' on hard times because the rituals weren't honored properly." She turned toward Conall. "And I suppose yer goin' to the bonfire tonight?"

"I wouldn't be missin' it fer anythin'," he said.

"'Tis wise." Mrs. Campbell nodded sagely. "Ye'd not want yer crops or animals to fall victim to disease." She looked back and forth between Conall and Mrs. Leslie. Her face took on a sly expression that nearly made Conall burst into laughter. "And doesna Aileen Leslie look bonny this mornin', Sergeant?"

Mrs. Leslie's eyes narrowed. She pursed her lips and shook her head again at Mrs. Campbell. This time more forcefully.

"Aye. Verra lovely," Conall said.

The older woman's brow bounced up and down, which Conall thought was both fascinating and rather unnerving. "I wonder, Aileen, have you anyone to walk wi' ye to the bonfire tonight?" She opened her eyes wide and pouted her lip as if hoping her question sounded innocent.

"Mrs. Campbell!" Mrs. Leslie hissed the words, trying to catch her friend's gaze. Unable to do so, she sighed and closed her eyes. Her cheeks flared red.

"I think Sergeant Stewart intends to go alone," Mrs. Ross put in with a shake of her head. "A pity, that." His housekeeper wore a mischievous look of her own.

Conall tipped his head to the side and tapped a finger on his chin, amused at the two women and their stratagems. "Well, now that ye mention it, I just had a thought." He put on an innocent expression of his own. "Mrs. Leslie, 'twould be an honor if ye'd accompany me to the bonfire tonight." He gave a small wink.

Her cheeks flamed even redder. She studied his expression for a moment, suspicion tightening her eyes. Finally, she nodded. "The honor would be mine, Sergeant."

Relief relaxed his shoulders. He was surprised to find he'd anticipated her answer with a fair bit of worry.

The older women smiled, apparently satisfied that their scheme had played out so well. They bid farewell and left, linking arms as they walked away.

Conall stood beside Mrs. Leslie, watching them go. "Until I saw the preparations today, I'd not realized how much I'm looking forward to the celebration."

She remained silent, but from the corner of his eye, he saw her pull her coat tighter. "Excuse me, Sergeant," she said. "I need to be leavin' now to get my house in order for the festival day." Her voice was soft and sounded uncertain. From the few short interactions he'd had with her, Conall knew uncertainty was not a characteristic typical to Mrs. Leslie.

"Until this afternoon then."

"Aye." She curtseyed without meeting his gaze and hurried away.

For the third time that morning, Conall stood beside the dry goods store and watched a figure walking up the muddy road. But Mrs. Leslie's departure left him feeling pleased and at the same time nervous. The unsettling feeling was one he'd not felt for a long time—or perhaps ever.

The two meddling women had released him from any vulnerability in offering to accompany Mrs. Leslie to the bonfire. If she'd refused, he could have played it off as only going along with their insinuation. But at the same time, their interference had given her the impression that their coercion was the only reason he'd asked.

Though she'd tried to hide it, he knew she felt slighted.

He rubbed his cheek, concerned as to how he'd handle the situation. After a moment, he smiled. 'Twas a good thing he'd a merry festival and a night of celebration to convince her otherwise. Conall tipped his hat to a passing group and whistled a merry tune as he crossed the road to the Stag and Thistle.

Chapter 7

AILEEN STOOD IN THE CENTER of her cottage and wiped her arm across her forehead as she surveyed the room. Over the last hours, she'd swept, scoured, and dusted every bit of the stone, wood, and dirt that made up her home. Even the goat's inside pen was spotless. The hearth was cleaned and fresh branches and peat placed inside, awaiting the holy fire. Yellow flowers adorned the sills of the two windows, and she'd woven a floral wreath for the door.

She opened it, glancing upward. Weak sunlight struggled to shine through the clouds. At least 'twasn't raining.

Looking to the north, she could see smoke from the field above the village and knew the Beltane fire had been lit. Mrs. Graham and Mrs. Ross would be supervising the feast preparations, and when Aileen closed her eyes, she imagined she could smell the mutton roasting. The thought alone made her mouth water. The men of the village would have created the fire in the most primitive manner possible, rubbing sticks or sparking rocks together to make the flames. This made the fire's protective power more potent. Mr. Graham, the minister, would no doubt have blessed the fire already. The combination of pagan customs and Christianity seemed at odds to some, but to her, it made perfect sense. The connection with the land and blessings from the heavens brought harmony to her world. For a moment, she watched the smoke rising in billows and knew the same sight was visible in wee hamlets and large cities throughout the country.

Stepping outside, she gave a smile as she looked at the May bush. She and Jamie had found a lovely flowering hawthorn tree high on a rocky hill, and they'd cut off a branch, thanking the sacred tree for the gift. Now the limb sat in a bucket outside the door with stones holding it upright. The mother and son had laughed as they tied on bits of string and painted shells to decorate it. She knew 'twasn't as fine as the bauble and ribbon-adorned bushes at many of the other houses, but her son's excitement had made the scraggly branch seem as magical as if 'twere made by faeries.

She surveyed the yard. Jamie had pulled out the dead plants from her flowerbeds and small garden. He'd turned under the soil as well as a wee boy with thin arms, bare feet, and a broken shovel was able, and now the lad was stuffing clumps of flowers between the skeps in the freshly swept winter apiary.

Aileen paused to watch him. Jamie's brow was furrowed in concentration as he attempted to make the flower bunches look as pleasing as possible. His face was smudged, his clothes dirty, and his curls wild.

In spite of his probable exhaustion from hours of labor, he grinned when he saw her. "Doesnae the yard look bonny, Mam?"

She couldn't help but smile in return. "Finer than any in the village."

Jamie brushed off his hands and gave a satisfied nod as he looked around the property.

Aileen thought of what Sergeant Stewart had said earlier that day, and she could see precisely what he meant. Jamie was a hard worker and took pleasure in a job well done. The sight melted her heart with a combination of love and pride.

The memory of the earlier conversation sent a flush up her neck. She felt humiliated by the sergeant's reluctant invitation. Of course the man didn't want to go to the festival with her. She'd hardly said a word to him that hadn't been accusatory or angry. The embarrassment spread, making her stomach turn sour. Perhaps she could send word, tell the sergeant she was ill, but of course, she couldn't miss the bonfire. She rubbed her eyes. Why had Dores and Mrs. Ross been so nosey?

"What else needs to be cleaned, Mam?" Jamie asked, leaving the hives and carrying the garden tools toward the house.

"Only ourselves, mo croí. Come inside."

Jamie refused her help to wash and dress but did allow her to rinse soap from his hair, pouring water from the bucket. He wore the new trousers and shirt she'd finished sewing just the night before. There'd been enough fabric for her to make a vest, which he delightedly put on, standing tall and puffing out his chest. "I look like a fine gentleman, don't I, Mam?"

"Aye. The verra handsomest, to be sure." His clothing made him look much older than he had a few moments earlier, and the sight made her eyes misty.

"I'll be back soon, Mam. I'm off t' admire myself in Mrs. Campbell's looking glass."

She couldn't help her smile as she watched him go. If only he'd a pair of shoes . . . But 'twould have to wait until the honey came in.

While Jamie was gone, Aileen washed herself and dressed. She shivered, hair wet and no fire to help it dry, but she shook it out and ran a comb through the damp strands before tying it back.

She pulled on her blue Sunday gown, wishing it were new and fashionable instead of practical and homespun. In the bundle of clothing from Dores, Aileen had found a scrap of lace that looked like it had once been part of a curtain. It was just long enough to wrap over her shoulders and pin at her neck.

Aileen glanced around the room once more, making sure everything was in place. Their sleeping pallet was rolled up tidily in the corner, and the dishes she was taking to the feast were tucked into a sack beside the door. She emptied the soapy water and hung up the washrag. Satisfied that the cottage was ready, she smoothed back her damp hair, tucked it beneath her bonnet, then repinned the lace beneath her collarbone a few more times, fussing over how the folds fell and wondering why on earth she felt so nervous. Sergeant Stewart wouldn't notice or care one bit whether she had a new collar. He was surely annoyed at the entire arrangement.

The sun was dropping lower, shadows from the windows lengthening over the hard-packed floor. Sergeant Stewart could arrive at any time. She decided to hurry across the road to fetch Jamie and perhaps have a glance herself in Mrs. Campbell's looking glass.

Aileen opened the door then gave a yelp and jumped back in surprise.

Sergeant Stewart stood in the doorway, his hand raised to knock. He drew back, a smile spreading over his face. "I beg yer pardon."

Aileen had only seen the sergeant smile a few times, and she didn't think the expression had ever been directed at her. She liked the way lines creased merrily from the corners of his eyes and how the left side of his mouth rose before the right. A quiver moved through her stomach, and she looked away to hide her blush. She was behavin' like a fool, acting as if he were here on a social call.

Sergeant Stewart wore a plaid kilt and leather sporran, traditional attire for the festival. The plaid at his shoulder was fastened with a brooch shaped like a leaping stag.

He looked very handsome indeed. Aileen directed her eyes to the ground, reminding herself that he wasn't actually here on his own preference. "Welcome, Sergeant," she said, stepping outside. She motioned with her chin toward the house across the road. "I was just on my way to fetch Jamie from Mrs. Campbell's." The thought of her neighbor and the woman's interference this morning made Aileen's neck heat again, and she made a point not to meet the sergeant's crinkling eyes as she passed.

When Aileen lifted her gaze, she saw Dores carrying a wooden bowl across the street with Jamie in tow.

Jamie grinned at Sergeant Stewart, and Dores appraised the man from head to toe in a manner that, even in a rural Highland village, was scandalous. She winked at Aileen, her left brow bouncing up and down.

Aileen had a sudden urge to run back into the cottage and hide until Samhain, at least.

"Good evenin', Mam." Jamie put his hand over his heart and bowed. "Ye look verra bonny."

"Thank you," Aileen said.

"That she does, lad," Sergeant Stewart said. "An ye look a true gentleman yerself."

Jamie grinned and straightened his vest.

"An' yer all ready to go then." Dores held out the bowl of milk.

Aileen took it then handed it to Jamie, grateful for something to look at besides her shameful neighbor or reluctant escort.

Dores pointed and waved her finger toward a spot beside the door. "Go on, lad, put it just there. The Fair Folk will be out in force t'night, returned from their winter hideaways." She slipped a string with a small biscuit hanging from it over the boy's head. "There now, and a wee pinch o' salt in yer pocket will keep ye safe from any mischief."

Jamie smiled good-naturedly as the old woman produced a bag and poured some salt into his pocket. He tucked the biscuit beneath his shirt then turned toward Sergeant Stewart. "Are we ready then?"

"Aye. We'll fetch my livestock then return for yer animals."

"We've only the goat," Jamie said. "And the cat, if we can find her."

"And yer bees?" Conall asked.

"They'll not abide the cold," Aileen said.

He nodded and lifted his elbow toward her. "Shall we then?"

She reached to take his arm, but Dores stepped between them. "Aileen, where's yer shawl? Ye'll not want to be catchin' a chill."

Aileen knew any argument would be futile; besides, her hair was still wet, and the spring nights were far from warm. Dores meant well—most of the time anyway. Aileen stepped back into the house and grabbed both Jamie's jacket and her mother's plaid. She'd not wanted to cover up her new collar, but of course, she was acting silly. She left the sack of dishes by the door to fetch as they passed through the village.

When she walked outside, she found Jamie laughing. Sergeant Stewart was backing away from Dores, holding up his hands in protest as she patted him, searching for a pocket. She finally sprinkled a bit of salt into the waist of his kilt. "Well, 'twill have to do, I suppose." She wagged a finger in his face. "Ye'll need to be especially careful tonight, Sergeant, struttin' around lookin' as handsome as Rob Roy. I'd not put it past an enchantress tryin' to lure ye away, or even the queen o' the faeries herself."

Aileen could have sworn she saw a bit of red in the sergeant's cheeks as he grinned at Dores, white teeth flashing. Of course he enjoyed flattery. What man didn't? She folded the jacket and plaid, holding them against her. "Thank you, Mrs. Campbell. I'm sure Sergeant Stewart kens to be vigilant when it comes to enchantresses." She started up the road toward the sergeant's house.

Behind her, she heard Jamie and Sergeant Stewart bid Dores farewell, and a moment later, the two joined her.

Once they'd gone a sufficient distance, the sergeant let out a hearty laugh. "Yer neighbor. She's quite . . ."

"Eccentric?" Aileen offered.

"Aye, there's a good word for it." He continued to chuckle, reaching for the bundle she held and folding the coat and shawl over his arm.

Aileen felt defensive of her friend. "Dores has her quirks, but she means well."

Conall nodded. "I've known my share of meddlesome relatives—though I've not seen any o' them for more than a decade. Hearts in the right place but ofttimes, their methods are . . . frustratin'." He laughed again and glanced at Aileen. "I can see that she acts out o' love. She's concerned for yer well-being and Jamie's. The two o' ye are auld friends?"

"Aye. We're from the same village. We came to Dunaid together. Mrs. Campbell, Jamie, and me, after our homes were . . . gone." She stuttered the last words and walked faster, heart pounding. The conversation had moved too close to the topics she avoided.

Jamie ran ahead as they turned up the path.

Conall took Aileen's hand and tucked it beneath his arm, resting it in the bend of his elbow. He slowed their pace. "Mrs. Leslie, I meant to tell ye before, ye look truly—"

"Mam, did ye ken Sergeant Stewart has three coos?" Jamie ran back to join them. "One is yellow, and the others are brown—a big one and a wee one. The wee one has no horns. None o' them have names, but Sergeant Stewart said I could call them whatever I like. I call the wee one Barney." He took Aileen's hand and pulled her from the path toward the side of the house.

She released her hold on Sergeant Stewart, following Jamie around the house to the byres where the animals were penned. Garlands of yellow flowers decorated the enclosures.

Conall handed over her clothing. He opened one gate, leading out two horses. One was bridled, and the other only had a rope around his neck. Both animals had bouquets tied in their manes.

Aileen nodded to herself as she wrapped her plaid around her shoulders. Mrs. Ross had done well.

Jamie kept talking. "The gray horse pulls the wagon and the plough, and the brown horse is for ridin'. She's a mare—that means a lady horse. Her name is Aranella, but Sergeant Stewart calls her Nellie."

Sergeant Stewart led the animals toward them.

Aileen cringed as they drew near, but she stood still, hands clenched at her sides, hoping the sergeant wouldn't see her apprehension. She'd no experience with horses, and up close, the animals were so large.

Sergeant Stewart stopped. He handed the plow horse's rope to Jamie then brought the mare toward Aileen. "Nay to worry. They're both as gentle as kittens." He spoke softly and took her hand, bringing her a few steps closer and standing behind her. He lifted her hand to rest on the horse's shoulder. "Yer quite safe wi' Nellie."

Sergeant Stewart's hand was large and warm, and his breath tickled her neck, giving her a shiver. Despite the large animal looming before her, Aileen felt calm. She nodded, glancing up at the man. His eyes were deep brown, and the brows above were pulled together and upward, furrowing lines across his forehead. The calm feeling left, replaced by a jittery sensation.

Aileen pulled her hand away and stepped to the side. She looked to where Jamie stood holding the plow horse's lead rope and patting the bridge of its nose. She took the reins from the sergeant.

One side of the sergeant's mouth pulled up in a smile. He gave a nod then moved away to open the other pen and lead out the cows. The three shaggy-haired beasts were tied in a line, floral bouquets stuck into the knots of the lead rope. The larger animals had long wavy hair covering their eyes, but the wee one's fur was curly, making it look soft and fluffy. *Barney*, Aileen thought, smiling at Jamie's name for the calf.

"Get on wi' ye, Jamie," Conall called. "Lead the way."

Jamie and the gray horse started toward the road.

Conall motioned with his head for Aileen to go next.

She took a step, and the horse moved, sending a burst of panic through her.

"Just pull on the reins. She'll follow ye," Conall said.

"Aye. Tha's what I'm afraid of," she grumbled. But she'd not kept her voice as quiet as she'd thought because Conall laughed.

"I'd never have taken ye as one to be afraid of anythin', Mrs. Leslie."

"I'm not afraid." She shot him a glare and tugged on the reins. The horse followed at a docile pace, and after a bit of trial and error, she settled into a rhythm—neither walking too fast and pulling the animal nor too slow to let the horse overtake her.

They walked in procession up the lane from the sergeant's house, and once they reached the wider road to the village, he stepped beside her, the cows following obediently. "I told ye. Naught to fear with auld Nellie."

He kept his eyes on Jamie as he spoke, and Aileen was grateful to him for allowing her son to feel confident but keeping a close watch on him. She glanced back at the horse and the string of cows.

"She likes ye, does Nellie," Conall said.

Aileen sniffed, giving him a flat look. "Horses don't evaluate people. They jes' do as they're told."

He made a clicking sound, shaking his head. "And that's where you're wrong, Mrs. Leslie. Animals are excellent judges o' character." He pointed forward with his chin, toward Jamie. "Look there. That auld plow horse would follow Jamie anywhere. He kens the lad'll not lead him astray. Trusts him." He nodded. "Nellie sees the same in ye."

She could feel his eyes upon her but couldn't quite lift her gaze to meet his. Her thoughts and emotions were all jumbled together:

pleasure at his compliment, embarrassment that he'd seen her afraid, gratitude at the care he took of Jamie, and though she was ashamed to admit it, resentment at how he'd captured her son's admiration so fully. Luckily, she was spared the need to respond when they arrived at her house. She left the horse with Conall and fetched the sack of dishes and the goat, and they continued through the village.

Jamie grinned and waved at people they passed, and Aileen's confusing emotions returned. She felt petty for resenting the sergeant's influence on her son, especially when Jamie was so happy and well behaved as a result. But she couldn't help feeling that *she* should be the person to bring out the best in the lad, not this person they hardly knew.

They drew near to the field and walked to a large, temporary enclosure that had been erected for the event. Aileen patted Nellie's nose. "There ye go," she murmured and turned over the reins to Conall.

Once the animals were safely inside the corral, Conall rubbed his hands together, a smile growing on his face. "Och, how I've missed this," he said. "Longed for it, truly. This feeling of a community workin' together, celebratin' together. There's nothin' like it in the world. Nothin' at all." He took the sack from Aileen and offered his arm, leading her toward where the feast was being served. Jamie ran ahead.

"I imagine ye worked together wi' other soldiers, surely," Aileen said.

"Aye, but a group of fightin' men plannin' an attack or foragin' for food, even celebratin' a victory . . . 'Tisn't the same as families gatherin' to honor auld traditions. Nay, this, 'tis somethin' special. And I'd not known until I was so far away that my heart ached for it."

Aileen was surprised that he would speak so sincerely. 'Twasn't usual for men to reveal their emotions so openly.

Conall seemed to have the same thought. He glanced at her, and his eyes tightened in a slight wince. He cleared his throat and patted his stomach. "And o' course, nothin' compares to Highland fare."

"Yer spoiled," Aileen said. "Mrs. Ross is the finest cook in the county."

The corners of his mouth pulled down, and he nodded solemnly, though a twinkle remained in his eye. "Aye, that she may be."

At the bonfire, the three filled their plates: haggis, mutton, herring, stuffed eels—all of it prepared skillfully under the direction of Mrs. Ross and Mrs. Graham. Aileen saw Mrs. Ross slide a few extra sausages onto Jamie's plate.

The trio found a spot to sit, a flat patch of ground close enough to feel the fire's warmth, and listened as Jamie chatted between mouthfuls of food. The meal was delicious, the food plentiful, and the company . . . Aileen peeked to the side. Perhaps 'twas the casual atmosphere or the cupful of warm caudle, but at the moment, she felt rather happy with her companion. She watched the sergeant scoop up some of the moist, crumbly haggis. He chewed slowly, closing his eyes and letting out a small moan.

Aileen laughed. "I dinna think I've ever seen a person so taken wi' haggis."

Conall opened his eyes, looking surprised.

Aileen blushed, wishing she'd acted a bit more refined, constraining her mirth within ladylike bounds.

He smirked and sighed dramatically. "Absence makes the reunion all the more sweet."

"Sweet, is it? There's a word I've never heard associated wi' Highland puddin'."

He took a drink and opened his mouth to reply but stopped short when a shadow fell upon them.

They looked up, and Conall rose to his feet, shaking hands with the minister. "Good to see ye, Mr. Graham." Jamie stood as well, and the minister shook his hand then bowed a greeting to Aileen.

A slender man, the minister stood much smaller than Conall. He put his hands together in front of his chest. "I came to thank ye again on behalf of the village for bringin' the sheep. We've nay had such a fine feast for Beltane in all my years. 'Twill make Dunaid all the more fortunate come harvest season."

Conall inclined his head. "Of course yer welcome. And I thank ye, sir, for yer fine sermon on Sunday. . . ."

Aileen didn't listen any further. Her mind whirled. Sergeant Stewart had brought the sheep? An entire sheep? 'Twould have cost more than most families in Dunaid saw in a year. The lightness in her heart dissipated, and her cheeks heated in embarrassment. Had she really thought . . . ? She shook her head, and her gaze moved to their dishes on her mother's homespun plaid. Conall's painted porcelain plate looked like it belonged in a palace compared to her rough wooden one.

As the men spoke, Sergeant Stewart shifted, the buckles on his well-made boots glinting in the firelight. She pulled in her legs tightly beneath her, making certain her own worn boots were out of sight beneath her skirts. She felt foolish, wearing an old bit of curtain around her neck and thinking the sergeant would be at all impressed with her. Had she truly thought he considered her as any more than a case for charity? She was deceiving herself to think he might have actually wanted her company. The food she'd eaten felt heavy in her stomach.

When the minister took his leave and Jamie hurried away to join his friends, Sergeant Stewart must have sensed her discomfort. He asked a few leading questions, but Aileen gave vague answers, evading his attempts to start a conversation.

After a moment, he set down his utensils. "Mrs. Leslie." His tone had changed, sounding much lower and more serious. Conall remained quiet until she looked up. His eyes searched her face. "I'm glad ye agreed to accompany me today."

The embarrassment was joined by a hot surge of anger. "And why is that, Sergeant? So the auld ladies o' the village would stop pesterin' ye?"

"Nay. It has nothin' to do wi' them. Or anyone else fer that matter. I'm glad because I wanted a chance to become acquainted wi' ye."

Aileen didn't respond. She looked down at her hands.

"You don't believe me." It wasn't a question.

"It's quite gentlemanly o' ye to say, but we both ken that's not why ye asked."

"An' yer sayin' 'twas because o' the pair o' interferin' hens?"

She pursed her lips. "Yer sayin' 'twasn't? Please, Sergeant. I've not delicate feelin's in need o' protection." Blowing a breath out of her nose, she started to gather up the plates. "And I certainly don't need yer charity."

"Och, an' we're back to this again." Conall laid a hand on her arm, stilling her movements and taking the dishes from her. "Let me ask ye, Mrs. Leslie. Do ye ever take honey to yer neighbor, Mrs. Campbell? Or walk with her to kirk of a Sunday? Or even just stop by for a visit?"

Her arm felt hot where he held it. She pulled away, folding her hands in her lap. "Aye, of course"

"And would ye say 'tis charity?"

She thought for a moment before answering. "Nay," she said finally.

"And why is that? Why is it different if I do the same wi' ye or Jamie?"

"Because Dores and I are auld friends. I care for her. 'Tisn't charity when ye care for someone."

His expression turned thoughtful, eyes squinting and the corners of his mouth turning down as he considered what she said. "Aye. I see what ye mean."

She looked up at him, surprised by the sincerity in his voice. He wasn't arguing nor was he angry. He seemed . . . thoughtful.

Conall slipped a hand between hers, lifting one away to hold as he spoke. "Today's Beltane. 'Tis the first day o' summer—a magical night, a new beginning. Perhaps that's what we need, Mrs. Leslie, you and I." He tugged on her hand, making her look up at him. "I realize our association started out, uh, less than amiable, but I hope we'll move past it. I want us to be friends and for ye not to feel like anytime I'm friendly to ye or Jamie that I'm doin' it out o' pity or because some auld wives convinced me to."

His eyes were wide, hopeful, and the sight made her skip a breath. She gave a small squeeze then pulled away her hand, afraid he'd feel it shaking. "I'll think aboot it, Sergeant."

He smiled slowly, the left side of his mouth rising before the right, and crinkles fanned from the sides of his twinkling eyes. "Ye do that, lass."

Chapter 8

As the evening cooled, the people of Dunaid began to draw closer to the warmth of the fire. Conall stood and helped Mrs. Leslie to her feet. He shook out the plaid shawl and placed it over her shoulders.

Aileen pulled it tight then took his offered his arm, and the pair followed Jamie around the bonfire. Conall noticed the darkness seemed to make some people speak in quieter voices and others grow brash and rowdy. A few of the younger men, no doubt emboldened by liquor, goaded each other into jumping over the edges of the fire, and Conall smiled, remembering doing the same as a youth. Usually the object of such a performance was to impress a young lady. He smiled, glancing at his companion, imagining how very *un*impressed she would be with such a display. Aileen was a practical woman, and that sensibility was something he found appealing. He disliked the games some women played. With Aileen Leslie, he did not anticipate confused guessing or misunderstood intentions. She was reserved with her emotions, but he did not think her deceptive.

Since their conversation during the meal, he'd noticed that Mrs. Leslie had become thoughtful. She was proud, he knew, especially when it came to taking care of her family, but he'd hoped that his words had softened her heart toward him, even if 'twas just a bit. Perhaps they could even develop a friendship. The idea made him hopeful. They made their way to a quieter part of the field where the majority of the villagers were gathered. Around him, Conall could hear murmured conversations. Deep tones, loud exclamations, and guttural sounds formed at the back of the throat—this is how language was supposed to sound, he thought. Not the rapid chatter of Spanish or the nasal tones of French or even the precise, clipped words of English. The Scottish tongue was warm and hearty, filled with feeling. The language was as rich as the land it came from, and throughout his travels, he'd missed it more than he could have imagined.

A boy called to Jamie, and he ran to a group of children, giving a gentlemanly bow to the young lassies.

Conall smiled, pleased.

Aileen glanced up at him, offering a wee smirk, which he took as approval of his advice to the lad.

Not straying far from Jamie and the other children, they continued moving among the villagers, greeting friends and neighbors. Conall noticed Aileen shiver, and he adjusted their path, moving them closer to the fire as they walked.

Mrs. Campbell was distributing the bannoch Bealltainn, oatcakes baked especially for the festival. As had generations of Celts before them, they saved one portion to leave for the faery spirits, another portion to feed to the animals, and then ate the rest with a special caudle. Conall had only known the residents of the villagers for a few weeks, but the traditions were dear, familiar, and the sharing of them gave him a feeling of belonging to something greater than himself.

Noticing that people were moving toward the livestock pen, Conall called Jamie over. He took Aileen's arm and led her and the lad to the corral, finding his animals and their goat.

The three of them joined the other villagers, leading the livestock in a slow circle around the bonfire. They made certain the smoke blew over the beasts then fed them a bit of oatcake and sprinkled cooled ashes on their fur.

Conall knew the upperclass Englishmen he'd served with would consider the rite archaic, arguing that a fire could not possibly have protective powers. But the educated British would never understand the heartfelt solemnity and faith that went into such a practice.

With the sounds of animals jostling, the smell of smoke and fur and ash, the memories from his childhood were strong and brought with them such a range of emotion that it caught him off guard. Conall shook his head, rubbing his eyes. When he opened them, Aileen was studying him. She turned away, bending down to touch a mound of cooled ash.

Conall stood near, watching Aileen daub ashes on Jamie's cheeks. The lad did the same for his mother then turned to Conall, holding up blackened fingertips. Conall bent down and allowed Jamie to smudge some ash onto his face, scratching over the whiskers of his cheeks. The lad gave a serious nod. "There now, Sergeant Stewart. 'Twill keep ye in good health."

Conall straightened and met Aileen's gaze. She reached up and brushed her fingers over his cheekbone, rubbing in the ash, then she pulled her hand away quickly, as if she'd acted without thinking, and returned her attention to Nellie.

He stood still, his cheek tingling where she'd touched him. Was he reacting to the memory of the custom? Or to the person who'd performed it? Had Mrs. Leslie been ensuring that her son did a thorough job, or was there more behind her action? The cattle moved restlessly, tugging on the rope, and moving to tend to them gave Conall a private moment to think.

A warmth spread through him. The feeling of belonging grew stronger, not only as to fellowship among the people of the village but the comfort of being with family. He shook his head. 'Twasn't *his* family, and he'd do well to remember it. He was letting the magic of Beltane affect him. "Jamie lad, we can leave the horses penned for a few more hours, but the cattle should be returned to the farm soon. Will ye go wi' me?"

"Aye, Sergeant."

"And Mrs. Leslie . . ." He spoke in a businesslike tone. Tending to practical matters did wonders to dispel the distractions that were taking over his thoughts. "Do ye mind waitin' here for a bit?"

He and Jamie left Aileen in the company of Mrs. Campbell and Mrs. Ross, and made the trip through the village. He was glad the boy wore a coat. Once they left the warmth of the fire, the air was damp and chilled. They walked through the darkened village—houses gloomy and vacant, awaiting their owners' return from the festival with holy fire to relight the hearths and candles.

They walked quickly and delivered the animals to their pens, but the trip still took the better part of an hour. The entire time, Jamie remained uncharacteristically quiet. On the return journey, the lad walked with his head down, hands in his pockets.

Conall slowed. "Is there somethin' botherin' ye, lad?"

He shook his head. "I'm just ponderin'." He glanced up at Conall. "Sergeant, how does it work? How does the fire protect the animals and farms and people?" His nose wrinkled, and he chewed on his lip. "Mam says 'tis the earth and heavens workin' together to look after us."

"Aye, I suppose she's right in that."

"But people still die, and crops too. And animals get ill, even with the blessin' and the ash. Does it mean the fire failed? Or that the people were wicked?"

Conall wasn't prepared for this line of questioning. He'd no experience teachin' doctrine to a child. Scratching beneath his ear, he considered before he answered. "I don't think it means either.

'Tisn't always a person's fault if bad things happen. Nor is God to blame, nor the fire." He glanced down and saw Jamie was watching him, listening closely. "We must have faith and do our best to be moral, honest people. And if misfortune does befall us, we pray for God's mercy, and we help each other. 'Tisn't enough to count on a fire or the Lord to keep everything in order. The most important thing is to care for others and to help them, ye ken? Thinkin' bad things happen because of somethin' we did or didn't do is useless." He stopped walking, turning to look Jamie in the eye, willing the boy to understand the weight of what he was saying. "Blamin' ourselves or others leads only to remorse and pain." Swallowing, he realized how often he'd done the very thing he was preachin' against.

Jamie nodded slowly. "And 'tis important to be part o' a village, like Dunaid, where we all watch over one another."

"Aye, Jamie. Sometimes that's how the Lord looks after us, through each other." Conall hoped his answer was reassuring. It sounded exactly like something his da would have said. And it sounded exactly like advice he himself should follow. But knowin' something and doing it were two very different things.

They walked in silence, each lost in their thoughts until Jamie jerked up his head. Conall darted a look around to find what had startled the child.

"Do ye hear the music?" Jamie pointed ahead. "There'll be dancin' now."

The droning sound of the pipes reached them. The two grinned at each other and quickened their steps.

They found Mrs. Leslie speaking to Davy MacKay and his wife, Catriona. A short woman with a square face, Mrs. MacKay wore a scarf around her hair. She was a cheerful person with gentle manners and a pleasant smile, much like her husband. Conall greeted the women with a bow. "Good evening, Davy. Mrs. MacKay."

"Good evenin' to ye, Sergeant," Davy said. "Good evenin', Jamie." He smiled as the boy followed Conall's example and bowed to the ladies. "From what yer ma's told me, ye've a right clever touch wi' the horses, lad. Perhaps ye should come work with me in the livery."

Jamie looked up at Conall, his expression uncertain.

Conall shook his head, placing a hand on the boy's shoulder. "Aye, and true 'tis. But the lad's far too happy workin' for me. I'll not have ye poach my best employee."

Davy gave Conall a wink and looked back at Jamie. He shook his head, clicking his tongue. "Poor Jamie. Ye must get tired o' hearin' the sergeant's war tales, surely?"

Jamie shook his head, eyes bright. "Not a'tall, Mr. MacKay."

"Well, more's the pity." He sighed. "My own stories o' tendin' animals and mendin' plows are much more captivatin'."

Catriona swatted her husband, rolling her eyes at his teasing. "And how are ye enjoin' Dunaid, Sergeant?'

"A lovely place with fine people. I like it verra much, Mrs. MacKay."

"Davy said ye've only taken the house for a few months. He worries ye'll be off once the harvest is in."

From the corner of his eye, Conall saw Mrs. Leslie turn toward him. He wondered if the news was a surprise to her. And if it was, how did she feel about it? "Aye, well . . . 'twill depend on what I discover about where my family's gone to, ye ken. Mr. Graham helped me to contact a minister in Fort William, a Mr. Douglas. And I'm waiting on word. Otherwise, I believe I'd happily settle in Dunaid forever."

"Well, we're glad to have ye bide here as long as ye will," she said. "'Tis nice to have the auld house occupied, and the mutton . . . Well, none o' us are complainin' aboot a full belly, now are we?"

He glanced at Aileen but couldn't discern anything in her expression. She simply watched him. "Leavin' the Highlands . . ."

He sighed, feeling an ache at the thought. "'Twouldn't be a simple decision, to be sure."

Catriona gave an understanding nod.

Davy winced and rubbed his knee above the wooden leg. "Och, if ye'll excuse us, I'll be needin' to sit a spell." He motioned toward the music and the more boisterous partygoers. "Jamie, if ye've a mind to join the dancers, I'm headin' in that direction. And perhaps Mrs. MacKay will need a partner, bein' that her husband's not disposed to doin' a jig. "

Jamie looked up at his mother, eyes hopeful.

"We'll keep an eye on him," Mrs. MacKay said. Once Aileen nodded her permission, Catriona took both Davy and Jamie by the arms and headed toward the dancers.

Conall and Aileen watched them go. The field wasn't large enough to worry about Jamie getting lost, but away from the bonfire, the night was dark and cold with folks consuming ale and getting into all kinds of mischief. Conall wondered if Mrs. Leslie was concerned about Jamie finding trouble.

He thought they could move closer to keep a better watch over the lad and turned to propose the idea to Aileen when a gunshot cracked in the night.

Sweat broke out over his skin. Conall jerked around to pull Mrs. Leslie to the ground, but he got no farther than laying a hand on her arm before his mind registered the source of the noise. A log snapping in the fire. He closed his eyes to calm his pounding heart and dispel the battlefield terror that had come over him. He could hear screams and cannons but knew the sounds were no more than memory. At least the rational part of him knew. Another part—the same that fed his nightmares—was frantic to take cover.

"Sergeant?"

He felt Mrs. Leslie's hand cover his and looked down to where he still held her arm. Releasing his grip, he winced. "I beg your pardon. I was—I was just caught off guard, startled for a moment."

Instead of backing away, Aileen stepped closer. She took his hand, which he realized was still shaking. Conall felt mortified. What must she think of him? He steeled himself, pushing the memories away and blowing out a breath. "Truly, I apologize. I—"

"I ken."

He looked into her face, and instead of pity or disgust, he saw understanding.

"It happens suddenly, for no reason." She spoke softly, holding his hand in both of hers. "Sometimes weeks will pass without giving it a thought, then a smell or a sound, and it's like bein' back there again."

He breathed heavily, studying her hands as his heartbeat calmed. Aileen's hands were small, the nails were short and her fingers calloused. Not a gentlewoman's hands, but those of a person who'd seen hardship, hands that labored each day to provide for her son.

She continued softly, "'Twas more than eight years ago, and the memories are still there, no matter how hard I try to forget." She looked up at him. "Do ye have the dreams too, Sergeant?"

"Aye." He nodded, wondering what 'twas that had happened to Aileen Leslie. Davy had told him the villagers came from all over the Highlands. Some after suffering terrible ordeals when they were driven from their homes. Eight years ago . . . Jamie must have been an infant or perhaps yet to be born. What kind of monster expels a young mother from her home? What had happened to her husband? Had he gone to the war? A number of scenarios moved through his thoughts, each worse than the previous. But he wouldn't ask. He had a feeling she'd already revealed more than she was comfortable with. He looked up and held her gaze. "And how do ye overcome it?"

"I've Jamie. Without him to care for . . ." She let the words trail off. She dropped his hands but didn't move away. Pulling the shawl tighter, she shivered. "And what about yerself, Sergeant? What keeps yer dreadful memories at bay?"

He shrugged. "The farm. I toil each day until I'm too tired to dream."

The corners of her mouth turned down, and she nodded. An expression he'd seen before when she was considering something he said.

She shivered again and took a step close to the fire. Turning her head slightly to the side, she spoke, keeping her gaze on the flames. "Davy tells me ye didna ken aboot the evictions until ye returned home." Her voice was a bit louder but not less concerned. "I'm sorry. Must have been devastatin' for ye."

He nodded, moving toward the warmth to stand beside her. "Aye. But I wager 'twasn't as devastatin' as experiencing it firsthand." He wanted to know more but had to tread carefully, fearing she'd close off completely if he asked questions that were too personal. "Where was yer home, Mrs. Leslie?"

She stiffened, and he cursed himself for not exercising more caution. "Northeast of here," she finally said.

The Duchess of Sutherland's lands. He didn't ask more.

After a long, uncomfortable moment, Aileen turned from the fire. She wore a smile that seemed a bit forced. "And where did ye serve, Sergeant? Ye mentioned Spain and Australia."

He was grateful for the change of subject. The question was asked in a casual tone, and he answered in the same manner. "I was mostly at sea, assigned to one ship or another. I spent a bit of time in the Mediterranean and Greek isles, but once I served on the *Bellerophon*, Captain Seymour requested I be assigned to the ship until the end of the war. He primarily sailed convict vessels to New South Wales."

She nodded. "My father served as well."

The way she said it, her voice low and shaking, told him all he needed to know. Like so many others, Mrs. Leslie's father hadn't returned from the war. One would think such news wouldn't affect a person after hearing it so often, but each time he thought of a dead comrade or heard tales of brave men who gave their lives for the Crown, Conall felt an ache. "I'm sorry," he said. "And yer mother?"

"Died when I was six. A fever and sickness o' the lungs."

Conall nodded, knowing without her saying that she didna want to speak o' her parents anymore.

They remained, side by side, watching the fire. The silence wasn't uneasy, but Conall still wished he could think of something to say.

Mrs. Leslie adjusted her shawl. Was she cold? Now that he thought of it, she'd shivered enough during the evening that he should have taken her home hours ago or at least found her a warmer wrap.

He nudged her arm with his. "Come, lass, if yer ready to leave, I'll fetch the horses and Jamie."

Chapter 9

THE DAY AFTER THE BELTANE festival, Aileen woke Jamie early. "Come, mo croí. We've hives to deliver." She sat for a moment in the faint dawn light, rubbing her neck. Her head and body ached. She'd stayed out far too late the night before, and scrubbed the house for hours as well. It would probably take a day or so to recover.

In spite of the chill, she made herself rise and dress quickly. She set out oatcakes and hurried outside to milk the goat, pulling on both her coat and the shawl. Even with the fire in the hearth, the cottage was cold. She hoped she'd warm herself by moving.

She and Jamie ate a hasty breakfast and loaded the skeps into the small handcart. The bees would be much calmer in the cool morning hours. But that wasn't the only reason she wanted to hurry. She'd prefer to deliver the hives to the orchard and move on before Sergeant Stewart awoke.

'Twasn't that she didn't want to see Conall again but perhaps not so soon, not until she gave herself time to think and come to a better understanding of why she'd allowed herself to be so vulnerable in the man's presence.

She'd contemplated the question as they'd walked home from the bonfire and late into the night as she lay on her pallet, trying to slow her thoughts so she could sleep.

The conclusion she'd arrived at was two-fold. 'Twas a magical night, Beltane, a night when the rules of etiquette were relaxed and the earth celebrated life and hope. In all her years, she'd never attended the festival with a man. She must have let the situation go to her head. The other reason she'd come up with was that it had been a relief to speak to someone who understood how she felt: the nightmares, the panic-filled memories. Sergeant Stewart had experienced horrific things as well. Since Mrs. Campbell believed that dwelling on the past only prevented a person from moving forward, Aileen hadn't told anyone about her terrors. The feeling of being able to share it with another person . . . it had felt like a weight lifting from her shoulders.

But the answers seemed lacking, and she didn't like the uncertainty of it all. The truth of the matter was, in her desire for empathy, she'd said things she'd promised herself never to speak of, and to a person she hardly knew. Sergeant Conall Stewart had a way of making her wish to confide in him. She felt as if he took her words seriously and would never betray her trust, but she couldn't risk speaking to him of her past, no matter how compassionate he seemed, not with Jamie's safety in the balance. Avoidance of the man seemed the surest way to be certain she'd not reveal any more.

Her memory traveled back to that night in the cold kirkyard: blood in the snow, the smell of their homes burning, a baby's cries, and Sorcha's face growing pale as she became too weak to even hold Aileen's hand. "Don' let Balfour find the lad." Her voice had been little more than a scratchy whisper. "Promise me."

She swallowed past a tight throat as she remembered giving a promise, holding the small body against her own to keep the infant warm, and watching her dearest friend lay back her head into the snow, never to raise it again.

Jamie walked around the handcart and took his usual place, hand on the handle's T-shaped crossbar, ready to pull when she joined him. He rubbed his eyes and gave a sleepy grin, white teeth interspersed with gaps.

Aileen remembered the day when he'd lost the first of his young teeth. They'd carefully rolled the tooth in paper lined with salt, then after a bit of searching, they'd found a mouse hole in a glen near the village.

Jamie had knelt on the ground, peering inside the opening. "Did ye hide yer wee teeth in a mouse hole when ye were a lass, Mam?"

"Och, aye. Yer grandmother wouldna ha' had it any other way."

He squished his tongue into the space where the tooth had come out, wrinkling his freckled nose. "And yer sure a big, strong tooth will come in?"

She'd nodded, kneeling beside him. "I'm sure."

He set bundle into the damp cavity, pushing it far inside with his short finger, then stood before her. His tongue explored the space again, then his face brightened, and he put his hands on her shoulders. "I'm glad ye did it, Mam. Yer smile is verra bonny."

At the memory, a surge of affection swelled inside Aileen. She scooted around the cart and pulled him into an embrace, bending down to kiss his cheek, but Jamie squirmed out of her hold. "Mam, I told ye I'm a man now. I'm too old for kissin'," he protested.

"Aye, ye told me." She tried not to let her hurt show. He *was* too old, she supposed, but the knowin' didn't make it easier. Grabbing the other end of the crossbar, she motioned toward the road. Her fingers ached where she clasped the wood, her legs felt sluggish, and the headache hadn't eased. She thought again of all the scrubbing and cleaning she'd done the day before. She must have worked herself harder than she'd realized.

Jamie pulled beside her through the morning mists, neither of them tugging too quickly— 'twouldn't do to jostle the bees.

They kept to the most worn parts of the road, making sure the ride was as smooth as possible for the hives full of wee passengers.

The lad put a hand in front of his mouth as he yawned. "Och, but I'm tired, Mam," he muttered.

She nodded. "I know it, love." If there weren't hives to deliver, she'd not have minded a nice lie-in this morning herself. Over the green hills and craggy rocks, the fog hung low, keeping the sunlight dim, and gray clouds filled the sky. Likely, the afternoon would bring rain. She hoped they'd get the hives sheltered before then.

Jamie walked with a scowl pulling his brow low over his eyes. The expression was the only one that reminded Aileen of the boy's father. She'd not seen Balfour MacTavish but a few times, even though he and Sorcha had lived only a mile away from the cottage Aileen had grown up in. He didn't accompany his wife to kirk, and Aileen's father wouldn't allow her to visit Sorcha when Balfour was there. She supposed her da knew more about Balfour's character than he'd told her. All she remembered of her friend's husband was that he was dark and handsome with a scar across his nose and cheek and eyes that seemed always to be calculating. Whether 'twas because of her father's warnings, Sorcha's plea, or her mind making him into a villain over the years, she couldn't be sure, but the thought of Balfour MacTavish terrified her.

Rumors suggested that Balfour had been involved in dealings of an illegal nature. Smuggling, Aileen thought, though she didn't know for certain. The man's business took him from home for months at a time. She remembered once hearing that he was imprisoned in the English garrison in Inverness, but it could have been speculation. She'd been too young to know what was true and what was gossip.

Balfour had been away when the Duchess of Sutherland conscripted men to the Highland Regiment, and again when her factor, Patrick Sellar, brought British soldiers to drive the people of her township from their homes.

She didn't know why Sorcha had begged her to hide the child from Balfour, but the fear in her friend's eyes was all the motivation she'd needed to agree to the course of action. In her opinion, the man's failure to do his duty for his country and clan and his failure to care for his wife and unborn child were enough reason to keep the boy from him.

The pair pulled the cart up the path and then around the side of the manor house, using the same route they'd taken the day before. But this time, they steered clear of the animal pens and continued into the orchard.

Aileen inhaled the damp air and smiled at the smell of apple blossoms. Some had bloomed, but the majority were still buds, nearly ready to open. Then would come the plum blossoms, and if she was not mistaken, she'd noticed a few pear trees. In a few days, this orchard would be fragrant and heavenly. 'Twould make the bees happy, and the honey fruity—tha' would make her customers happy.

Jamie guided her along a path that followed a rock wall, chasing away wisps of fog on the cold ground, then he stopped, pointing to a stone structure with a sod roof. They carefully pulled the cart from the path and led it closer.

The apiary had been built by someone who knew what he was doing. 'Twas nicely situated with the open side facing southeast, Aileen saw to her approval. Perfect for warming the bees in the morning. The roof overhung the shelves to keep the skeps dry, giving the bees shelter and sunshine. She laid her hand on the stone shelf. Still a bit cool but not too cold, she judged. She glanced over the structure, noting how clean the apiary and the area surrounding it were. "Ye did this yerself, Jamie?"

Jamie's wee chest puffed out. "Aye, I fixed the stones and cleaned the shelves. And Sergeant Stewart showed me how to use clay beneath the sod to repair the roof, just like I did at home."

"I couldna have done better myself." She smiled at his obvious pride in the task. "And is there water nearby?"

Jamie pointed. "Aye, a stream on the other side of the wall, near those trees there."

She put fists on her hips, turning in a slow circle to survey the spot. The water was near but not too near. And the land sloped slightly away from the apiary. 'Twould keep the lower shelf dry in a storm. A well-chosen location indeed. She could find nothin' to complain about. "Shall we be introducin' the hives to their new home then?"

The two put on protective gloves, tying strips of cloth around the openings of their sleeves. The insects seemed to find the gaps and wrinkles in clothing irresistible, and once they were trapped inside, they panicked and stung the wearer. At home, she'd tucked her underclothing into long socks and now made sure Jamie's trousers covered the tops of his boots. Kneeling, she bound his leg openings with strips of cloth as well as the tops of her own boots.

Hearing the whinny of a horse, she looked toward the direction of the sound, squinting into the fog.

Jamie waved his arms, calling out, "Sergeant Stewart! Good mornin' to ye!"

Even with the hazy sun behind him and wisps of fog before, she'd have recognized the man's broad shoulders as he sat atop his horse. The sergeant changed direction, riding toward them through the haze. "I'd not expected to discover fae in my orchard this mornin'," he called.

The sergeant's face was hard to make out, but Aileen could still hear a smile in his words. She rose and curtseyed. "Good mornin', Sergeant."

He reined in on the other side of the low wall and dismounted, Nellie's breath puffing out in white clouds. He bowed. "So early, Mrs. Leslie?"

"Aye, 'tis best for the bees. And we've more hives to be deliverin' today." She'd intended to avoid the sergeant and felt frustrated that he'd found them. And she felt even more frustrated at being pleased that he'd found them. She shook her head, thinking herself a foolish lass, and the motion made her head slosh like it was filled with thickened.

She set to work unpacking the supplies from the cart and stole a careful glance to see Sergeant Stewart looking with a furrowed brow at the buzzing skeps. Was he afraid of the bees? The thought made her smirk to herself. The broad-shouldered military veteran with his medals and dangerous library full o' weapons was wary o' wee insects.

Jamie was striking flint into the smoker to light the pine needles.

"Ye might want to be movin' Nellie away," Aileen said, slipping a wide-brimmed hat over her head, leaving the mesh veil up for the time being. "Bees don't care for the smell o' horses."

She took the smoker from Jamie and gave the bellows a trial squeeze, sending billows of gray smoke out through the nozzle. "Well done," she said then handed the boy a hat similar to her own.

"Jamie lad, would ye mind returnin' Nellie to her corral? Ye can take her for a bit of a ride first if ye care to." Conall glanced at Aileen. "That is, if yer ma can spare ye."

The boy's face shone with anticipation. "Could I, Mam? I'll not be gone long."

She felt hesitant, not only out of worry for Jamie's safety, but she liked working with him, liked having him beside her. The sergeant's offer was so enticing to him, however, and she felt ashamed of the jealousy turning her stomach bitter. She pursed her lips. "Will he be quite safe with yer horse, Sergeant?"

"Aye. Jamie and Nellie rub together splendidly. Nothin' to worry about. He knows what he's doin'."

Aileen would have to have a heart of stone to say no to Jamie's freckles and hopeful eyes. "Then off with ye, lad. I'll finish here and fetch ye at the corral."

Jamie grinned. He pulled off the gloves, untied cloth strips, then scrambled over the wall and allowed Sergeant Stewart to help him into the saddle. He pulled on the reins and kicked his heels into Nellie's sides. The horse moved and Aileen gasped. Jamie looked so small atop the animal. She watched, tensed as Nellie turned, bobbed her head, and walked down the path toward the house.

"Nay to fear, lass. I'd not allow it if I had even a wee bit o' concern."

She started when she realized Conall had moved to stand beside her on the other side of the wall. He tapped her hand, and when she looked down, she saw the smoker clenched tightly in her fingers, the bellows compressed. She forced her hands to relax and gazed back at the horse, noting how Jamie sat tall in the saddle. He was in control of the animal and not afraid in the least.

The sadness she'd felt earlier returned, along with a fair amount of resentment toward one Color Sergeant Conall Stewart. Why was he able to make her son happy and confident? The resentment grew. As did the guilt. She should feel grateful to him. And part of her did. He made Jamie happy. She glanced to the side and saw that he was watching Jamie as well. Aileen put a hand to her aching head, frustrated with herself. The man planned to leave Dunaid soon enough, but instead of pleasure that she'd have Jamie to herself again, she felt anger. Jamie would be devastated, and she . . . She rubbed her forehead.

She was a bit dizzy from being so tired, and the confusing mixture of thoughts and the ensuing emotions—most of them in direct opposition to each other—threatened to make her headache unbearable.

She moved away from the low wall and turned to her work, setting out shallow dishes and opening a burlap sack to reveal the sweet fondant inside. She sliced chunks off the thick, white slab and set one into each dish.

"And what's this then?" Conall asked, pointing to the dishes.

"Bee candy." She brought the dishes to the apiary, placing them on the stone shelves.

"I didna' realize ye'd have to be feedin' the bees." He remained in the same spot, craning his neck to watch instead of venturing closer, she noticed with amusement.

"The food tides them over until the blossoms are in bloom." She lifted a dish, pointing to the three pegged feet on the bottom. "These here are to keep the wee builders from stickin' the dish to the shelf with wax." Aileen wasn't sure why the man remained. Did he think that as a woman, she was incapable of tending the bees? Well, she had nothing to prove to him. Let him watch or not. 'Twas no concern of hers. Perhaps he'd become bored and leave.

She pulled down the veil, covering her face and neck, then squeezed the bellows, sending a cloud of smoke over one of the wicker skeps. When she figured the bees were sedated, she hefted it carefully from the cart and carried it to the apiary. She set it on the dirt ground and turned it over, blowing more smoke over it as she worked. A gauze cloth was pinned to the straw to keep the bees inside as they were being transported while still allowing the air to circulate.

Unpinning the cloth, she pulled it off and set it aside. She glanced up and saw the sergeant take a step back when she opened the hive. She pressed her lips together to hide her smirk, though she thought the man couldn't see it beneath the veil anyway. "See here, Sergeant Stewart, the new comb built beneath the darker, older comb?" She tipped the skep's open bottom toward him.

He had to take a step forward for a look. His eyes were tight, and the sides of his mouth pulled in a grimace. "Aye."

"This hive's got a good queen, ye see. She'll be layin' eggs in the new comb, and storin' honey in the old." Aileen turned the skep back over, moving it to the shelf and resting it over the dish.

She returned to the cart and offered the other veiled hat to the sergeant. "If ye'd care for a closer look . . ."

He shook his head, leaning back against the wall. "I've a fine view from here. Thank ye, Mrs. Leslie."

"Just as well, and ye smelling o' the horse." She felt a bit wicked, knowing he was nervous but, she had to admit, also rather vindicated. She continued to work, unloading the other skeps, inspecting the combs, and making occasional comments. The task took longer than it should have, thanks to her achin' joints and head, but finally, each of the eight hives was in place in the apiary, and she pulled out the grass she'd stuffed into the openings. "Off ye go now, explore yer new home," she muttered then stepped back to watch—not just because she loved observing the bees and their orderly ways, but she was also very tired, and the thought of pulling the cart back to fetch another batch of hives was discouraging to say the least.

At least she'd have Jamie's help.

She turned toward the cart but must have moved too quickly. The motion made her unsteady for a moment, and she swayed, reaching out a hand to clutch the apiary shelf.

"Mrs. Leslie." Conall hurried to her side, putting a hand on her arm. "Are ye unwell?"

"Excuse me." She touched her forehead. "I'm just a bit dizzy."

Conall didn't release her arm but held on tighter, just above her elbow. He led her toward the cart. Once they reached it, she shook off his grasp. She removed the hat and put it into the cart then put on her bonnet, fumbling as she tied the bow. "Thank you, sir, but I can manage." She took hold of the cart handle. "I've more hives to deliver today." She tried to remember which farms had requested hives. Only three. Or was it four? She blinked, frowning at the confusion.

He didn't speak but grasped the other end of the cart's handle and pulled alongside her.

Though she wouldn't admit it, she wasn't certain she'd have been able to do it alone. Even with the skeps out of the cart, it was heavy. She certainly needed to rest once she reached her cottage.

"Mrs. Leslie, I can't help but wonder if yer feelin' well. Perhaps the hives can wait until another day."

"Thank ye for the concern, but I'm quite well."

He made a sound in the back of his throat. "In that case, is somethin' else the matter? Ye seem . . . troubled. I hope I'm not the cause of yer distress."

She thought for a moment but had a difficult time coming up with a reply. The thoughts in her head seemed not to want to form into words. And she was so cold.

"I should have asked yer permission before sending Jamie with Nellie," he said after a moment. "I apologize for the presumption."

"He doesn't allow me to kiss his cheek or smooth his hair." She felt a tear on her cheek and wiped it away with a gloved finger, wondering where the words had come from. What happened to her resolve to stay away from personal topics?

"I'm not sure—are ye speakin' o' Jamie?"

Aileen closed her eyes and forced her mind to focus. "What I mean is 'tis difficult to see the lad growin' so fast. In no time at all, he'll be a man, and . . ." She wiped another tear, humiliated at the outburst of emotion. "I ken I'm pamperin' him, treatin' him like a wee bairn, and then ye arrived in the village—a soldier, handsome, strong, and he without a da. Ye've made him feel sure o' himself, and—" She closed her mouth, realizing she was prattlin' on without any thought as to what she was saying.

Conall stopped, turning toward her. "Mrs. Leslie. I never meant to offend ye or come between ye and yer son."

For some reason, his words made her tears come faster. She drew in a breath that turned into a sob and felt mortified. What was she doing? She didn't feel this upset.

He pressed a handkerchief into her hand, and she was too humiliated to even raise her gaze to his. "I'm so sorry, sir. I'm being silly. I must be tired from the festivities. Please don't pay me any mind." She dabbed her cheeks and gave a smile, trying to appear as if her mind were clear and her body didn't ache. She tugged on the cart, and with an uncertain look, Conall clasped the handle as well, pulling beside her.

They arrived at the byre and found Jamie hauling a bucket of water, which he dumped into the horse's barrel. "I took off the saddle and rubbed her down just like ye showed me," the boy said.

"And fed and watered all the animals, I see." Conall nodded toward the fresh straw in the troughs. "Fine job, lad."

Jamie grinned and puffed out his chest as he had when Aileen complimented his work at the apiary. "What tasks do ye have today, Sergeant?"

Conall glanced at Aileen. "I think the first task is to get yer ma home."

Jamie's eyes widened as he looked at her, and she saw a flicker of panic. "Are ye ill, Mam?"

The fever last year had frightened the boy. Aileen gave a reassuring smile. "No, mo croí. Just a bit tired. I'll feel better after a rest."

"We'll not be deliverin' any more hives today?" Jamie asked.

Aileen shook her head then immediately regretted it as pain erupted behind her eyes.

"Then might I stay and help Sergeant Stewart?"

"I've plantin' to do, if ye can spare Jamie," Conall said. "Since ye'll be restin'."

His voice sounded tentative, as if he were nervous to ask. Aileen felt like a silly fool. Of course he was nervous, worried that anything he said would cause her to break into tears and indiscriminate blatherin'.

"O' course he can," she said.

"Jamie, take the handcart home, and I'll bring yer ma in the wagon." Conall helped her climb up onto the wagon bench, and then he set to harnessing the horse.

The journey home was hazy. Aileen remembered feeling chilled, giving in to a fit of coughing, then riding with her head in her hands. Conall held her arm to keep her steady, and sometime later, she was being helped out of the wagon and into her cottage. But surely she must have been drifting in and out of dream because as she lay down on her pallet, she thought she felt a blanket pulled up over her shoulders. A finger brushed her cheek, and she heard a familiar deep voice: "If ye're ever needin' a cheek to kiss or hair to smooth, Mrs. Leslie, I'll gladly oblige ye."

Chapter 10

CONALL RAN HIS FINGERS THROUGH his wet hair, watching the storm through the dining room window. He was glad he'd sent Jamie home before the torrent began. The rain had fallen on and off throughout the afternoon, hardly uncommon for the eastern Highlands, but within the last half hour, a full raging thunderstorm had developed. Before Mrs. Ross had left for the evening to practice with the kirk choir, she'd prepared a warm meal, set a fire (bless the woman), and put together a basket with venison stew and warm bread for Jamie to take home for himself and his ailing ma.

Conall couldn't believe Mrs. Leslie had been working in her condition. Her usually bright eyes had appeared unfocused and tired, her cough was rough and jarring, and she'd fallen asleep on the short ride home. She needed to be abed, not haulin' hives around the countryside. Especially in such weather.

Once he and Jamie had returned her home and put away the bee cart, Conall sent Jamie inside to check on his ma while he himself crossed the road to speak to Mrs. Campbell. The older woman had promised to keep a watchful eye on her neighbor. She was a peculiar auld bat, Mrs. Campbell, but he knew Aileen would be safe under her care. And luckily, Jamie had repaired the cottage's leaking roof.

Conall couldn't help a smile as he thought of the lad and his cleverness when it came to fixing things. He seemed to have a genuine knack for it. And seein' Jamie master a new skill and the child's resulting pride was more satisfying than anything Conall had done in years.

He considered what it was about Jamie Leslie that made Conall look forward to the lad's company. Not since he was a child himself had he truly spent time with a young person, and it surprised him how much he enjoyed it.

But as he'd come to care for the lad, something else had happened, another thing Conall had not expected. He'd grown fond of Mrs. Leslie as well. In the beginning, the reasons for that were rather obvious, he thought. She was a beautiful woman, full of spirit, and not one to mince words nor hold back when she felt wronged. She was brave—one would have to be when driven from her home and forced to raise a child alone. All of that and seeing her affection for her son made Conall's attraction natural, but 'twas the understanding she'd shown at the bonfire that had sparked a deeper regard. She'd not given pity nor downplayed his reaction, but she'd asked about his experiences, listened, and told of her own in return.

And seeing her today. She'd been so competent with the hives, and though *he* didn't particularly care for the topic, he liked hearing her speak about something she was obviously passionate about. If only 'tweren't bees. He winced, remembering the pain of all those stings and the fright of being chased by thousands of angry insects.

Perhaps when she felt better, he'd ask if she'd like to attend the choir practice with him. The Dunaid congregation was filled with fine voices, and she may enjoy—

A banging on the door pulled him from his thoughts. Who was calling on such a night? The banging continued, and he heard a child's voice accompanying it—Jamie's voice. Conall felt a burst of worry as he hurried to the front hall. He pulled open the door to reveal the boy, soaked through and shivering.

As soon as Jamie saw Conall, he ran forward, grabbing his arm. "Sergeant, 'tis Mam. She's gone." His eyes were wide and his face pale.

Conall glanced out into the dark. "Perhaps she's only at Mrs. Campbell's."

Jamie shook his head, spraying drops from his curls. "I ran to Mrs. Campbell's straightaway, but 'twas nobody at home. She singin' at the kirk. Mam's nowhere. Not in her bed, not in the bee shed or the midden, not at Mrs. Campbell's . . ." His hand clamped tighter. "Has a faerie taken her?"

Conall shook his head, a tendril of worry working its way inside his thoughts as he remembered Mrs. Leslie's condition earlier that day. He pulled loose from Jamie's grip, closed the door, then found his coat, insisting the boy put it on. Though 'twas much too large and still damp, it was better than only the soaked linen shirt the boy wore. "Come, lad. We'll take Nellie."

As they rode over the muddy road, Jamie's arms tight around his waist, Conall tried to think of what could possibly have happened to Mrs. Leslie. There was a chance the lad was mistaken. Maybe the cottage was dark and he simply hadn't seen her when he'd gone inside. Based on how much time had passed since Jamie left the manor, he couldn't have been home for more than a few minutes before running back to Conall's house. Perhaps he'd simply not looked thoroughly. Or his ma could be at Mrs. Campbell's drinking tea in front of the old woman's fire or even at the kirk listening to the choir. But Conall was forced to admit that each of the scenarios seemed unlikely. The idea that Mrs. Leslie would have gone out in the heavy rain while in such poor health worried him. What could have drawn her from home?

When they reached the cottage, a quick glance was all it took to verify 'twas deserted just as the boy'd claimed. The blankets were pulled back, and the pallet was empty. Conall lit a lantern and followed Jamie into the bee shed, but there was no sign of her there either. He was glad to see the handcart in place. At least she'd not attempted to deliver more hives.

In the pouring rain, they searched the small yard but quickly realized she wasn't there. The lad stood beside him, shaking in the oversized coat and looking up at Conall with rain dripping on his frightened face.

They crossed the road, splashing through muddy rivulets, to Mrs. Campbell's cottage, but the windows were dark, and banging on the door brought no answer.

Jamie sniffed and wiped a sleeve across his eyes.

Conall place a hand on the boy's shoulder. "Let's look at the kirk then, lad. She could have jes' gone to hear the choir, and ye fretted for nothin'."

They hurried back to Nellie, climbed into the wet saddle, and rode through the village. Conall dismounted and helped Jamie down, and the two hurried through the kirkyard and inside the heavy wooden door. They must have been a sight, dripping water as they moved into the dim candlelight because Mr. Graham hurried over to them directly.

"We're lookin' for Mrs. Leslie." Conall kept his voice low so as to not disturb the practice. "Have ye seen her?"

Mr. Graham shook his head. "Nay, not since the bonfire. She's gone missin'?"

"Surely a misunderstanding." Conall laid a hand on Jamie's shoulder, shaking his head slightly. The last thing he wanted was for the lad to become more panicked. "We thought she might ha' come to hear the singin'."

"What's this then?" a woman's voice said.

Conall turned to find Mrs. Campbell had joined them.

"Wha' are ye doin', Jamie? Bargin' in and disruptin' the singin'? I've half a mind to tell yer ma. And Sergeant. Yer a man grown. Ye should know better, and that's the truth."

"Mrs. Campbell," Conall said, his voice sounding sharper than he'd intended, "the lad and I are lookin' for Mrs. Leslie."

"Well, she's at home where I left her." A look at Jamie's tears and Conall's serious expression made her eyes wide. "What do ye mean? She's gone off? Where?" Her brows pulled together.

"Tha's what we'd like to know. Weren't ye watchin' over her?" Conall asked. "I told ye she's unwell."

"Och, aye. I checked in on her this afternoon, and she was sleepin'. Then, when I left for the kirk, I saw her in the yard talkin' to Mr. MacKenzie." Mrs. Campbell jerked a thumb over her shoulder, indicating a man in the choir seats. "She looked well enough then."

A few other members of the choir joined them in the aisle.

"What's happened to Mrs. Leslie?" Davy walked toward them, his wooden leg clunking on the floorboards.

"We canna find her anywhere," Jamie said, sounding helpless and very young.

"Oh, dear." Mrs. Graham put fingers over her mouth, looking as if she'd be ill.

Conall squeezed Jamie's shoulder. "Stay with Mrs. Campbell, lad. I'll speak with Mr. MacKenzie. We'll clear this up quick enough."

By this time, the music had stopped and the remainder of the choir was craning their necks to see the source of the commotion. The kirk was an old stone building with high windows, converted from a Catholic house of worship, and instead of a choir loft, the singers sat in a small alcove on the opposite side of the altar from the lectern-pulpit.

Conall stepped across the room and approached the man Mrs. Campbell had indicated. "Mr. MacKenzie?"

"Aye." Mr. MacKenzie was an older man, broad with cropped hair and a ruddy complexion. He surveyed Conall with the gaze of a person who is immediately distrustful of any newcomer.

"Do ye ken where Mrs. Leslie has gone?"

"Who are ye?"

Conall didn't have time for niceties. He was starting ty feel the tingling in his chest that accompanied dread. "Sir, ye were speakin' with Mrs. Leslie earlier today. What was the nature of the conversation?"

Mr. MacKenzie's scowl grew darker, deepening the lines between his bushy brows. "Don' see as tha's any o' yer affair."

Conall's jaw tightened. "Mrs. Leslie is ill, and she hasn't been seen since she spoke with ye." He gestured toward the boy with the minister and the rest of the group in the aisle. "Her son is worried aboot her." Hearing Davy's uneven steps behind him, Conall glanced back then moved to the side to include him in their conversation.

Seeing Davy seemed to ease some of the tension in the older man's face. Mr. MacKenzie sucked at his teeth. "I talked to her aboot a swarm in the hills above my farm. Likes to know aboot these things, does Mrs. Leslie."

Conall had difficulty drawing a breath into his tight lungs.

Davy spoke up. "A swarm? Did she go after it?"

He gave a slow nod. "I assume so. Looked up at the sky and said she'd fetch it before the rain came."

Conall leaned forward. "Can ye tell me exactly where the swarm is?"

The man described the location, and Davy nodded. "Aye, I ken just where ye mean." He turned to Conall. "I'll take ye there."

Conall gave a grateful nod. Davy MacKay was one of the few men in Dunaid who owned a horse. Most didn't have the means and only leased the animals as needed—typically for plowing or during the harvest season.

They thanked Mr. MacKenzie, who looked worried instead of angry now, and made their way back to Mrs. Campbell and the others.

"Jamie, yer ma may have gone after a swarm. Davy and I will—"

Jamie spoke before Conall could finish. "I'll go with ye."

Conall knelt down to the lad's height. "I'll ride faster alone, and we've no time to waste, ye ken?" A crack of thunder sounded, and Conall's stomach roiled with anxiety, but he put on a calm face for Jamie.

"But—"

Mrs. Campbell put an arm around Jamie, exchanging a worried look with Conall over the boy's head.

"Don' worry yerself, lad. We'll find her." He spoke the words, but he had a hard time making them sound convincing. He rose and hurried with Davy out into the night, glancing upward. The rain and darkness would make a search difficult, nearly impossible.

"'Tis a chance she's taken shelter somewhere until the rain stops," Davy said as they rushed down the muddy street to the livery.

Conall grunted in acknowledgment. 'Twas a possibility, he supposed. Maybe she'd not even made it as far as the farm before finding cover. But he thought of the open heatherlands and craggy hills between her house and the MacKenzie land, and the hope was fragile at best.

Chapter 11

AILEEN PRESSED A HAND TO a wet rock as a fit of coughing came on. She shivered and continued up the craggy hill to the spot where Mr. MacKenzie had described seeing the swarm. 'Twas becoming dark, and based on the sound of distant thunder and the approaching low clouds, soon enough the rains would start in earnest.

She paused, wrapping her coat tighter with one hand and struggling to remember why she was on the mountain. Were she and Jamie to have a picnic? She looked down at the supplies in her arm: her veiled hat and a wicker skep. *Oh yes, of course. The swarm.*

The bees must be near, though she couldn't hear them. They'd not like the rain, she thought, and would find a new hive quick enough, perhaps an old log or a deserted burrow. She needed to find them before they moved on.

She walked a bit farther and shook her head, wincing at the aching. Where was her da? Was he to meet her? She couldn't remember. Looking up, she saw a mass of black writhing on a high branch. Da would be here soon enough with a ladder. He'd know just where in the mass to find the queen, and his clever fingers would work gently to gather the wee insects into the skep.

Another fit of coughing took her, and she bent over. Once the spell had passed, Aileen stood back up, but the motion made her dizzy. She sat, laying her arms on a rock and cradling her head, finding it difficult to get a deep breath. She shivered, but the cool stone felt good against her cheek. Da would come soon enough.

Jerking upright, she gasped. Her father didn't know where to find her. He'd gone to fight in France, and she and Dores had taken Jamie as far away from the deserted township as they could. If her da had returned, he'd have found the other tenants of Glencalvie in the eastern costal villages not all the way in Dunaid. A tear slipped down her hot cheek, and she laid her head back down, thinking of her father either dying on the battlefield alone or returning home and finding his family gone. But she couldn't risk attempting to contact him. Not when Balfour MacTavish might get word of where she had taken his son.

No, not his *son. My son. Jamie is* my *son.*

She coughed again, the action hurting her chest. More tears. But no, they weren't tears, rain. The rain poured down, each drop making her skin ache. She lifted her head and saw it was dark. How long had she been here? She should scoot closer beneath the tree, but she felt so tired. And Da would be here soon. If she moved away, he'd not know where to find the swarm.

Lightning lit the sky, and Aileen closed her eyes against the brightness. Thunder followed, making her wince at the pounding in her head. The storm would certainly frighten the bees.

She coughed again, too tired to worry about the pain in her lungs. She just wanted to sleep.

Aileen blinked. She thought she heard voices. Had her father finally found her? She couldn't raise her head to call out.

"Over here!" Someone lifted her head. It felt so heavy. Her eyes wouldn't focus. "Da?" Hands cupped her cheeks.

"Oh, lass, yer burnin' up." She thought she recognized the voice, low and deep, but as soon as the thought flickered into her mind, it was gone.

The coughing returned, wracking her body, and arms wrapped around her. The voice spoke softly until the fit finished.

"She doesna sound good." Another voice joined the first.

She was lifted and held against a strong chest. "Da, I missed ye so."

"Hush ye now," he said.

But she had so much to say. She needed to tell him what had happened to their cottage in Glencalvie, the kirkyard in Croick, the swarm, the war. She tried to speak, but her words and thoughts muddled together, and soon confusion was overcome by exhaustion. Aileen laid down her head and slept.

Chapter 12

CONALL RODE NELLIE AS QUICKLY as he could down the mountain. The rain made it difficult to see, and the mare was nervous slipping over wet rocks with the storm crashing around them. He held the reins tightly in one hand and Aileen closely against him with the other. Her head bobbed as they rode, and he worried the horse's movements were shaking her too roughly. But getting her out of the rain and into the care of Mrs. Ross was more important than a comfortable ride, he decided.

Hearing her deep, hacking cough made his stomach rock-hard with worry. He'd heard coughs like it before—from men in long, cold campaigns—and knew it didn't bode well. Combined with the cough, her shallow breathing and heated skin led him to believe she had an ailment of her lungs. He had no idea how to help her. He felt helpless, a sense of panic making his own breathing tight. "Ye must get well, lass," he murmured into her wet hair.

Occasionally she'd seem to wake and start to speak, muttering words he couldn't hear over the rain. Conall realized she didn't know what she was saying. 'Twas the fever talking. Her raving seemed frantic, and he wished he could calm her. The best he could do was speak in a soft voice that he thought might sound reassuring. His ma had done the same with him or his sister when they were ill or frightened.

Once he and Davy reached the manor house, he rushed Aileen inside. Mrs. Ross was waiting in the entry hall. The housekeeper took charge immediately, directing him to one of the upstairs bedrooms and following close on his heels.

He laid Mrs. Leslie on the bed, noting in the candlelight how flushed she was. Her hair had come loose and long tendrils stuck to her face and neck. She looked so small and so vulnerable, shivering on the pillow. He felt helpless, like a large oaf, just standing there with no idea how to help her.

Mrs. Ross elbowed him out of the way and pressed her hands to Aileen's forehead and cheeks. She brushed the hair off the woman's face. "Och, my dear, how did ye come by such a fever?"

Aileen's eyes opened, and she stared vacantly. "Da? Did ye return to Glencalvie?" The horrible cough returned, choking her words, and she curled up on her side.

"Mrs. Ross, ye must do somethin'." Conall could hear desperation in his voice. "Shall I go for a doctor?"

"None close enough. Ye'd be away for days, and she needs succor now." Mrs. Ross stood straight, her eyes squinting as she assessed the situation. "We must be gettin' the fever down and soon." She turned to Conall, lips tight and face set in a decisive expression. "Fetch Mrs. Campbell. Tell her to bring meadowsweet and elderberries—she'll ken what else we need. And nightclothes for Mrs. Leslie. Goodness knows I've none that will fit her."

He turned, glad someone knew what to do, even though it meant his housekeeper was ordering him about. He needed to have a job, anything to keep his mind from worry.

Davy stood in the bedroom doorway. "My Catriona kens a bit aboot curin' herbs. I'll bring her straightaway as well."

Mrs. Ross nodded. "The pair o' them are the best healers in the county." She made a shooing motion with her hands. "Now away wi' ye while I change Mrs. Leslie out o' her wet clothes."

***

An hour later, Conall stood before the hearth in his library, knowing his pacing was making Jamie and Davy nervous, but his apprehension wouldn't allow him to sit still. The other two were seated in the leather armchairs, both staring into the fire. Attempts at conversation had been futile, and they'd stopped trying. Aside from the crackle of the flames and an occasional sniff from Jamie, the room was silent. Above, Conall could hear the murmuring voices of women working to bring down Aileen's fever and occasional bouts of coughing that made him wince.

During a particularly loud attack, Jamie's eyes darted toward the door. He clutched the arms of the chair, his face paling.

Conall stepped to the side table and lifted a decanter of rum, pulling out the stopper and tipping it to pour before he realized he couldn't give the lad the strong spirits. He left the room and searched in the kitchen, finding the tea kettle still hot from the medicinal concoction Mrs. Campbell had brewed. A moment later, he had a saucer and cup filled with peppermint tea, his personal favorite. He added a healthy amount of cream and sugar then delivered it to the lad.

"Thank ye." Jamie's voice was quiet. He held the cup in his lap.

Conall patted the boy's shoulder, but Jamie didn't look up. He stared down at the tea, and Conall wished he knew what to say. He stood a moment longer then returned to the side table.

Needing something stronger after their long night, Conall poured a drink of rum for himself and Davy. He handed the glass to his friend and sat facing the pair o' them on the sofa, just now realizing how tired he was.

Davy lifted his glass, offering a half-hearted smile. Conall returned the gesture and sipped the strong drink. At sea, he'd developed a taste for the sweet liquor, and he welcomed the warming as it flowed down his throat. He'd still not changed from his wet clothes. Nor had Davy, he realized.

Conall glanced up at the man then studied his drink, turning the glass to catch firelight in the golden liquid. Though they'd known each other less than a month, he considered Davy MacKay to be as loyal a friend as he'd had. He was cheerful and always willing to lend a hand. He'd not hesitated an instant to ride out into the precarious hills during a raging storm. Conall hoped that in a similar circumstance he would act as honorably.

Another attack of coughing drew all three pairs of eyes toward the door. The noise sounded so painful that his own chest ached in sympathy. The feeling of helplessness returned, bringing both a weariness and surge of nervous energy that made him feel like he should be doing something—but having no idea of what.

He thought of Aileen's flushed cheeks, her burning skin and vacant eyes, and a deep sorrow filled him. He'd seen men with similar afflictions, and more often than not, they'd not recovered. Up until now, he'd avoided these thoughts, but 'twasn't practical to pretend her condition was any less than dire. And the realization hurt. The depth of his ache surprised him. He didn't know Mrs. Leslie well, and the thought was accompanied by one of intense regret. He'd hoped to know her better, to think of clever things that would bring out her smile. He'd wanted to tease her to make her bright eyes flash. Aileen and Jamie were forefront in his thoughts a good amount of the time. Thinking of ways to make their difficult life easier—but without their knowing, of course—was something he'd considered almost constantly since his first meeting with the passionate, independent Mrs. Leslie.

But now . . . Were those opportunities to pass before he'd even had a chance to implement them? Would he ever again see the tick of her brow when she pretended to disapprove of something he said or the way she pulled down the corners of her mouth when she was thinking?

Conall's throat tightened, and he glanced at Jamie. What would the lad do without his mother? Conall was certain the village would care for him. Mrs. Campbell would likely take him in, but nobody could replace his mother. And Conall realized he'd do anything to keep Jamie from experiencing that pain.

Looking down, he was surprised to see his glass empty. He stood to refill it, reaching for Davy's glass as well. Davy shook his head, declining more liquor. But Conall filled the man's glass anyway and set it on the table beside him. As he walked back to the sofa, his eyes lighted on a framed map of Scotland. He stepped closer, looking at the place Aileen had mentioned in her fevered ramblings. Glencalvie. He studied the region at the head of Strathcarron.

Davy had told him the story of the tenants in that area: driven from their homes and forced to shelter in the snowy kirkyard of Croick town. Had Aileen and Jamie been among them? Had her husband been alive, or was she alone? Had she tried to keep the infant warm without walls or family to help her? His eyes prickled as he imagined it. He'd no idea if the story even pertained to her, but some things she'd said made him think there might be some truth to it. She'd told him she was from the Duchess of Sutherland's lands, and in her fevered confusion, she'd thought her father had returned to Glencalvie. Was it possible that he'd survived the war and returned to discover his home ruined and empty as Conall had? What if he had no way of finding out where his daughter and grandson had gone? What if she didn't know how to contact him?

His thoughts were interrupted when Catriona MacKay entered the library.

Jamie sat up, and Davy crossed the room to his wife. "How is she?"

"We've done all we can. Now we've just to wait and hope." She turned to Conall. "Dores will sit with her tonight, and I'll be returnin' in the mornin' if I may."

"Thank ye." He stepped across the room and took her hand, giving a bow. "I canna thank ye enough for all ye've done." He turned, clasping Davy on the shoulder. "And ye, Davy. If not for yer knowin' the hills as ye do . . ." He had a difficult time finishing the sentence as he thought of Aileen lying alone on the wet mountain, shiverin' in her thin coat.

Davy, perhaps seeing Conall's emotions, gave a smirk and shrugged one shoulder. "Sometimes 'tis difficult, bein' the hero." He winked. "But I bear the burden wi' grace."

Conall appreciated him lightening the mood, even though he could tell the joke was forced. They all felt the weight of Aileen's illness like a heavy cloud pressin' down.

Mrs. Ross appeared behind the MacKays and walked with them to the front door. Conall himself retrieved Davy's horse from the barn, and once the couple was safely away, he stepped back inside with Mrs. Ross.

"How is she?" He kept his voice low, not wanting it to carry to the library where Jamie was.

"She's in good hands. The fever seems to be easin'." Mrs. Ross shook her head, her lip trembling. "But och, she's ill."

"Do ye think . . . ?" He grimaced and left the question hanging in the air, not quite sure how to finish it.

The plump woman squeezed his hand where it rested on the rail. "I think we're needin' to pray."

Conall closed his eyes, letting out a breath.

Releasing his hand, she patted it. "There's nothin' more to be done tonight. Get ye to yer bed, Sergeant. I prepared the chamber beside Aileen's for the lad. Poor dear." She shook her head, making a tsking noise, then turned to return to the chambers above. "Mrs. Campbell will let us know if anythin' changes."

After bidding the housekeeper good night, Conall returned to the sofa in the library, not quite knowing what to say to Jamie but wanting to reassure the lad he wasn't alone.

Jamie was leaned forward, elbows on his legs and hands dangling between his knees.

Connall sat on the sofa. "Jamie lad, perhaps ye should get some sleep. Come. Mrs. Ross has prepared a bed for ye."

Jamie looked at him. His eyes were red and held more worry than a young child should have to carry. "Sergeant, can we stay here a bit longer?"

"Aye, lad. We'll remain as long as ye like."

"And can I sit by ye?"

Conall slid to the side, patting the cushion next to him.

Jamie scooted into the spot. He slipped his hands under his legs, feet dangling a few inches from the floor. "Sergeant? Will my mam get well?"

Of course she will. Conall opened his mouth to reassure the lad but stopped. Jamie deserved the truth. No matter how difficult 'twas to hear. "I dinna ken, lad." He blew out a breath through his teeth. "She's verra ill."

Jamie pursed his lips tightly, looking down at his knees. After a moment, he spoke in a soft voice. "'Tis like the last time. She's hot and shiverin'. And the cough." He pulled out his hands and clasped them together in his lap. "Sergeant?"

"Aye, Jamie?"

"Ye told me 'twasn't a person's fault when somethin' bad happens."

Conall thought of the conversation they'd had walking toward the Beltane bonfire. Had it truly been only a day earlier? "I spoke true, lad. If yer thinkin' ye are in some way to blame for yer ma's illness . . ."

"I chased Mr. MacKenzie's chickens and hid the minister's glasses so we didna' have to read anymore aboot Revelations."

His hands clenched tighter. "Sometimes I tell Mam I behaved at school when I didna behave at all. And one day I took away Robena's bonnet jes to see what she'd do." His small shoulders slumped. "I'm a wicked lad, Sergeant."

"Och, Jamie, yer a good lad. I've seen ye takin' care o' yer ma. And feedin' Barney and Nellie withoot bein' asked. Ye patched Mrs. Campbell's wall and prepared my apiary." He patted the boy's hands. "None o' us are perfect lad."

Jamie looked up at him, the corners of his mouth pulling down just as his mother's did when she was thinking.

"This"—Conall pointed toward the stairs—"tisn't yer fault. Yer ma's not bein' punished because of things ye've done."

Jamie's face pulled into a scowl. "Whose fault is it? God's?"

Conall shook his head. "I ken ye're wantin' to understand why bad things happen. We all are. But searchin' for someone to blame will make ye angry and unhappy, and that's not the type of man God wants ye to be, is it?"

Jamie shook his head.

Conall scooted around so his knees faced the lad, and he laid his hand on the back of the sofa. "Ye feel frustrated and helpless, I ken. And ye want to fix everythin'. Make yer ma well again. But some problems canna be fixed, ye see. Not by worryin' nor by blamin'. The only thing to do is pray and trust in God's mercy."

"And will God make Mam well?"

Conall sighed. "He might, Jamie. Or he might not."

"Then why bother prayin' if 'twon't do any good?" Jamie grumbled.

Conall gave a wry grin. He'd asked the same question often enough. "I don't have all the answers, lad, but I believe prayin' will ease yer fear. 'Twill bring ye peace."

Jamie sat still, watching the fire as he considered. Conall hoped something he'd said had comforted the child. He imagined brokenhearted people had asked the same questions for thousands of years. He wished he knew the answers.

Finally Jamie shifted. He rubbed his eyes and leaned his head on the sofa's arm. "Sergeant, will ye tell me a story?"

Conall's eyes stung as he regarded Jamie. Though at times he spoke like a much older person, Jamie was still just a wee boy. "Aye, lad."

He yawned and spoke in a sleepy voice. "Do ye ken aboot Fionn mac Cumhaill?"

Chapter 13

AILEEN SAT FORWARD IN THE soft bed feeling discouraged as Dores fluffed the pillows behind her and smoothed the bedding. She blew out a sigh, hating that her breathin' still pained her, and leaned back against the pillows. Even the simple movements of adjusting her position made her tired.

"No need to be givin' me yon look, lass. I ken 'tis frustratin' to remain abed, but ye'll nay mend if ye move about too quickly."

"Aye, I know it. But I thought I'd be well by now." She knew she was pouting but couldn't help it. "Beltane 'twas over a week past, and here I am still sleepin' all hours o' the day and keepin' the household awake at night with the cough."

"I'll have ye know, none o' us is bothered in the least by yer noise. Not when yer finally healin'. Ye had us worried, lass." Dores patted Aileen's hand where it rested on the quilt. Then her thick brow rose, and she smirked, giving a knowing look. "*All* o' us."

Aileen blushed at the reminder of Sergeant Stewart and the tales Dores and Mrs. Ross had delightedly related of his pacing for long hours in the library and sitting on a hard chair in the passageway outside the bedchamber while the ladies tended to her over these past days.

"I feel terrible aboot bein' such a bother to the man," she said in a low voice, a blush moving up her neck and into her cheeks. Not that she thought he could hear through the bedchamber door. Besides, he was likely off workin' the fields with Jamie.

"Nonsense." Dores flicked her hand. "'Tis good for him to be worryin' a bit. Men need a nudge now and then. Forces them to acknowledge the feelin's they'd rather keep concealed."

Aileen shook her head, thinkin' her friend had been too long beside her sickbed, conjurin' up fanciful stories. "His feelin's are likely annoyance at havin' an unwelcome houseguest eatin' his food, occupyin' his servants, and barkin' like a beached selkie at all hours o' the night."

Dores gave her mischievous smirk. "We'll see aboot that, won' we?"

Aileen didn't have the strength to argue. She was having a difficult time sitting up. The discouragement returned. She needed her strength back. There were bees to care for, she'd hardly seen Jamie for days, and her cottage . . . She closed her eyes for just a moment. Thinking of all the work she had to do was nearly overwhelming.

"Now, don' go fallin' to sleep wi'out takin' yer tea."

Aileen opened her eyes. She reached forward and obediently sipped the warm drink from one of Sergeant Stewart's lovely porcelain cups, recognizing the taste of the herbs that made up Dores's sleeping draught. She didn't need help falling asleep, of course, but Dores told her the concoction kept the cough from waking her. Both Dores and Catriona agreed that now that the fever was gone, sleep was the best cure for her ailing lungs.

Aileen's eyelids grew heavy before she finished the tea, the herbs already taking effect. She handed the cup to Dores and sank down into the soft pillows, imagining she heard the creak of footsteps in the passageway. The thought of the sergeant's concern, fantasy though it might be, brought a smile to her lips, and a comforting warmth wrapped around her heart.

***

Two days later, Dores and Mrs. Ross helped Aileen to bathe and wash her hair. She dressed, giving Brighid a chance to clean her nightclothes. Though the simple tasks drained her strength, she insisted she was well enough to leave the room and wait for Jamie to return from his morning studies. Dores and Mrs. Ross each held on to an arm as they helped her down the stairs. Nearing the bottom, Aileen found herself leaning heavily on the women. Her breathing was labored, and her lungs ached. She gritted her teeth, tired of her body refusing to heal more quickly.

She could feel rather than see the concerned expressions that passed between the women as she stopped in the entry hall, wheezing, and wished she could show them that she didn't need their worry. But she felt too exhausted to do much of anything but lean on the banister and try to catch her breath.

"Come to the library," Mrs. Ross said. "There's a fine view o' the road. Ye'll be able to see the lad approachin'. And the sun shines warm on the sofa this time of day."

Aileen nodded, too out of breath to speak, and allowed herself to be led to the library.

The women sat her on the sofa and, after making sure she was settled with a good view through the window, covered her with a blanket and left her to herself.

Mrs. Ross was right. The sun shining through the large windows felt divine. Aileen leaned back her head and closed her eyes, enjoying the warmth on her face. Perhaps once Jamie returned, she'd move to the other side of the house, where the windows faced the orchard. Surely the blossoms were out in full bloom. It must be a glorious view, and the bees would be busily building comb and storing honey. A fretfulness made her open her eyes. She should be tending to the bees. She still had hives to deliver. She must recover.

Once her breathing felt less labored, she looked about the room. During her illness, she'd had plenty of time to think about the man who'd so graciously opened his house to her and Jamie while she convalesced. From her position on the sofa, she allowed her gaze to wander around the shelves, studying the rows of leather-bound books, wondering which were the sergeant's, if any, and which had come with the house. Did he enjoy reading? she wondered. She herself had never had occasion to learn letters, but she made certain Jamie attended the minister's lessons. 'Twas important for the boy to be schooled. He would do grand things with his life, she was sure of it, and reading was the first step.

Aileen rose and made her way around the room. She stopped to look at a framed map hanging on the wall, recognizing the shape of the country. She'd always thought Scotland resembled the flame atop a melting candle. She had a general idea where Glencalvie was, of course, on the east coast, but she wasn't certain of much beyond that. They'd traveled southwest from Strathcarron to Dunaid. That she knew, but she couldn't locate the village. 'Twas on a deep-ocean firth, but she didn't know exactly where, and looking at the lines and letters, she couldn't tell one from another. Not that it mattered. Seein' one's location on a map wasn't necessary when she could look out the window. She and Jamie were safely in Dunaid, away from the Duchess of Sutherland and her factor and, of course, Balfour MacTavish. She looked back to the east side of the map, wondering how far 'twas across the ocean to France. The sergeant's tales of war only increased her longing to know what had befallen her da.

Footsteps sounded behind her, and Aileen went stiff. The clapping noise on the wooden floor wasn't made by a woman's soft shoes. Her cheeks flushed when the steps paused.

"What a delightful surprise 'tis, Mrs. Leslie, to see ye up and movin'."

His voice was the same she'd heard in her dreams, comforting her through her sickness and speaking gentle words in a low tone. She didn't know what of that was memory or what was fantasy, but the thought of him holding her, murmuring in his deep voice made her stomach do a slow roll and her heartbeat speed up. *Get ahold o' yerself, lass.* She turned and curtseyed. "Good mornin' to ye, Sergeant."

His expression took her aback. His eyes were soft, and the right side of his mouth pulled up the slightest bit. He reached forward but then pulled his hand back. "Och, but I'm glad to see ye in fine fettle, lass. I didna think . . ." He blinked and shook his head, stepping closer. "And how are ye feelin' then?"

"Much better. I canna begin to thank ye for yer hospitality. And for comin' after me in the rain. Jamie told me—"

He raised his hand, cutting off her words. "No thanks necessary." His tone was too intimate, and he stood too close.

She folded her arms, resorting to practicality to keep her grounded. "Aye, but I'll be thankin' ye all the same." She kept her voice detached, which gave her a sense of control. "Ye've done more for me—for us—than I can repay. This house . . ." She thought of the fragile dishes and her worry that one would smash to bits in her clumsy fingers, the soft sheets and bed with down-filled pillows. She'd never before known such luxury. The gap between the elegance of the manor and her simple cottage life seemed a chasm too wide to cross. This book room alone was larger than her entire home.

Sergeant Stewart wasn't put off in the least by her manner. When she dared a glance up at him, she saw he still regarded her with warm eyes. "But a wise woman once told me 'tisn't charity when ye care for someone."

Aileen opened her mouth but couldn't find words to reply. The man's gaze held hers so completely that she couldn't have looked away if she'd wanted to. For an instant, she was suspended, seeing nothing but deep-brown eyes and not fully understanding what she read in their depths.

A shuffling noise came from outside the library door: footsteps and whispers that she realized came from two nosey auld women.

Aileen rolled her eyes and saw the sergeant's expression mirrored her own. The moment passed, and she took a step back. "Be tha' as it may, Jamie and I will be out o' yer hair as soon as—"

"Not until yer hale and hearty, Mrs. Leslie. And I'll brook no argument on tha' account."

She gave a small smile, feeling suddenly quite bashful. "Thank ye, Sergeant."

"Conall." He raised a brow as if daring her to disagree with him. Aileen glanced at the door, aware of the listening ears in the passageway. "Conall." She spoke the name quietly.

He narrowed his eyes and shook his head then shrugged, and she understood his meaning. He wouldn't allow the meddlers to bother him, and she shouldn't either. "Ye look pale, Aileen." His brow tapped upward at the use of her name as if wondering if he'd overstepped. When she didn't correct him, he continued, "Do ye need to sit?"

"Not just yet," she said. "Will ye show me yer book room?"

"Aye." He lifted her hand and pulled it around his arm but didn't release his hold on her fingers as he led her toward the bookshelf. "'Tis my favorite room. Perhaps because o' the great windows or the carved wood mantle. But I canna take credit for the furnishings. 'Tis just how I found it when I moved in. The owner o' the house, a Mr. Roberts, died near ten years ago, so I'm told. His son lived here for a bit. Did ye know him? Hamish Roberts."

Aileen shook her head. "Nay. The house was empty when Jamie and I arrived eight years ago."

"'Tis Hamish I'm rentin' from," Conall said. "He'd prefer to be sellin' the auld place, but I wasna ready for a commitment o' that sort."

"The village is glad to see it occupied again. 'Tis too fine a home to sit empty."

"That 'tis."

He looked pensive as he spoke, and Aileen wondered if it had to do with the possibility that he'd be leavin' soon. The thought brought with it a swell of sadness. She wondered if his thoughts were on the same path, but she could not discern his feelings and so turned her gaze to the bookshelf. "And have ye read all these books, Serge—Conall?"

"Not even close." He smiled, perhaps at her use of his name. "I have found a few new favorites though." He looked down at her, tipping his head. "And what about yerself? What books are ye fond of?"

"I've . . . I don't ken many books. I don't read." Aileen felt her cheeks heat at the admission. "I am fond o' stories though."

Conall nodded. "I didna learn myself until a few years ago. A midshipman on the *Bellerophon* befriended me and spent months showin' me letters and teachin' me words." His eyes looked far away as he spoke, and Aileen wondered about the man who'd taken the time to teach Conall to read. Had he survived the war? She was about to ask when he turned to her. "Would ye wish to read?"

She shrugged. "I haven't given it much thought. I suppose I would one day." Truthfully, she'd always wanted to learn. Wanted to know the mysteries hidden away in books. The knowledge, o' course, but the stories were what she truly longed to know. She imagined stories from all parts of the world—Arabian tales with magic jinn, ancient Greek epics telling of heroes. It all sounded so wonderful. But, she told herself, she'd no time for readin'. And though she didn't want to admit it, she worried she'd not understand it if someone did try to teach her. What if she couldn't learn?

She looked away from the books, changing the subject. "I am a bit disappointed not to see yer war medals. Didna ye say the library was filled with dangerous weapons?" She gave a smile to show she was teasing. "I don't see anythin' more deadly than a sharpened quill."

He glanced around the room. "I'd intended to display my uniform and weapons and some o' the treasures I picked up in my travels—a rainstick from Australia, a folding fan from Spain, things o' that nature." He shrugged. "But they don't hold the same importance for me now. I canna explain it." He rubbed his thumb over her knuckles. "I suppose I'm a different man in Dunaid than I was in the war, and sometimes I don't want to be rememberin' him."

His expression was serious, perhaps more so than she'd seen before. And pensive. She didn't know what memories he was trying to evade, but she understood his need to hide them away. She often wished to escape her own. "I ken what ye mean." She spoke softly and turned toward the window, giving a gentle tug on his arm as an invitation to accompany her.

She looked down the road, hoping to catch a glimpse of Jamie, but didn't see him and so turned away, facing Conall. "So yer a farmer now and not a soldier any longer?"

"I suppose I am." He looked out the window, but she didn't think he was seein' anything. He seemed lost in his thoughts. "'Tis strange how life plays out. My da wanted me to be a farmer. Loved the land, he did, and wished the same for me. But I resisted. Fought with him over the topic daily. I wish I could take back those words." He closed his eyes then opened them with a wry grin. "And now here I am. As much as I tried to escape it, I've become just what he'd hoped. Strangely, I understand now why he wanted it for me. It took goin' to the other side o' the world to realize what I had right here at home." He looked down at her, his eyes pained, but a smile pulled up one side of his mouth. "I'm verra stubborn, ye see."

"He'd be proud of ye, Conall."

"I wonder if he'll ever know. I dinna ken if he still lives. And if he does . . ."

"Ye'll go to him. To yer family."

He lifted her hand, studying it as he spoke. "I don' yet know."

"'Twill be difficult on the village if ye leave. And Jamie. 'Twould devastate him." Aileen felt bold, speaking so plainly, but she wished for Conall to know he was needed here in Dunaid. Her son needed him.

"And what aboot his ma?" Conall tipped his head. His eyes seemed a deeper brown. He squinted, looking vulnerable. "If I were to leave Dunaid, would ye miss me too, Aileen?"

She blinked, her mouth going dry, and turned down her eyes, unable to look directly at him as her mind became muddled. "Aye, I would."

His hand tightened, and when she looked up, she saw his crooked smile.

Heat flooded her cheeks. "Now don't ye go gettin' conceited." Scolding seemed the best strategy to keep her feelings from being exposed. She heard another scuffle outside the door and, along with the women's whispers, Jamie's voice.

A moment later he burst into the room. "Mam! Yer mended!" Jamie ran toward her, throwing his arms around her waist.

Aileen couldn't stop her grin. She'd hardly seen Jamie aside from the few short visits to her sick bed permitted by Dores and Mrs. Ross. She embraced him, kissing his curls. That he didn't struggle away attested to how worried he'd been. He held her tight, pressing his face into her stomach as his shoulders shook. He sniffed.

Aileen's throat constricted, and she felt her own tears prickle her eyes. "Och, Jamie, ye've nay reason to fear any longer. I'm well now."

"I worried for ye, Mam," he said in a tight voice.

Conall touched the small of her back, and she glanced up to see his expression filled with affection as he looked down at the lad.

"Well, there's no need to worry any longer, mo croí," she said.

Jamie nodded. He pulled away, wiping his sleeve over his eyes. She thought he looked a bit embarrassed that Conall had seen his emotions. He cleared his throat, swallowing. "Mrs. Ross says we can all take luncheon together if ye feel well enough, Mam."

At the sound of her name, Mrs. Ross entered, followed by Dores. Both women looked as though they were endeavoring innocent expressions but could not fully keep from smiling at what they'd overheard.

A wave of exhaustion washed over Aileen. 'Twas difficult to remain standin', and she knew she hadn't the strength to sit for a meal. "I think I need to rest, love."

"Perhaps later this evenin', ye can read a story to yer ma, Jamie?" Conall said. "But only if she's properly rested." He winked at Aileen.

"Shall I, Mam?"

"I'd love that."

Dores came forward, arm outstretched to assist Aileen back up the stairs.

Aileen bent and gave Jamie a kiss on the cheek, quickly before he could move away. She took a step toward Dores then stopped, feeling brave. She turned and kissed Conall as well, feeling the scratch of his whiskers as her lips brushed over his cheek. The rush of courage passed, leaving her horrified at her impulsive act. She took Dores's arm and hurried from the room, not daring to look back.

Chapter 14

CONALL BREATHED IN THE CRISP morning air, watching the tendrils of fog dissipate from the hills above him as he folded the paper and slid it back into the envelope. He'd read the letter from Mr. Douglas in Fort William enough times that he'd memorized the words, but he kept reading it, perhaps in hopes that he'd know what to do with the information. His parents' names and he believed his sister's—if Elspeth had truly married Dougal Fraser, the blacksmith's son—were listed on a copy of a ship's manifest. The *Dorothy* had departed from Greenock more than a year earlier destined to land in Quebec, Canada. Mr. Douglas knew the ship arrived safely but had no further information on the passengers.

There 'twas. The answer he'd waited for. But now his course didn't seem so clear. He tapped the letter against his leg as he paced back and forth over the rocky ground. Nellie looked at him curiously then returned to munching meadow grass beside the creek. Conall had thought once he discovered where his family had gone, he'd join them, but things had become complicated here in Dunaid. And the majority of the complication could be attributed to a lovely beekeeper and her ginger-haired son.

When he thought of Aileen and Jamie, warmth filled him like a cup of peppermint tea. Aileen's healing had been a relief, a miracle if he was to believe his housekeeper. He and Jamie had sat up late night after night, worrying. Conall had paced the upstairs passageway in the wee hours, hearing the boy's weeping and the woman's body-wracking cough. Day after day, Catriona MacKay and Dores Campbell had mixed and administered herbs. Mr. Graham prayed for her in kirk on Sunday. For those weeks, a heaviness had hung over all of Dunaid. 'Twas as if everyone held their breath, cringing as they awaited news, worrying for one of their own.

But when he'd walked into his library a few days earlier, there she was. He'd been taken aback by the sight. She'd stood before the window, her honey-colored hair glowing in the sun. Her creamy skin had looked a bit pale, and her cheekbones were more pronounced, but she was recovered and smiling, her eyes bright and more beautiful than he'd remembered. And he'd felt . . . something. Something different than the fondness he'd felt before. Something deeper. Perhaps the feeling came because, in her fevered state, he'd seen past the sensible, strong woman to the frightened lass she kept concealed. The seein' triggered his instinct to protect her—though he didn't think she'd be pleased if she knew. Aileen Leslie wasn't one to appreciate a man thinkin' she needed watchin' over.

A small twist of guilt pulled inside as he wondered if she'd appreciate the inquiries he'd written to Inverness and Fort William on her behalf. Or would she be irritated at his interference? She'd been incoherent, cryin' out for her da, burnin' with fever, and Conall had felt desperate to do anything to help, even if, in the end, the efforts might amount to nothing.

He hadn't had much information to give the recipients of his letters—Jamie knew his grandfather's name was Fearghas but didn't know a surname—but Conall sent the inquiries all the same, hoping someone would know what had become of Fearghas the beekeeper of Glencalvie, member of His Majesty's Ninety-Second Highland Regiment, tenant of the Duchess of Sutherland, father to Aileen Leslie, and grandfather to James.

Perhaps an old neighbor or a military comrade or a church man would come forward. Someone like Mr. Douglas. His thoughts came again to the letter in his hand. He tucked it into his coat pocket, returning to his original dilemma. Should he leave Dunaid and journey to find his family in Canada? Merely the thought of leaving the Highlands pained him. And how could he say goodbye to Jamie? He loved the boy like a son. And his mother—Conall stopped short, his outstretched hand nearly to Nellie's reins. He stood for a moment as the question in his mind settled and he could see the quandary clearly for what it was. He no longer wondered whether he could leave the *Highlands* but whether he could leave *them*. Her.

Would she join him? His heart pounded in his chest as he came to the realization: he wanted Aileen and Jamie in his life whether here in Scotland or in Canada. They were his family. Or would be if he could convince her. He, of course, wouldn't take her away until the questions about her father were answered.

Conall felt a sudden burst of energy—of purpose. He mounted Nellie and rode toward the house. The course of action was not one he'd previously considered, not consciously anyway, but it felt right. Perhaps it had been there all along, waiting for him to see it for what it was. He loved Aileen Leslie. Whatever his future held seemed optimistic.

His heart felt light as Nellie followed the path along the orchard wall. Now that he had a plan, he was eager to see it through. He reined in when he spied a flash of plaid fabric in the orchard. Dismounting, he walked closer. His smile spread when he saw Aileen at the apiary, one of Mrs. Ross's shawls around her shoulders. She stood with her back to him, bending slightly as she watched the bees.

Conall stopped, not wanting to get too near the wee stinging devils. "Good day to ye." He took off his hat, leaning forward in a bow.

Aileen turned quickly spreading her fingers over her breastbone. He'd obviously surprised her. She must have been intent on her observations. "Oh. Good morning." Her cheeks went pink. She dipped in a curtsey, seeming not to know where to look. "I was jes' watchin' the bees."

Her shyness reminded him of their last meeting, most specifically the kiss that preceded her departure. He smiled, amused that he could cause the practical woman to become so flustered. "And what are the bees doin' that has ye so interested?"

She pointed to the small opening on one of the hives. "They're expellin' the drones."

Conall pretended to look interested while maintaining a good distance. "Why would they be doin' that?"

She looked back into the small opening, obviously seeing something in the bees' behavior. "The nectar stores must be strained, but I won't know for sure until I've my equipment and can open up the hive. See here?" She pointed toward some bees that, from Conall's view, looked the same as all the other bees. "Drones are larger than worker bees, with big eyes. They don't contribute to carin' for the brood nor do they retrieve pollen." She squinted, turning her head to peer through the small opening. "They just loll about eatin' all day," she muttered. "Rather like unwelcome houseguests." Aileen straightened and turned to him with a self-conscious smile. "I suppose I'm one to talk, aren't I?"

"Jamie and yerself are *welcome* houseguests." Conall mustered his courage and took a few steps closer. "In fact, I'd call the both of ye *delightful* houseguests."

"Ye're a verra considerate host, but we've outstayed our welcome."

He pulled off a glove, touching her forehead with the backs of his fingers in the pretense of checking her temperature. Her breathing sounded shallow, and she wheezed a bit. "How are ye feeling, Aileen?" He brushed her soft cheek and rested his hand on her shoulder.

Her face flushed a fiery red. "Much improved." She looked down, lashes spreading over her cheeks.

From this close, he could see a small freckle near the corner of her eye that he'd never noticed before. "I told ye I expect ye to stay until yer fully mended."

"Aye, but I've still hives to deliver—"

"Nay to worry aboot tha'. 'Tis done already."

She looked up, her brows pulling together over her bright eyes. "Done?"

"Aye. Jamie and I delivered them a week ago."

Her mouth rounded. "I didna know that."

He shrugged, his thumb brushing her collarbone.

She appeared to be rattled by his nearness but attempted to keep a detached manner. "I'll still be needin' to leave. Even with Mrs. Campbell here, 'tisn't appropriate for me to stay in a single man's household."

"I'll be sorry to see ye go." Conall moved even closer, and Aileen tentatively laid a hand on his chest. He settled his other hand on the curve of her hip. Her eyes closed as he bent forward, touching his lips to hers. Aileen's lips were soft and warm, and—

A buzzing sounded in his ear, and Conall jerked back, his hat falling to the ground as he swatted the air. He rushed away from the apiary and uttered some very unromantic obscenities as he shook his head, fearing the insect had landed in his hair.

He was nearly to the wall when he turned and saw Aileen's wide eyes. In an instant, understanding dawned, and her confused expression turned to a wide grin. She put a hand over her mouth as she let out a small giggle then drew in a breath that sounded far too shallow. She picked up his hat as she came to the wall and sat, holding it on her lap as she breathed in then giggled again. "Oh, my lungs aren't well enough for this." It took a moment for her breathing to calm—especially as she fought against laughter.

Conall sat beside her and fixed her with an exasperated gaze. "I don't think 'twas *that* amusing."

"I am sorry. I—" She shook her head, another giggle bursting forth. "'Tis just . . . yer so large and strong, and the bees. Och, I should no' have laughed, but if ye'd seen yer face. And how fast ye leapt away." Another small laugh escaped. "Truly, I'm sorry."

Conall gave a wry smile that made her laugh again. "Careful, lass, ye'll hurt yerself," he said dryly. But he couldn't hold in his own laughter and shook his head at the absurdity of his reaction.

She stood and faced him, setting down the hat and turning his head to the side. "Ye know, swatting at them just makes them angry. Now where were ye stung? Mrs. Campbell will have some lavender oil to . . ." She squinted, studying the side of his face and running her fingers over his cheek and behind his ear. "I don't see . . ."

"It didn't sting me," he confessed. "I just thought 'twas goin' to."

She pressed her lips together, and he thought she was stifling another laugh. But the corners of her mouth turned down, and he realized she'd become serious. Her hands were still holding the sides of his head, and instead of pulling away, she brushed back his mussed hair with her fingers. Her eyes softened. "And why are ye so frightened o' the wee creatures?" she asked. "Were ye stung as a lad?"

"Aye. An entire swarm chased me after I threw a rock at their hive." He shivered at the memory. "I was covered in stings."

Aileen moved back to sit beside him on the wall. She slipped her hand into his. "I imagine 'twas terrifyin'." She rested her head on his shoulder. "And ye still delivered my hives with Jamie."

"I was more o' a cart puller than a hive deliverer," he said, enjoying the feel of her beside him. He didn't mind her sympathy in the least, not when it meant she nestled up against him. He tightened his fingers around hers, liking how her small hand was completely enveloped within his. Even though he was confessing to a fear of something she dealt with without a bit o' apprehension, he felt strong with her hand in his.

"Well, I'm all the more grateful, knowin' how difficult it must have been for ye. Ye made a sacrifice, and 'twas verra considerate."

Conall smiled. He released her hand and put his arm around her shoulders pulling her close against him. Making a fool of himself was a small price to pay for a pleasant moment such as this one. She shifted, and the paper in his pocket rustled against his chest. He thought again of his purpose in coming to find Mrs. Leslie and was more certain than ever about his decision. But 'twould be best not to rush the matter. He'd do things in the correct order, and before anything else, there was someone he needed to speak with.

***

A week later, Conall hefted his shovel and walked along the drainage ditch to where Jamie was working. The lad didn't have the strength of a man, but what he lacked in strength, he made up in sheer determination.

Jamie lifted another shovel full of dirt, tossing it to the side. He saw Conall and smiled, wiping his hand across his forehead and leaving behind a muddy streak. The boy stepped out of the trench and came to stand next to him.

The sun was getting low. "Fine work, lad. I think 'tis enough for today." Conall dug his fist into the small of his back, wincing at the stiff muscles. "We'll worry aboot drainage on the other side o' the field tomorrow."

Jamie balanced the shovel's wooden handle in the bend of his elbow as he rubbed his fingers over his palm. He looked across the field and squinted in what he must have thought was a very adult-like manner as he nodded.

When Conall looked closer, he could see open blisters on the boy's hands. Why hadn't he thought to find the lad some gloves? Yet there had been no word of complaint. Just the idea of another day of digging must fill Jamie with dread, but Conall knew the lad would agree to any chore without protest. "Although the diggin' could wait a few days. Come. Let's go home." He patted Jamie's shoulder and started down the path toward the manor house.

Jamie lifted the shovel over his shoulder and walked beside Conall. The boy's lack of chatter indicated he must have been more tired than usual, and Conall was annoyed with himself for continuing on so long without giving the lad a rest. His mind had been so occupied that he'd not noticed the time pass.

Once they'd returned the tools to the shed and Jamie'd paid a visit to Barney, they walked around the side of the house toward the road. Conall missed the two o' them heading into the house to have supper with Aileen, but true to her word, she'd departed, returnin' to her cottage with Jamie.

"Good evenin' to ye, Sergeant," the boy said in farewell, giving a salute.

"Jamie lad, if ye please, there's somethin' I'd be speakin' with ye aboot." He pointed with his chin toward the front door of the manor house.

"Are ye angry with me, Sergeant Stewart?" Jamie asked, following him up the path.

Conall realized his brooding might be mistaken for irritation. "No, 'tis nothin' like that. I . . ." He opened the door, stepping aside for the boy to enter. "I'd jes like yer advice."

Mrs. Ross met them in the entry hall, but Conall sent her away, telling her he'd take supper later. He led the way to the library, closing the door behind them. "Sit down, Jamie."

Jamie sat in his usual chair near the fire.

Conall glanced toward the side table, thinking he could use a bit of a drink for courage but decided against it and sat on the sofa facing the boy.

Jamie's face was confused, and Conall thought he looked rather uneasy. But the boy's apprehension was nothing to what Conall was feeling. He'd sat in war councils, punished prisoners, and faced reprimand from commanding officers, but the discussion he was about to have with this small, curly-haired lad made all of those other exchanges seem trivial.

Conall had thought for days of how best to approach this but, in the end, decided there was nothing to do but to jump straight in. "Jamie Leslie, I wish to marry yer ma. I hoped ye'd give me yer blessin'."

Instead of looking surprised or pleased or even irritated, Jamie's brows drew together, and he chewed on his lip. He remained silent so long that Conall started to worry he wouldn't answer.

"Do ye love my mam?" he finally said, speaking slowly, as if choosing the words carefully.

"Aye."

Jamie nodded, continuing to chew on his lip as he looked down at his hands. "And will ye have babies?"

Conall hadn't expected that question, but he hadn't fully considered what his mother's marriage would entail from the lad's perspective. Of course 'twould be of concern to him, wonderin' about the changing roles in the family. "I hope we might . . . someday. If yer ma agrees . . ." He ran a finger around the inside of his collar.

"And ye'd be their da, and Mam would be their mam."

"She'll always be yer mam first of all. Havin' more babies won' change that."

"But ye won't be my da."

Conall studied the boy's face but, for the life of him, couldn't make out his expression. Was he insisting that Conall could never be his father? Or wishing he would? Was he feeling jealous? Resentful? Conall wished more than ever that he'd taken a drink. As much as he'd thought he was prepared for the conversation, he hadn't realized how delicately he needed to tread.

"Jamie lad, the reason I came to ye before yer ma was because I know how the two o' ye care for each other, and I want ye to know that'll not change. Not with her married or with babies or anythin'." He watched the boy, hoping for some clues as to how he was receiving the words. "I want ye to feel comfortable. If ye prefer to call me Sergeant Stewart or Conall, ye can do that. 'Twon't hurt my feelin's if ye don't consider me to be yer da."

The wee lad looked even smaller with the high back of the chair looming over him and his feet dangling above the floor. His forehead was creased, and his mouth turned down into a pensive frown. Again silence stretched, and Conall felt like a misbehaving child awaiting a reprimand.

Jamie looked up. "Remember that day when ye showed me how to mix mortar and stick together stones?"

"Aye, I remember." Conall's stomach sank, remembering the day before that, when he'd dragged Jamie home and told Aileen the lad was a criminal in the makin'. He didna think he'd ever been more wrong in his appraisal of a person. No wonder the lad was unsure about accepting him into his family.

"When we were sittin' on the wall eatin' sausages and ye told me about Napoleon?" Jamie looked down at his hands. "Tha' day, I wished ye were my da."

Conall blinked. He slid forward to the edge of the sofa then knelt in front of Jamie, tippin' his head to the side to see the boy's downturned face. "And do ye still wish it, Jamie?"

The boy nodded then glanced up. "Aye," he whispered.

Conall's throat grew tight. "Then I shall be." He held out his hand. "And we'll shake on it. A gentleman's promise."

A small dirty hand slid into his, and Conall shook it, careful not to press on the blisters. He pulled the boy forward into an embrace, blinking his eyes against their stinging. Jamie rested his head on Conall's shoulder, and he leaned his cheek against the red curls. His heart felt near to burstin'. He'd no idea he'd ever come to love a child so much. Suddenly, a new concern entered his heart. What if Aileen were to refuse him? He feared losing the two of them would be more than he could bear.

Chapter 15

THE SUN SHONE THROUGH THE high windows of the kirk, catching dust mites in its rays and heating the Sunday service. Aileen stifled a yawn as her gaze roamed over the congregation. She'd intended to sweep her eyes past Conall—of course, 'twas happenstance that she'd even looked in his direction at all—but at just the right time, he glanced over his shoulder, catching her eye. He gave a wink, and she smiled reflexively, heat spreading over her cheeks.

She snapped her gaze away, certain the entire congregation had seen the exchange, and returned to watching the minister.

Dores poked an elbow in to her ribs. *She'*d seen the wink.

Aileen poked her back, schooling her expression and looking piously toward the minister's pulpit. Her face continued to burn as she tried to concentrate on the sermon. Had Conall looked her way on purpose? Or was he just becoming distracted in the hot building?

More than a week had passed since Aileen had returned to her home. She'd kept busy with the hives and her regular household duties and had only seen Conall a few times in passing. He didn't seem to be avoiding her—he was happy enough to stop for a moment and engage in small talk—but she felt there was something different between them. And 'twasn't difficult to identify exactly what.

The kiss.

Though it had lasted only the briefest second, she'd thought of little else since that morning at the apiary. 'Twas the first time a man had kissed her. And it had been every bit as magical as she'd imagined. His lips were warm and soft—she hadn't realized a man's lips would be soft. He'd smelled nice, and in spite of his size, his touch had been tender. She'd felt a nervous fluttering inside her ribs that made her breath hitch and her knees tremble. Even now the memory was enough to set her heart racing.

She supposed it hadn't been the same for Conall. He'd acted polite but a bit distant toward her since, and the thought that the kiss had disappointed him made her feel like hiding away from him.

Had her laughter about his fear o' the bees been more than his manly pride could take? She worried she'd ruined everything. But the village was small, and she couldn't avoid him forever. Besides, she was a woman grown not a silly young girl with romantic dreams. If he could act unaffected, so could she.

The congregation rose, startling her as they began to sing. Aileen hadn't realized the sermon had ended. She stood quickly, joining in the hymn. Without even looking, she could feel Dores's smirk. She glanced down at Jamie and realized she'd not had to remind him once to pay attention. It seemed he was more well behaved during the service than she'd been.

Once the meeting ended and the wooden doors were opened, letting in a breeze of delicious cool air, Aileen followed Jamie out of the pew, stepping into the aisle and not glancing back once to see if Conall was approaching. In spite of her impulse to hurry away, she took her time. 'Twouldn't do to rush home, not when the other villagers remained behind visiting of a Sunday afternoon. She stopped to thank Mr. Graham for his sermon and moved on to join Dores and Mrs. Ross in the kirkyard.

Instead of finding his friends, Jamie remained beside her, making her wonder if he was hungry and eager to get home to eat. He seemed quieter than usual. She turned toward him, pulling on a glove. "We'll not remain long if ye'd rather—"

Her words were cut off when the other glove was snatched from her hand. Turning, she saw Dores, grinning wickedly, brows moving up and down. She held the glove in one hand, her index finger raised in front of her mouth.

Mrs. Ross stood beside her, lips pulled to the side in an attempt to restrain her smile. Both women's expressions were so obviously conspiring that a feeling of dread settled over Aileen.

"And what mischief are the two o' ye plannin'?" she hissed.

Instead of answering, Dores grabbed on to Aileen's arm and pulled her across the kirkyard. Mrs. Ross walked on the other side, making an observation about the warm weather that was much louder than necessary. The two women conducted Aileen along, speaking casually—though in a strange, forced manner—and excusing themselves as they passed through a group of people visiting with the minister. They stopped beside the cemetery wall.

"What on earth was that?" Aileen asked. She pulled away her arms and turned to make sure Jamie was still beside her. "Have the two o' ye lost yer—"

A voice sounded behind her. One she recognized all too well: Conall Stewart's. "I believe ye dropped this, Mrs. Campbell." He held out the glove toward Dores.

Aileen's mouth opened, but she was speechless. Did the two women truly conspire to drop her glove, hoping Conall would retrieve it? She needed to give the superstitious meddlers a talkin' to.

"Oh no, 'tisn't mine." Dores's eyes were wide in feigned innocence. "Does this glove belong to you, Mrs. Leslie?"

"Aye." Aileen reached for the glove, but Conall pulled it away.

"Och, in tha' case, I'll be keepin' it for a bit if ye don't mind." He tucked it into his vest pocket then offered her his arm. "Would ye walk with me, Mrs. Leslie? I've a matter I'd like to discuss wi' ye." His eyes twinkled.

Aileen glanced at the women, seeing by their surprise and confusion that their design had taken a different direction than they'd intended. She didn't know whether to feel angry or flattered or embarrassed. The situation was so absurd that she was left with an overall bewilderment.

She slipped her hand into the bend of Conall's arm, and with his other hand, he took ahold of her fingers, reminding her of the day they'd met in the library. Her skin tingled beneath his touch.

"I'll deliver her home safely," he said to Jamie then gave the boy a wink.

Jamie grinned then winked in return.

Aileen didn't understand what was transpiring between the two and started to ask, but Conall led her away before she had a chance.

He led her from the kirkyard and across the road. They passed between buildings and came out on the hill overlooking the waterfront. Beneath, fishing boats bobbed in the water or rested on the shore, idle on the Sabbath.

Conall led Aileen along the top of the hill away from the village. He didn't seem to be in a hurry, and the pace was leisurely. She wondered if he had a destination in mind or if he simply intended to walk. Would he mention the kiss? What if he planned to apologize for it, telling her 'twas a mistake? She glanced back, wondering if she should make an excuse to leave, but he'd likely offer to escort her home, so 'twouldn't save her from the inevitable.

They walked in silence nearly as far as the Beltane field and stopped at a grassy spot beneath a flowering crabapple tree. The hill was much higher here, nearly a cliff, and with the clear sky, they could see all the way to the ocean. Seabirds soared over the water, their cries mingling with the crashing of waves. She and Jamie had walked this cliff often in the fall and winter, hoping to spot gray seals—selkies.

Conall stopped walking and turned toward her. "How are ye feeling?"

The question sounded abrupt, and she wasn't certain if he were asking out of concern or just acting polite. His manner was tense, and she felt a trickle of worry. "I think I am fully mended, sir. Thank ye."

"I'm glad." He stepped back, releasing her and clasping his hands behind his back. He scratched beneath his ear then stepped forward again, leading her to the crumbled remains of an ancient wall where he indicated she should sit. He stood before her.

"If ye don't mind," he cleared his throat, "I want to ask ye somethin'."

"Aye, of course." Her mouth was dry. What could be making him so nervous? Had Jamie done something deservin' of a reprimand? She didn't believe so. Not with the way the two had exchanged winks. It had to be the kiss he was thinkin' to discuss.

He ran a finger around the inside of his collar then dropped his hand. "Aileen Leslie, would ye do me the honor of bein' my wife?"

"Oh." She touched fingertips to her lips. He wished to marry her? She'd not expected . . .

Aileen's mind was a whirl. Fluttering started in her stomach as his words sank in. Marry Conall Stewart? The man who'd saved her life, cared for her son, opened his house to them. He loved her Jamie, brought out the best aspects of the lad. He was gentle and thoughtful, handsome, a hard worker. Conall made her feel safe and happy. He embodied all the qualities she could desire in a husband.

She twisted her fingers together, one gloved hand winding with her bare one. She didn't dare to look up. Marriage to Conall would be everything she could ask for. But what of him? He was educated; well traveled; and now lived in a grand house with carpets, a book room, and delicate china. What could Aileen possibly offer him?

She knew plenty of women who married with the sole objective of improving their circumstance. So why did the idea make her uneasy?

She laid her palms flat on her legs. Conall obviously liked her company, but did he love her? Would he come to regret marrying her? He was a generous man when it came to caring for those less fortunate. He'd proven it time and again by sending home food and other necessities with Jamie. She'd heard of various generosities he'd performed for members of the village, and he'd bought an entire sheep for the Beltane festival. Was he proposing to her out of a sense of chivalry or philanthropy? Her stomach soured at the thought.

Conall cleared his throat again, and she looked up, realizing she'd remained silent far too long. "Conall, I—"

"I worried ye'd need convincin'." He knelt in front of her, taking her hand in his. "'Tis difficult for ye to consider, I understand. I ken ye loved someone before—yer first husband—and I'm not meanin' to diminish that."

Aileen closed her eyes, the sick feeling in her stomach getting stronger as it was joined by guilt.

"I promise I'll be a good husband to ye. I don't mean to replace him. I—"

She tugged on his hand to stop his words. "Nay, 'tisn't that at all." She let out a heavy breath and looked at him directly. "Sir, you've no need to convince me to accept you. I would love nothin' more than to marry ye. But I worry yer not considerin' everything properly. I've nothin' to offer to ye: no dowry, only a small crofter's cottage, a goat, and some hives." She felt ashamed admitting it, but to remain silent felt like deception—and not telling the truth pertaining to her widowhood and Jamie's parentage was already deceiving him enough. But she'd kept the secret for so long, and Jamie's protection was still her strongest motivation. "Conall, a marriage between us seems to be beneficial to only one party. I'd not be wantin' ye to regret yer decision one day because ye showed compassion to a poor woman and her son."

Conall stood. "And is that what ye think this is? Charity?" He removed his hat and pushed his fingers through his hair. "Ye think I'm proposin' marriage out o' the goodness o' my heart?"

"I would hope 'tisn't the case. But . . ."

Conall sat beside her. "Listen to me, Aileen. I fret about ye in tha' drafty cottage, I do. When it rains, I worry ye'll take a chill and yer fever will return. I care about Jamie and hope the two o' ye have enough food so ye don't go to sleep hungry. I'll not apologize for my worryin', but I'd not marry a woman out of sympathy. No matter how I agonized when she was ill." He cupped her chin, lifting her face toward him. "I love ye, Aileen. Tha's the reason I wish to marry ye." He dropped his hand, his gaze not leaving hers.

He looked vulnerable, eyes soft and brows drawn together, but there was also a determination in the set of his mouth. He'd laid out his feelings, and now the matter was left up to her.

Aileen stood. She stepped around until she stood before him. Conall's broad shoulders were tense, but he didn't hunch. He sat straight with a confidence that she admired. He held his hat dangling between his knees and just watched her, waiting.

"Do ye love me truly?"

"I do."

A jittery feeling spread through her. He was in earnest, and she . . . "I'll need to be speakin' with Jamie of course."

One side of his mouth drew up in a smile. "I spoke to him already. The lad gives his blessing."

Aileen felt like her chest was expanding as her heart grew light. Every argument she could think of floated away leaving her with a warm contentment. She smiled. "Then, Sergeant Conall Stewart, nothin' would make me happier than bein' yer bride." Once the words left her mouth, their significance grew, taking up the world. Everything would be different from this moment on. But it felt . . . right.

The other side of his mouth rose, and his eyes darkened. "Come here, lass."

Aileen pulled off her glove, one finger at a time, and let it fall to the ground. She stepped forward until she stood before him. He rested his hands on her hips.

She felt brave and nervous as she brushed her fingers through the curls that fell over his forehead and ears, smoothing his hair. Placing hands on both sides of his face, she tilted his head back, and her thumbs smoothed the lines between his brows. A jagged white scar stood out on his forehead, and she drew a finger over it, wondering if an enemy bayonet had caused it or perhaps he'd simply fallen as a child. The idea of, over time, learning the details about his life gave her a thrill. The whiskers on his cheeks were scratchy on her fingertips as she traced the line of his jaw and touched the cleft of his chin. She drew her finger up the shallow crease and along his lower lip, surprised again by the softness.

Conall made a noise deep in his throat. His hands slid up her back, tipping her forward to press their lips together.

And time stopped. 'Twas exactly how she remembered. Her heart racing, nerves tingling, but this time, the kiss wasn't a question but an answer. A commitment between the two o' them. A promise.

When Aileen finally drew back, her legs felt shaky. Her skin was flushed. She stooped down to pick up her glove, but Conall clasped her hand, stopping her. He lifted the glove and stood, pulling her up with him. Taking the other glove from his pocket, he placed the two together and set them in her palm.

His motions seemed meaningful, and she looked up at him, brows furrowed in question.

"I waited to return it to ye until after we'd talked. I didna want ye to think the auld hens' tricks were the reason behind anythin' I said today."

She smiled, looking down as she drew on the gloves.

Conall waited for her to look back up at him. "From now on, trust that everythin' I do or say is because I love ye. Not out o' pity or auld women's manuverin'. Do ye understand?"

Aileen nodded. "Aye."

Conall touched the back of his fingers to her cheek. "That's my lass."

Chapter 16

CONALL KEPT NELLIE TO A slow pace. Aileen would be returning from the heather hives at any time, and he didna want to miss her. He scanned the hills as he rode, a pleasant anticipation stirring in his belly. Though the engagement had lasted longer than a month, he'd not grown tired of the feeling, the skipping of his heart when he saw her, nor the heat that moved through him with her simplest touch.

The banns had been called for three successive Sundays, and at Dores Campbell's insistence, they'd delayed another week for the new moon. Waiting to marry Aileen had been an exercise in patience. If Conall had his choice, he'd have taken her before the blacksmith and married her the very day he'd proposed, but he knew the deed should be done respectably. Not only for Aileen's sake. In the back of his mind, he wanted to make his ma proud. And at long last, the day had nearly arrived. June 25 was tomorrow. At last.

Tomorrow he'd not have to bid her farewell of an evening and return to his own home. He'd not have to invite Mrs. Campbell or Jamie along if they went for a picnic. He could finally toss aside the blasted rules of decorum and hold her hand in kirk, stay awake talking to her late into the night, kiss her for as long as he wished—for Aileen Leslie would be his wife.

He thought back to the past ten years, realizing in all his hopes for the future, he'd never imagined he'd be so happy. After years of travels and fighting, tomorrow he'd have a family of his own. The knowledge filled him with a joy that surpassed any he'd known.

He rounded a hill and saw her, raising a hand in greeting.

She smiled, her bright eyes visible from even this distance. The wind lifted the veil of her beekeeping hat, and she swatted it back out of her face.

He urged Nellie forward. "What a surprise. If 'tisn't my betrothed." He dismounted and took her hand, bending forward in a bow.

Aileen curtseyed. "A surprise, is it?" She smirked, raising a teasing brow. "Ye jes happened to be out ridin' toward the moors this evenin' then?"

He took the basket holding her beekeeping tools and put it over his arm. "I jes returned from deliverin' Jamie home." He'd fetch the lad back in a bit for his stag-night party. "Since my fiancée was still out tending her bees, I thought I'd take a wee ride in search of a kiss. Maybe one of the *Aos si* would oblige."

Aileen covered his mouth, her eyes looking around nervously. "*Bi sàmhach.* Ye shouldna name the folk aloud, even in jest."

He smiled, her superstitions reminding him of his childhood. His mother would have punished him for teasing about "the good neighbors." His own belief in the faery folk had weakened in his travels, and he found Aileen's convictions of the mythological creatures to be charming. "Ye remind me so much o' my mother at times."

Aileen raised her brow. "I don't ken if 'tis a good thing or nay."

"I said sometimes, not all times." He set down the basket, pulling on her fingers to draw her closer, then he untied her hat, pulled it off, and slid his hand beneath her ear to cradle her head. He pressed a kiss to her mouth, the heat from her touch filling him nearly to bursting. Pulling back, just a bit, he whispered against her lips. "Like now, ye don't remind me o' her a'tall."

Aileen rolled her eyes. "I should hope not." He saw a smile on her lips as she turned toward the horse. She patted the bridge of Nellie's nose. "And how are ye, bonny lassie?" she murmured as the horse nuzzled her cheek.

"'Tis still undecided whether she favors ye or Jamie the most," Conall said. "Lately, I think she leans in yer direction." He tucked the hat into the basket and laid a hand on Nellie's neck. "Would ye care to ride her home?"

Aileen shook her head, declining the offer as she always did. He knew the idea of sitting so high off the ground on a large, moving beast frightened her, but he'd hoped her concern would decrease as she spent time with the animal. He was certain she'd develop a love for riding if she could overcome the initial anxiety.

He gave her the reins, letting her lead the horse, which he knew she enjoyed doing, and took her hand. They started back along the road toward Dunaid.

"I know ye miss yer ma," Aileen said after a moment. "Ye mention her often. And yer da. I'm sorry ye still haven't any word from yer family."

He'd yet to tell her about the letter from Mr. Douglas, fearing she'd think he'd manipulated her into marriage with the intent of whisking her away to Canada once they were wed. Which, of course, he'd no intention of. He knew her heart was here, in Dunaid. She loved the village, belonged here. They'd taken her in as a young widow with a baby. How could he ask her to leave this behind? And as for himself, this peculiar little village with its unpredictable residents had siezed hold of his heart as well. He felt an attachment to this place. Perhaps because 'twas less than a day's ride to Glengarry. Perhaps because it reminded him of his childhood. Whatever the case, he wasn't anxious to leave. But the draw to find his family still pulled at him.

He glanced down at her, bracing himself for her reaction. "I did receive a response."

Aileen stopped, holding her arm out behind and pushing back on the reins to keep Nellie from running into her. "When?"

"Over a month ago."

"And are they . . . alive?" She winced.

"Aye, my parents and likely my sister are all alive and well in Nova Scotia."

"Well, tha's good then." Her eyes squinted, and her mouth drew down into a frown. "Why did ye no' tell me?"

He shrugged, his thumb rubbing over the back of her hand. "I thought ye'd worry I'd try to take ye away from here."

"And would ye?"

"I don't know. I want to find them. I need to. When I left— well, I wasn't the courteous gentleman I am now." He attempted to smile, but it fell flat. "Words were spoken. There are things I need to say that canna be written in a letter. Apologies mostly."

"And ye thought I'd object to leavin'?"

He turned toward the cliffs. "'Tis far away—across the sea."

"Would we return?" Her voice was soft, and he heard a bit of a waver.

"I dinna ken."

Aileen slipped her arm around his waist, unable to move closer and still hold the horse in place. He took the reins from her hand, dropping them and then pulling her against him.

"It doesna matter where we go, Conall, as long as we go together."

He pulled back to see her face. "Ye'd really leave Dunaid?"

She drew in a quick breath and smiled, though she couldn't quite hide the pain the idea caused. "I'd leave if my husband wished."

His heart swelled with love. "Don't fear. We'll not be goin' anywhere, at least for a while. I wrote to Mr. Hamish Roberts, tellin' him I was interested in purchasin' the manor house."

Aileen nestled beneath his arm, resting her cheek on his chest. With his hand on her back, he could feel her relax in relief. "Dunaid is home, isn't it?"

He rested his chin on her hair. "Home is where ye are, Aileen. Ye and Jamie." She tightened her arm around his waist, and he held her in a blissful embrace that was disrupted when Nellie bobbed her head, telling them 'twas time to be returnin' home.

They continued on through the village, walking in a pleasant silence until they reached the cottage.

"'Tis the last time I'll be biddin' ye good night and walkin' away," he said.

A blush stole over her cheeks, turning them a lovely pink. She laid a hand on his shoulder and rose on tiptoe to kiss him.

This time, he ignored the horse and pulled her in tight, savoring the moment: the feel of her arms around him and soft lips moving over his.

"Will I ever tire of this?" she whispered.

"Of what?"

"Kissing ye."

He lifted a loose tendril from her cheek and tucked it behind her ear. "I hope not, lass, or I'll have to go in search of—"

She kissed him quickly, likely trying to prevent him from bringing ruination on them all by naming the fair folk.

Conall turned his head, deepening the kiss and eliciting a small noise from Aileen that set his blood aflame. He pulled her tighter.

"If the two o' ye are quite finished tryin' to swallow each other, I've a bride to prepare." Mrs. Campbell's reprimand sounded loudly from Aileen's cottage.

He closed his eyes, letting out a calming breath. He couldn't find it in his heart to be angry with the woman—not when she and Mrs. Ross had put such effort into wedding preparations. And, he was pleased to find, when the two had an occasion to plan, they'd much less time to be nosey aboot his personal life.

"Jes' a moment, Mrs. Campbell," Aileen said.

"Davy already fetched Jamie to yer house, Sergeant," Mrs. Campbell said. Apparently she was not going to allow them any more privacy. "Now haste ye back home. Ye'll have plenty o' time for slousterin' tomorrow."

Aileen's eyes widened, and her pink cheeks flamed red. She pecked a quick kiss on Conall's cheek and took her basket, thrusting the horse's reins at him.

Conall called a farewell, but she'd already hurried into the house, with Mrs. Campbell closing the door behind. He mounted the horse and turned toward home, unable to hold back a laugh at the outspoken auld woman and Aileen's reaction.

He was still chuckling when he turned up the lane that led to the manor house. Lights glowed inside, and he imagined the men of the village were already startin' on the drink. Hopefully, they'd save him some rum. They'd surely be waiting to blacken his feet and legs with some difficult to remove substance such as boot black or soot mixed with egg. 'Twas a silly tradition, but he didn't mind a bit, not when tomorrow was so promising.

When he reached the corral, he found Jamie sitting on the fence waiting for him.

"I'll tend to Nellie if ye want to go inside to yer party."

Conall shook his head. "The party can wait." He and Jamie worked quickly, removing the saddle and tack. He returned from the storage building and found Jamie brushing Nellie, just as he'd been shown. Conall leaned his forearms on the fence rail, watching the lad.

After a moment, Jamie moved to the other side of the horse and continued brushing where the saddle had been. "Are ye nervous, Sergeant?"

"For the stag-night party?" Jamie must have seen what the men were planning. He hoped they'd not use something sticky like tar.

Jamie shook his head. "For bein' married."

"Why would I be nervous?" Conall asked.

Jamie looked thoughtful as he put away the horse brush. "I know the men are jes bein' playful, but they say ye'll be shackled and that marriage, 'tis like a lifetime punishment with no chance of parole."

Conall placed a hand on Jamie's shoulder as they walked to the house. He could see preparations already in place for the feast on the morrow—tables and chairs were set in place throughout the yard. Mrs. Ross had the women of the village baking cakes and tarts while she herself had prepared fowl, mutton, and endless scones. "I'm not nervous, Jamie. In fact I've never been so happy aboot anythin' in my life as I am about marryin' yer ma and bein' yer da." He opened the door, standing aside to allow Jamie to precede him inside.

"I'm happy too," Jamie said. "And Mam—she's singin' and smilin' all the day long. She loves ye, Sergeant."

The lad's words touched him, and Conall swallowed hard against the constricting of his throat.

Jamie took a few steps into the kitchen then turned around, wrapping his arms around Conall's waist. "We both do," he said then whirled and hurried inside.

Conall stood in the kitchen doorway. His heart was full, and he thought again that he could have never imagined being so happy.

Chapter 17

AILEEN STOOD IN THE MIDDLE of the cottage as Dores fastened the buttons on the back of her dress. The bride skimmed her hands over the cream-colored silk, savoring the feel of the soft fabric. Conall had delivered the gown a few weeks earlier, ignoring her protests that the price must have been very dear and she certainly did not need such a fine dress to wear for only one day. He'd also brought shoes for Jamie, insisting the boy could not attend his own mother's wedding unshod.

"There." Dores held on to Aileen's shoulders, turning her around. She reached up and adjusted one of the flowers she'd arranged into Aileen's hair then stepped back, looking over her masterpiece with a critical gaze. She touched a hand to Aileen's cheek. "I never saw a more bonny bride."

Aileen was surprised at the soft tone and even more surprised at the tears in her friend's eyes. Her own eyes prickled as she reached for Dores's hand. The woman had been the closest thing to a mother that Aileen had known. They'd been together when they'd been turned out of their homes and 'twas with her help that Aileen had been able to care for Jamie as they fled Strathcarron. "What would I do wi'out ye, Dores?"

She wagged her finger. "Ye'd never ha' ensnared tha' handsome sergeant, an' tha's certain."

Aileen knew the auld woman well enough to recognize when Dores was concealing her emotions beneath an abrasive exterior. She pulled her friend into an embrace. "Thank ye, Dores, for everythin'."

Dores returned the embrace, just for a moment, then pulled away, bustling about the cottage, picking pieces of stems and fallen petals from the dirt floor. "Enough o' that. Ye'll crumple yer dress, an' we've no time to press it. Yer groom will be here any moment."

Aileen's stomach turned over, every nerve in her body feeling overly sensitive. The time had come at last. Conall was probably right this moment on his way, leading the wedding procession to fetch her and Jamie. She imagined him wearing his kilt and sporran, looking devastatingly handsome as he strode through the village. She strained her ears, listening for the sounds of the pipes. Her hands started to tremble, and her head felt light.

"Och, but yer pale, dearie." Dores led her to a chair, fussing with the skirts before helping her to sit. "Please tell me ye've had a bite to eat this mornin'."

When Aileen shook her head, the older woman rolled her eyes. "On a day such as this? What do I do wi' ye? Can ye imagine if ye were to faint away before the minister?" Dores took a small loaf from the cupboard and set it on the table in front of her. "Now eat, lass."

Aileen obediently tugged off a piece of the bread, chewed, and tried to swallow it past a dry throat.

Jamie came inside carrying a fresh pail of goat's milk and looking like the perfect young gentleman in his Sunday best. "I didna get my shoes dirty, Mam." He held out each foot in turn to demonstrate.

"Ah, but ye look handsome, mo croí."

He set down the pail, and Dores snatched it up and poured the milk into a pitcher.

Jamie stood before her. "Mam, wha' aboot when ye're married? Will ye call Conall mo croí then? He'll be yer love and not I."

Aileen pulled Jamie toward her, not caring if it crumpled her dress. She brushed his hair to the side, letting the curls spring back, then kissed his cheek. "Ye'll always be mo croí, Jamie. Bein' married won' change tha' one bit. Do ye ken?"

"Aye, Mam."

She held him tight a moment longer until he wiggled from her embrace. She considered it a victory that she'd gotten him to tolerate both an embrace and a kiss, so she'd not complain.

She'd just taken a drink of the milk and stuck another bite of bread in her mouth when a knocking sounded at the door. *He's here.* She stood, brushed crumbs from her lap, and ran her tongue over her teeth, hoping no remains of the hurried breakfast lingered.

Jamie started toward the door, but Dores stopped him. "Tarry ye a moment, lad." She lifted the bouquet she'd made and handed it to Aileen, pushing the sprig of white heather in tightly. "Ye've a sixpence in yer shoe?"

Aileen nodded, gripping the stems of the flower arrangement, her breath coming in nervous gaps.

Dores brought a horseshoe and hung it on Aileen's elbow. "Now dinna forget to cross the threshold wi' yer right foot, dearie." She placed a kiss on Aileen's cheek and nodded for Jamie to admit Conall.

The lad grinned and pulled open the door but then stepped back.

A man with thick, dark hair covered by a smashed cap loomed in the doorway, the light behind casting his face into shadow. From his silhouette, she could see 'twasn't Conall.

"Well, if 'tisn't little Aileen Leslie. I've been looking for ye." The tone of his voice sent a shiver over her skin. He stepped inside and was followed by two other men. One shut the door.

Now that he was out of the doorway, Aileen could see the dark-haired man's face clearly. *Balfour MacTavish.*

No. Her stomach dropped. How had he found them?

Dores gasped, and Jamie moved closer to Aileen.

"Mam, who is it?"

"Who is it?" Balfour strode toward them, a deep scowl pulling his dark brows low. "Why, 'tis yer father, lad."

Jamie looked at Aileen. "My father?"

Aileen finally found her voice. "What are ye doing here?"

He sneered. "'Tis rather obvious, I'd think. I've come for my son."

"No." She held on to Jamie, feeling him shrinking away from the stranger.

Balfour's scowl deepened. "This is Sorcha's doing, hidin' him away from me. Did ye truly think I'd never find ye?"

Aileen looked at the other two men. They stood blocking the door, looking exactly how she pictured evil villains from a story. The smaller was lean, dressed in clothes that must have been fashionable at one time but now were worn and stained. He had a pointed beard, and his face bore the marks of hard living: red-rimmed eyes, blisters around his lips. The other man was exceptionally large, bald-headed, with a nose that looked as though it had been broken multiple times. Aileen ached to get Jamie away from these men, through the door to safety, but they looked as if they both knew what she was thinking and remained, blocking her only exit.

Balfour continued toward her.

Aileen backed away, dropping the bouquet as she scooted to the other side of the table and pushed Jamie behind her.

Balfour continued to scowl as he watched her. "Truthfully, I'd nearly given up until a kirk man came around Inverness askin' if anyone knew where to find Fearghas Leslie. His daughter, Aileen, and grandson, James, were living in Dunaid." He rounded a corner of the table tapping his chin comically. "Fearghas Leslie, I thought. Wasna his daughter, Aileen, my wife's dear friend?" He gave a shrug. "I asked at the Stag and Thistle, and it turns out the boy's eight years old with bright red hair, just like Sorcha's."

"Mam?" Jamie's voice shook as she pushed him back into the corner of the room.

Balfour continued toward them. "I thought 'twas too much o' a coincidence to be ignorin', ye see." He stopped right before them, dirty lip curling in a sneer as his gaze moved over her. "Och, but little Aileen Leslie, ye've grown up nicely."

His leer made her skin crawl. She held out her arms, shielding the lad behind her and trying to look brave. "Ye canna take Jamie."

His scowl hardened, and the anger in his eyes shot ice through her core. "I mos' certainly can." He motioned to the two men, who came toward them. "And if ye resist, I'll return wi' the constables. Even in an isolated village like this, kidnapping is a crime."

"Ye'd not dare." Dores stepped in front of the men, wagging a finger. "Now away wi' ye scoundrels, and stop botherin' decent folk."

The men hesitated, perhaps unused to being chastised by an auld woman with a sharp tongue.

Balfour barked out a laugh, planting fists on his hips. "Dores Campbell, as I live and breathe. Yer still as much of a busybody as ye ever were." He took ahold of her arm and pulled her away roughly. Leaning close to her face, he hissed through his teeth. "Keep yer nose oot o' my business, or I'll have to teach ye a lesson, ye auld bat." Still holding onto Dores, he snapped his fingers, jerking his head toward Jamie.

The smaller man grabbed ahold of Aileen, pushing her aside, and the large one seized the lad.

"Mam!"

The terror in her child's scream pierced her heart. "No! Mr. MacTavish, please don't take him." She grasped Balfour's arm. "Please."

Jamie kicked out his legs, overturning a chair and knocking the pitcher from the table. It hit the floor with a crash.

"Famhair. Stop the brat from hollerin'," Balfour said. "Do ye want to alert the entire village?"

The man called Famhair—'twas obvious why his mother had given him a name that meant "giant"—grabbed the back of Jamie's neck. "If yer not quiet, lad, I'll hurt yer ma." His voice was a low rumble.

Aileen shook Balfour's arm. "No, please. Ye canna—"

He gave a wrench, flinging her across the room. She hit against the kitchen cabinet and fell, head swimming. She tried to get up but was too dizzy.

"That'll teach ye to take what doesna belong to ye." Balfour's voice came from far away.

Aileen felt Dores lifting her head as the door slammed, leaving them in silence.

Chapter 18

CONALL STOPPED IN FRONT OF Aileen's cottage. He turned to survey the crowd that had joined him as he'd walked through the village. Smiling faces looked back at him. Some he'd never met, but most were people he'd grown fond of in his months in Dunaid: Davy and Catriona, Mrs. Ross, the crotchety Mr. MacKenzie. He gave a nod of thanks for their well-wishes and stepped to the door, his heart light and a grin spread over his face.

He smoothed down his shirt, flattened the lapels of his jacket, and made sure his plaid was fastened properly at his shoulder. He took a deep breath, letting out slowly, and knocked.

The wait was longer than he'd expected, and he began to grow uneasy. Was Aileen havin' second thoughts?

He tugged on his collar, feeling warmer than he should until, finally, Mrs. Campbell opened the door.

Conall smiled, but it dropped, and his muscles tensed in warning when he saw her face. Something was wrong.

Hearing sobbing, he pushed past the woman and found Aileen lying on the sleeping pallet. She was curled up, hands fisted, arms covering her face. The flowers in her hair were crushed, her dress crumpled. The sobbing was accompanied by a keening. Conall's stomach went rock hard. "What's the matter, lass?" He pulled her arms away from her face and discovered blood on her temple. He saw more blood on her dress and on a rag beside her. "Aileen, what the devil happened here?" He sat, pulling her against him and pressing the bloody rag to her head.

Her sobbing continued. "Jamie. He took Jamie."

Her voice was muffled against him, and he was reminded of when she'd carried on with the fever madness. He rubbed his hand on her back. "Lass, 'twill all be well."

She shook her head, sitting up and pulling away the rag. Her face was pale, streaked with blood and tears. "Balfour. He was here."

Conall glanced around the room, seeing for the first time the broken pitcher and overturned furniture. Had a man been here? The thought filled him with rage. He took ahold of her shoulders. "Aileen, ye must tell me what happened. Did someone hurt ye? Where's Jamie?"

"Balfour took him away." Unlike when she'd suffered from fever, her eyes were clear, her speech lucid. In spite of the fear in her voice, he believed she understood what she was saying.

"Who is Balfour?"

"Jamie's father."

The words struck him with a force that seemed tangible. Conall froze, replaying the sentence in his head, and bit by bit, the warmth he'd felt earlier retreated to be replaced by ice. He pulled his hands away, looking at the woman he'd been holding and realizing he didna know her at all.

Dores reentered, followed by Catriona.

Conall rose, still unable to comprehend what was happening.

Catriona turned Aileen's head to allow light from the open door to shine on her wound. She picked up the rag Conall had dropped. "There ye go, dearie," she said, putting the rag back in place. "'Tisn't deep. Head wounds jes tend to bleed more than they should."

Aileen pulled her knees to her chest. She sobbed as she reached out a hand toward him. "Conall?"

Conall backed away, unable to produce words from the jumble in his mind. He stepped outside to where the villagers awaited. Whispers and questions sounded around him, but he couldn't focus on any.

The piper stood by, mouthpiece between his teeth, anticipating Conall's signal.

Conall pushed the blowpipe down. "Nay, there'll be no weddin' today."

He started away, but Mrs. Campbell pulled on his arm, stopping him. "Sergeant, ye must tarry."

"Did ye know?" he asked. He could see from the guilt in her expression that she did. Pulling away his arm, he continued toward his house.

"Ye don't understand." She hurried beside him, nearly running to keep pace. "Balfour MacTavish is wicked. Aileen hid Jamie away to protect the lad."

Conall held up a hand to stop her. "Aileen lied." He increased his pace, storming up the lane to his house. He closed the door behind him; the ice forming around his heart helped to dull the pain. He thought rum would do a suitable job as well. The last thing he wanted was to feel—anything.

He didn't think he'd ever felt so betrayed, and it hurt. He made his way to the library, lifting the decanter from the side table. He picked up a glass but set it back down, taking a drink straight from the crystal bottle and carrying it up the stairs.

He entered the master's chambers, and the pain hit him full force. Mrs. Ross and Brighid had spent the morning preparing the room for his wedding night. A vase of flowers sat on the dressing table, and fresh bedding was pulled tight over the mattress between new fluffy pillows. He pushed the pain away, focusing instead on anger—'twas a much easier emotion to endure—and on the drink in his hand. He took a deep drink and looked away from the room, turning toward the closet. He'd come to this blasted place with only a few things, and that was all he intended to take with him. He pulled out the military pack that held his uniform, musket, and a few items he'd picked up in his travels. Then he opened another pack, stuffing in the clothing he'd purchased in London.

He tipped his head back for another drink from the decanter, frustrated when it came up empty.

"Sergeant Stewart?" Mrs. Ross entered the room. "What am I to do? We've all this food, and—"

He slammed down the decanter on the dressing table. "Have the feast. Celebrate all ye like. 'Tis of no concern to me henceforth what anyone in this blasted village does."

He hefted the two packs, pushing past her into the upstairs passageway.

"Sergeant, where are ye going?"

"Canada." He marched down the stairs and out of the house, planning never again to return.

***

That evening—or perhaps 'twas the next day, he didna know or care—Conall sat on a tavern stool in a roadside inn, leaning over a dirty glass. He also didna care about the number of times the balding bar man had filled the drink. He'd lost count hours ago, and yet his heart continued to ache.

This morning, he'd had a family, but now he had nothing. Nobody. Aileen lied to him. Jamie was gone. The thoughts scrolled through his mind, repeating again and again, no matter how he tried to drink them away.

He twirled the ring on the bar, a simple bit of jewelry, but he'd imagined Aileen would love it. He'd seen it when he traveled to Fort William for the wedding gown, and—

He grunted and held the empty glass toward the man behind the bar.

The stool beside him scraped over the wooden floor and groaned as someone sat. "Don't ye think ye've had enough?" Conall recognized Davy MacKay's voice but didn't turn.

He slipped the ring back into his pocket. "No' as long as I'm still conscious." He reached for the newly filled glass but misjudged the distance and knocked it over.

"Yer guttered."

"Not yet," Conall said. "But wi' any luck, I'm well on my way." He nodded a thanks to the man who wiped up the spilled drink. "How did ye find me, Davy?"

Davy sipped on a glass of his own. "Well, 'twasn't difficult. There's only one road out o' Dunaid, and I figured ye'd stop in the first tavern ye came to."

"Why are ye here?"

"I missed Nellie."

Conall snorted at his friend's joke and accepted a freshly filled glass from the bar man.

"What happened?" Davy asked.

"Ye've not heard?" Conall was surprised. If there was one thing a village the size of Dunaid was good at, 'twas gossipin'.

"Nay. By the time I left, Aileen and Dores hadna come oot o' the cottage."

Hearing her name sent a fresh shard through Conall's heart. He took a deep drink.

"Catriona tol' me somethin' about Jamie bein' taken away," Davy said.

Conall set down the glass, wiping a thumb over his wet lip. "She convinced me she was a widow, then on our weddin' day, who should show up but her *husband* to take away his son. *Their* son."

"Her husband?" Davy twisted on the stool to face Conall. "But I thought . . . I've known the woman eight years now. Aileen Leslie's a widow."

"Aye, tha's what she claimed."

"Why would she lie aboot a husband?"

Conall shrugged. "That's the question, isna it?" He gulped another drink and slid his glass forward to be refilled. "I've thought aboot it all day and reached two possible scenarios. Either she's married and attempted to trap me into an illegal union, or she's not, in which case, she hoped to hide the boy's origin by legitimizin' his parentage. Usin' my good name to protect her sullied one." His stomach twisted at the harshness of his words. He thought of Aileen as a young lass, not yet out of her teenage years, tryin' to raise an infant on her own. The shame and fear she must have felt. But with an effort, he shoved away the sympathy. Aileen had played him for a fool. "Either way, I was deceived."

"Do ye blame her for keepin' such a thing a secret?" Davy said. His voice was soft, the compassion Conall refused to feel apparent in his friend's tone. "With her son's reputation hangin' in the balance?"

Conall planted an elbow on the bar and rested his forehead in his palm. His mind and heart were in chaos. "I could ha' forgiven her anythin', Davy. Blast, but I love the woman." He slapped down his hand, feelin' the alcohol loosening his tongue. He fought to keep his emotions under control. The last thing he wanted to do was to start weepin' in a roadside tavern. He swallowed down the hurt that came from a deep shame that she'd not trusted in him enough to confide the truth. His shame grew, but he stifled it. *She* was in the wrong, not he. "I canna forget tha' she lied to me." He motioned the bar man toward them. "If 'twasn't for Balfour MacTavish, I'd be wedded right now, blissfully unaware o' her deception."

"Balfour MacTavish?"

Both Conall and Davy looked up at the bar man when he spoke.

"Do ye know him?" Davy asked.

The man filled their glasses and set them onto the bar. "Nay, not personally. But he was in here earlier today with a man called Famhair on his way to Fort William. Best to be stayin' away from *that* one if ye know what's best for ye." He bent closer, glancing to both sides to ensure they weren't overheard. "Works for Sim MacRob."

Conall's gut clenched. During his time in the marines, he'd heard the name spoken in whispers by convict felons destined for Sydney and soldiers whose petty crimes had been forgiven on condition of military service. Sim MacRob was a notorious criminal with rumored connections to various smuggling ventures. Tales of his involvement with human trafficking were rampant, though he somehow managed to evade capture by allowing lesser men in his organization to take the blame for his crimes.

Apprehension made Conall's mind alert. "Did they have a child with them?" he asked the man.

"Aye, a wee lad with gleamin' shoes. Red hair."

Conall jumped to his feet, fumbling in his jacket pocket for his billfold. "Davy, I have to go."

Davy rose as well. "I'll come wi' ye."

Conall set a pile of bills on the bar and started toward the stairs to fetch his bags from an above room. As he'd learned to do during a battle, he was able to hone confusion into a sharp focus. All he'd needed was a mission, and now he had it.

"I'll be ready in a moment," Davy called behind him. "I'll need to send a letter to my wife."

The ache Davy's words produced surprised Conall. His wife—Conall had thought to have a wife by now. But 'twas easier to push it aside now that he had an objective. He concentrated on the objective, letting distractions fall away. He needed to find Jamie before Sim MacRob got a hold of the lad.

Chapter 19

"YE CAN'T STAY INSIDE FOREVER, dearie." Dores opened the cottage door, letting in a breeze and a shaft of sunshine.

Aileen held up a hand to shield her eyes. She turned over on the sleeping pallet to face the wall, not caring if she never got up again. She *could* stay inside forever. The two people she loved were gone, and 'twas all her fault for keepin' a secret so large that it couldn't help but grow too big to be contained.

Jamie was gone—who knew where—and she'd no way of finding him again. Was he even now crying for her? Hurting? She heard his screams in her head and squeezed her eyes shut, but no more tears came. She felt hollowed out, empty except for the pain. The aching filled her, growing and stretching until her skin hurt as well.

And Conall. She couldn't erase the memory of his face when he'd realized her lie. Betrayal, anger . . . If only she'd a chance to explain. Surely he'd understand and remain with her. But she hadn't. And he hadn't. He'd left thinking her a liar, and in truth, she was.

The pain inside increased, becoming so strong it hurt every inch of her, and she felt that she might shatter. 'Twas worse than anything she'd felt before. Worse than when her da had gone away. Worse than when she'd been forced from her home and watched it burn. Those times, she'd hurt. She'd mourned but continued on. Now she felt broken. She hadn't the will to go about tending bees, smilin' at her neighbors, and milking the goat as if everything was fine.

Because 'twasn't. In just a few moments, her world had changed. Everything she'd loved—her hopes for the future, her heart—gone.

"Mo croí," she whispered, touching the space beside her where Jamie had slept. She thought of how he'd wake with one side of his curls flattened down and a grin on his freckled face. How he'd cuddle against her on cold nights, his freezin' wee feet pressing against her legs for warmth as she told stories and sang him to sleep. The memories that had once brought such joy now hurt, and she curled tighter, pressing on her stomach, trying to contain the pain.

She heard voices that she dimly registered as belonging to Catriona and Dores, but she didna have the energy to care what they were sayin'.

Footsteps approached.

"Aileen, come, lass." Dores spoke with her typical tone, one that brooked no nonsense, but 'twas softened a bit. "Ye must stop yer wallowin'. Sit up now." The auld woman pulled on Aileen's arm, tugging her into a sitting position.

Aileen complied, not having the will to fight against it.

"Listen now," Dores said. "We've somethin' to tell ye."

"First things first." Catriona squatted down, inspecting the cut on Aileen's temple. She sat back, a pleased expression on her face. "Och, 'tis much better. I'd wager ye'll nay even have a scar." She gave a nod to Dores, giving her permission to continue with what she'd planned to say.

Aileen leaned to the side, intending to lie back on the pallet.

"Catriona's had word from Davy. He's with yer sergeant."

Tears that she'd thought were long dried up welled in Aileen's eyes. "He's nay *my* sergeant." She laid her head down, and the tears overflowed, dripping over her nose and into her hair.

But Dores yanked on her arm, pulling her back up. "Aileen, ye must listen. Jamie is in danger."

Aileen opened her eyes. That got her attention. "Tell me."

Catriona pulled a folded paper from her apron pocket. She spread the paper out on her knees.

All Aileen saw were lines and squiggles, which she supposed, formed a message. She looked at her friend, waiting for her to decipher it.

"Davy and the sergeant are off to Fort William." Catriona ran her finger along the markings as she spoke. "He said somethin' they heard in the Glenfinnan inn led them to believe the lad might be in danger. His father"—she winced and glanced at Aileen apologetically—"they believe he's travelin' wi' a dangerous man, Famhair."

Famhair was the name of the giant man that grabbed Jamie. Aileen looked at Dores. "We must go after him." She started to rise.

Catriona laid a hand on her arm. "Davy and the sergeant will find Jamie," she said. "Ye've seen what kind of man this Famhair is." Her eyes darted to the cut on Aileen's temple. "'Twould be best if ye remained here, out o' harm's way."

Aileen patted her friend's hand then stood. "He's my son," she said simply.

Dores left the cottage abruptly, but Aileen didna have time to worry aboot the woman. She tugged at the silk dress she still wore, reaching over her shoulders to unfasten the buttons.

"Fort William is two days' journey," Catriona argued, stepping behind her and taking over the button unfastening. A moment later, they lifted the dress over Aileen's head. Aileen felt a pang of regret, lookin' at the beautiful gown, now quite ruined from her bleeding and weepin'. But she'd no time for such worries. Her son needed her.

Based on the blast of sunlight that had filled the cottage when Dores had opened the door a moment earlier, Aileen figured 'twas still mornin'. "If I hurry, I can catch the mail coach." She prayed it had arrived on schedule—Wednesday morning—and that it'd not left early. She didn't know if the driver would bother to wait around. 'Twas a rare thing for the coach to take a passenger from as far away as Dunaid, and 'twasn't a rare thing for the coach not to arrive at all. Sometimes it was days or even a week late.

She pulled on her homespun dress and shook the crushed flowers from her hair, pulling it back into its standard twist, then tied a bonnet beneath her chin.

On the top of her kitchen cabinet, Aileen had kept a box of ready money for emergencies. She hoped 'twould be enough. Dragging over the chair, she climbed up and took down the box, opening the lid. As she looked inside, she felt a twinge of disappointment that the sum was so small. She'd no other choice; 'twould have to do.

"Ye'll care for the goat, won't ye, Catriona?" Aileen filled her coin purse, folded her mother's plaid over her arm, and started for the door.

"Aye."

The door opened, and there Dores stood wearing a coat and carrying a purse o' her own. "Yer nay going alone, Aileen." She lifted her chin as if expecting an argument. She narrowed her eyes. "I'd no' mind another go a' those scoundrels."

The sight of her friend standing there, willing to accompany her into possible danger filled Aileen's aching heart with the deepest gratitude.

She kissed the older woman's cheek then linked her arm with Dores's, pulling her toward the center of the village. "I canna imagine goin' anywhere without ye."

Chapter 20

CONALL SLOUCHED IN HIS SEAT. His ears strained as he listened to the men at the tables around him. He'd heard enough complainin' in the past hours aboot torn fishing nets, nagging wives, and irritable warehouse overseers to last a lifetime. He glanced up, recognizing the look of concentration on Davy's face as his friend listened at the tables on the other side of the tavern. Conall shifted, feeling restrained by the borrowed clothes he wore as a disguise. What he wouldn't give for a good stretch. The jacket was tight across his shoulders. The holey trousers also fit poorly, and he itched to loosen the waist.

He rubbed his eyes, lifting the mug of the tavern's strong coffee. Three days had passed since the cancelled wedding, and in that time, he'd hardly slept. The journey from Glenfinan had taken all night and most of the following day, but he'd pushed himself and Davy, only stopping for short rests as they made their way to Fort William.

Once they'd arrived, he'd spent every waking moment searching for Sim MacRob. He'd spoken to Mr. Douglas, the minister who'd sent him the letter about his parents, and an old military companion who lived on a farm a few miles out of town, but the men could tell him nothing that he didna already know.

He finally had a stroke of luck when he inquired at the local garrison. The commander, a Colonel Fredrick Ravenwood, was a man he'd served with in Andalucía. The colonel had invited Conall into his office, delighted to see an old war companion and, over the course of their conversation, provided Conall with new information regarding Sim MacRob. None of it good.

With the approaching emancipation of slaves in British territories and the growing division in America, the African slave trade was winding down, and slave owners were looking elsewhere for labor. MacRob supplied "indentured servitude"— not illegal if entered into on one's own volition, but according to rumors, the man dealt in mostly women and children, abducting and selling the poor souls to crooked ship's captains who smuggled the human cargo abroad.

"And how is it that he's not been apprehended?" Conall had asked Colonel Ravenwood.

The man tugged on his graying mustache, leaning back in his chair. "He preys on orphans, prostitutes, and beggars, those who are invisible to the law, you see. People with no family, nobody to testify before a magistrate or bring a case against him. All we have are rumors, and that's not enough to convict a man."

With every word, Conall grew more worried about Jamie. He tapped his fingers against his leg, frustrated that this evil crook might have the lad.

"The main problem, of course, is we're unable to procure any evidence," Colonel Ravenwood continued. "No one knows whence he operates or even where he lives. It seems impossible in a town of this size, but Sim MacRob has managed to conduct his illicit business in utter secrecy." He leaned forward, resting his elbows on the desk and steepling his fingers. "If you were to find his lair, Sergeant, you'd have the appreciation of the Crown. And the help of the garrison and the local constables." He shrugged looking unapologetic. "To be honest, I'd not mind the most notorious criminal in Fort William being brought to justice on my watch." Conall didn't blame him. For that, the man would receive a commendation at the very least.

He bid Colonel Ravenwood farewell, unsure of exactly how to use the information, but glad for it all the same. Anything that gave a better understanding of the enemy was advantageous.

It took hours of bribing and cajoling street urchins and beggars, but in the end, Conall discovered the tavern Sim's men were said to frequent. He and Davy had spent the day trying to blend in with typical wharf workers, watching and listening for anything that could lead them to the mysterious criminal.

He scratched the back of his neck, hoping the clothes hadn't become infested with fleas, and turned his head when the door opened.

An extremely large man entered. Conall wondered if they'd found Famhair. He certainly fit the description.

The giant swept off his hat, revealing a bald pate, and strode through the crowded tavern, not offering any apology to any so unfortunate as to get in his way but barreling in a direct line to the bar.

When Conall glanced across the room, Davy gave a slight nod—he thought they'd found Famhair as well. Conall rose and dodged between tables and bodies as he made his way to the back of the tavern. He didn't want to call any attention to himself, and so he stood with his back against the bar, watching the man from the corner of his eye.

Famhair seemed to have been headed to meet a thin man with a pointed beard. The two whispered for a moment, then signaling to the man behind the bar, they made their way down a hall that led to what Conall assumed to be private rooms.

He moved to where he could see down the hall. The men entered a room, closing the door behind them. Conall glanced around to make sure nobody was watching, then followed.

The door didn't fit perfectly into the doorframe, leaving a small gap where Conall leaned his ear, watching down the hall toward the crowded tavern to ensure he wasn't discovered eavesdropping.

Someone moved to the end of the hall, just next to the bar. Recognizing Davy, Conall let out a relieved breath, grateful for a partner to act as a look out.

"And ye took care of it then?" a nasally voice said from inside the room. Conall imagined the high voice belonged to the smaller man.

"Aye. Balfour MacTavish'll not be botherin' anyone again." This voice was much deeper, likely Famhair's. "Exceptin' perhaps the fishes in the harbor." The low voice chuckled. "Mr. MacRob wasna impressed wi' him assumin' one skinny lad was worth enough to repay all that he owed."

Had Conall heard correctly? Balfour was dead? Jamie had been used to pay off a debt? Conall felt sickened hearing the men speak so cooly about murder and the selling of a child. He leaned closer until his ear was just inches from the gap.

Davy took a step into the hallway and waved a hand. Conall pulled away quickly. Someone must be coming. He walked to the end of the hall, joining his friend, but didn't see anyone approaching. "What is it?" He spoke from the side of his mouth.

Davy jerked his chin, pointing without looking at Conall. Two women were walking through the tavern.

His chest clenched in dread.

Aileen.

Forgetting caution, he rushed toward her.

Aileen and Mrs. Campbell were speaking with a group of men seated around a table. "Sim MacRob," she said, pulling her shawl tightly around her shoulders. "If ye'd please tell me where I can find him. He works with a man named Famhair."

The men offered only lewd responses and jeers.

Aileen gasped, drawing back.

"Well, I never—" Mrs. Campbell began but stopped when Conall grabbed her arm. He grabbed onto Aileen's as well, towing the women from an establishment where upright, respectable ladies certainly didna belong. Pushing through the door, he dragged the pair outside, turning to face them.

"Sir, unhand me if ye please." Aileen jerked her arm away. Her face was red, whether from the indignation of being hauled from the premises or the taunts of the men in the tavern, he didna know.

"Aileen."

She looked closer. His disguise must have been better than he'd realized. Her eyes grew wide in surprise. "Conall?"

"Ye shouldna be here."

Aileen lifted her chin, eyes flashing. "I've come for my son, Sergeant. Now if ye'll be movin' oot o' my way."

Dores folded her arms, sneering as she looked Conall up and down. "I see ye've done well fer yerself since we saw ye last." The look in her eye could have cut glass. She took Aileen's arm and moved as if to shoulder Conall aside and return inside the tavern.

He stood firm, blocking their path. "Jes' listen."

Mrs. Campbell's brows rose then pinched together in a scowl. "An' why should we be listenin' to ye?"

No one could claim the woman wasn't loyal. Conall turned to the more rational of the two—though based on her matching glare, 'twasn't by much. "Aileen, this place is dangerous, these men . . ." He gave a pointed look to the side as two tavern patrons began to brawl in the street.

"I ken," she said, and he noticed dark smudges beneath her eyes. "But Jamie." Her voice cracked, and the desperation in her eyes nearly made him forget her betrayal.

"I'm lookin' for the lad," he said. "And I've a lead to follow." He glanced back at the tavern door. "I'll meet ye soon." The fighting drew closer with more pugilists joining in. Conall pointed to the side of the building. "Wait back there, in the alley."

Aileen stepped toward the door. "I'm coming wi' ye."

He shook his head. "I want to find him too. Ye must trust me."

Aileen's eyes grew hard, leaving him with no doubt that she didna trust him at all.

Mrs. Campbell shot him another icy look and muttered somethin' he was certain he didna want to hear, but the women started toward the alley.

Conall went back inside, passing Davy with a nod and returning to the spot outside the hallway door.

The voices had stopped.

He leaned closer, still hearing nothing, then put his eye up to the gap, but he couldn't get a broad enough view to discern whether the men remained in the room.

After a long moment, he decided to go inside. He'd pretend to have stumbled on the room by accident. *If all else fails*, he thought wryly, *act like a simpleton*.

Conall looked back at Davy then put his hand on the knob, twisting slowly to see if the door was locked. 'Twasn't. The door swung inward, and he followed it, finding the room empty.

Davy would have told him if the men had left through the tavern, and so Conall crossed the room to another door, leaning close and listening as he'd done before.

Again he heard nothing. He thought 'twould be much more difficult to convince anyone that he'd entered two different rooms by accident, but he'd gain nothing if he didna take the risk. And Jamie's very life could depend on it.

He took a deep breath, hand closing around the handle of the sheathed dirk at his waist and pushed open the door. The smell of refuse met his nose, and he stepped out into a filthy alley behind the tavern. He looked in both directions, seeing nothing to indicate which way the men might have gone, so he moved toward where he'd told Aileen and Mrs. Campbell to wait. He stepped around piles of trash and broken crates, frightening a family of rats that scampered out of his way with irritated squeaks.

When he reached the side alley, he found it empty.

Frustrated, Conall smashed a fist through a rotten barrel. He'd lost the men—possibly his only means of finding Jamie—and now the two women had run off when all he'd tried to do was keep them safe. Hopelessness mingled with exasperation as he walked back toward the tavern's main entrance, wondering how much time he had to find the lad. Or was he already too late?

Chapter 21

AILEEN WRINKLED HER NOSE AT the alley's smell. She and Dores stood against the side of the building, hoping to avoid the notice of the tavern's patrons. She winced at the noises of the men fighting and the crude jeers of those cheering them on.

She fumed. What gave Sergeant Conall Stewart the right to tell her what to do? Jamie was *her* son, and she'd spent the last days travelin' in an uncomfortable coach then begging for information from anyone in the grand town of Fort William who'd even take notice of a country lass. They'd learned from an innkeeper in Glenfinnan that the man called Famhair was employed by a suspected criminal named Sim MacRob, but the people she asked either didna know of him or pretended not to.

At last, Dores had taken charge, scolding a fisherman within an inch of his life until he told them of this tavern, where Sim MacRob's men were known to spend time.

And then, after all their work, who should happen to be inside but the very man who'd deserted her in her hour of need. She clenched her fists, angry at the reaction from the men in the tavern and humiliated that Conall had seen it. But in truth, her petty feelings didna matter. She had to find Jamie.

Dores was in the middle of a muttered tirade. "An' him tellin' us where we can and canna go. Who does he think he is?"

Hearing a door close behind them, Aileen laid a hand on her friend's arm, shushing her, and turned. Voices sounded from behind the building. Someone was approaching. She glanced toward the far end of the alley, but 'twas still blocked by the fighters, so she pulled Dores back against the wooden wall, hoping the shadows would conceal their presence.

Two men rounded the corner, and when Aileen saw them, panic jolted her insides. 'Twas Famhair and the man with the pointed beard, Balfour's companions. Her grip tightened on Dores's arm.

The smaller man stopped, a grin spreading across his face. "Well, look who we've here. I didna think we'd be seein' this lass again. Did ye, Famhair?"

The large man shook his head, then seeing his friend's expression, he grinned as well.

Aileen's legs trembled, and she shrank away. But in spite of her terror, she had a realization. These men, threatening though they may be, could lead her to Jamie. She stepped forward, and Dores moved with her, sticking to her side like she'd been plastered there.

"Gentlemen, if ye please, I'm looking for my son." Her voice sounded high to her ears.

"Did ye hear tha', Famhair? She called us gentlemen."

"We're nay gentlemen," the large man said, shaking his bald head. The pair closed in on the two women.

Their nearness made Aileen's trembling worse, and she felt tears itching her eyes. She lowered her shoulders, trying to appear brave. "Please, will ye tell me where Jamie is?"

They acted as if they'd not heard her.

"MacRob'll like this lass, to be sure," the lean man said.

Dores stepped in front of Aileen. She stuck a fist on her hip and leaned forward, wagging her forefinger at the villains. "Now see here. Have ye no manners a'tall? The lady's asked ye a question, expectin' an answer."

"Ye can leave the auld biddie," Pointy Beard said.

In a flash of movement that Aileen wouldn't have believed possible considering the man's size, Famhair snatched her up and tossed her over his shoulder. The air flew from her lungs with a whoosh. Instead of exiting the alley, the man spun, heading back in the direction he'd come.

Aileen fought to hold her head still as the man's steps bounced, disorienting her as he ran through the back alleys of the town. From her position, she tried to see where they were going, keep track so she could find her way back, but she only caught glimpses of buildings, wooden fences, clotheslines, and piles of refuse. Her back and neck were growing tired from the effort of keeping herself from bouncing against Famhair's back, and hanging upside down for so long was making her head pound.

Just when she thought her body couldn't endure the strain of hanging in such an uncomfortable position any longer, the large man stopped. She tried to twist around, lifting her head as much as she could, but could only see the dirt ground and more rubbish. She heard a creaking, like a metal gate opening on rusted hinges, then Famhair continued forward, slower now as he descended stairs. The metal creak sounded again behind them, followed by a clatter as the gate shut. The air around grew cold and damp, and she could see the pathway was dark. Occasional circles of light that she assumed were torches flickered on stone walls.

Famhair moved much slower in the underground tunnel, and Aileen went limp, letting her head hang loose. She rubbed her fingers against her eyelids, hoping to ease the pressure.

They stopped walking, and at a word from the other man, Famhair set Aileen on her feet. She held one hand to her aching head, the other pressed against a cold stone wall as dizziness nearly caused her to swoon.

The man with the beard did not wait for the spell to pass. He clasped her wrist and pulled her forward along the passageway. Aileen stumbled behind, followed by the large Famhair.

After a few more turns, they came to a wooden door that seemed newer than the rest of the tunnels. A man stood in front of the opening. When he saw them, he nodded and stepped aside.

The smaller man knocked and waited. When they heard a voice call out from within, he pushed open the door.

Aileen could hardly believe the room they entered. She paused, amazed, as her gaze traveled around the space. Plush carpet spread over the floor, and the walls were paneled in wood with artwork hanging in ornate golden frames. Silk-covered chairs were placed tastefully about. Wooden tables held sculptures and vases of fresh flowers. Suspended between the ceiling's engraved tiles, a chandelier hung down, lighting the room with a dazzling display of color.

On a far wall, flames crackled in a hearth fireplace surrounded by a wooden mantle. *There must be a chimney leading somewhere,* she thought.

Amidst the unexpected splendor of the underground cavern, Aileen's eyes were drawn to the desk of dark wood that adorned the center of the room—or more specifically, to the man sitting behind it.

He didn't rise when they entered or offer them a seat, but he sat, hands clasped calmly, his forehead wrinkled and his head tipped in a curious look, as if asking politely why they'd disturbed him. His clothing was finer than any Aileen had seen. He wore a colorful waistcoat beneath a black coat, which, she assumed by its sheen, must be made of silk or satin.

"I see ye've brought a guest," the man said, his voice pleasant. He nodded at Aileen.

"Sir, are you Sim MacRob?"

"Aye, lass. In the flesh."

"If ye please, Mr. MacRob, my son, Jamie was taken away by"—she glanced at the two men, one of whom still held her wrist—"by these men, and Balfour MacTavish."

Sim MacRob's lip curled at the name, but other than that, he didn't change his patiently interested expression.

Aileen wasn't certain exactly what he was thinking based on his reaction—or lack thereof. "Can ye tell me where he is?"

The man with the pointed beard released her arm and stepped closer to the desk. "Balfour's taken care of, Mr. MacRob."

Sim MacRob gave a nod of acknowledgment. "A pity he didna think to bring this lass as well. 'Twould have gone a long way to repayin' his debts." He sighed. "Ah well, nothin' to be done aboot it now."

Aileen looked between the men, trying to decipher their meaning. Balfour was taken care of? What did that mean?

Sim MacRob set down his hands, pushing himself to his feet. He walked around the desk in an unhurried manner and came to stand before Aileen. He bent close—too close—but she didn't shrink away, not wishing to do anything that might upset the man who could tell her where to find her son. He took hold of her jaw, pulling her mouth open, squinting as he looked inside at her teeth. Then he strode around her in a slow circle.

Aileen's skin prickled, and her heart pounded loud in her ears. She needed to get away from this place. From these men.

"Skinny, isna she?" He tapped a finger on his lip. "But she's a fair one." He shrugged and walked back around the desk, speaking without looking at any of them. "She'll fetch a good price." He waved his fingers in dismissal.

Aileen bolted toward the door, but Famhair caught her around the waist before she'd even gone more than a few yards. She scratched and kicked, hoping to make him drop her, but his arms were like iron bands.

"My son," she cried out, despair covering her like a cold fog. "Please."

Sim MacRob lifted a piece of paper, reading over it, as if unconcerned by the woman being dragged from his office or her screams. "Ye'll be seein' the lad soon enough, lassie. Don' ye worry."

Chapter 22

CONALL SAT NEXT TO DAVY at a table in the back of the rowdy tavern. He'd debated over the past half hour whether remaining was fruitless, but in truth, he'd no other leads. Their best chance of finding Jamie lay in this dodgy building, which, as the afternoon grew later, was filled with increasingly foul-smelling and foul-mouthed vestiges of humanity. Though he'd been angry that Aileen and Dores had ignored his instructions to wait in the alley, he was glad the women were at least away from this place.

Remembering Aileen's coolness toward him brought a pang. He figured thoughts of her would always be laced with regret, but he hoped the achin' would ease. Perhaps one day.

"Wha' do ye think?" Davy asked. "Should we separate and move among the tables?"

"Aye." Conall tugged at his jacket's tight sleeve. "Unless ye can think o' a better idea."

Davy made a grunting sound far back in his throat, apparently indicating that he considered this course of action to be as good as any. Davy rose, but instead of moving away, he stilled, looking toward the doorway.

Conall leaned forward to peer past him and saw Dores standing just inside, her gaze scanning the tables.

Davy waved to her, and she hurried over.

Where was Aileen? Conall wondered. He didn't like the idea that she'd been left alone in this town.

Dores reached them and slid into a chair. Her face looked pale, and her normally tidy hair was disheveled, strands pulling free from the net that held them.

"Yer arm," Davy said, sliding closer to the woman and inspecting a tear in her sleeve.

Conall noticed blood soaking through the fabric above her elbow. He felt a burst of alarm. What had happened?

Dores swatted Davy's hands away. "There's not time for that now. Aileen's been taken." She held up the plaid shawl Aileen had been wearing.

"Taken?" Conall repeated. "Taken by whom?"

Davy tore a strip from his ragged shirt and tied it around Dores's arm.

"By that hairless giant and his wee rat friend." She scowled, her dark brows forming a *V* above her nose.

Conall leaned toward her. "Did ye see where—"

"O' course I did." She huffed as if irritated he'd had the audacity to question her competence. "Takes more than a shove to the ground to keep me out o' the game. Should ha' done me in if they didna want me following." She jumped to her feet and motioned toward the door. "Come on wi' ye then. 'Tisn't the time to be sittin' around on yer bahookies. Are ye plannin' to help me rescue the lass or nay?" With a quick stride, she left the building.

Conall and Davy looked at one another then scrambled to follow.

Dores led them around to the back of the tavern then past the rear door, navigatin' through back alleys, around rickety fences and beneath clotheslines as if the route were one she'd traveled daily. Conall couldn't see what landmarks she might be using to find her way and, after a bit, stopped trying to guess and just followed.

They walked along the side of an old wooden warehouse, and Dores slowed. She waved her hand for them to stop, then she crept forward, peeking around the corner. She ducked back, and at her beckoning, the men gathered close to her.

"'Tis jes' there." She spoke in a low tone and jerked her head toward the corner. "Ye'll think 'tis jes' an ol' grate leanin' against a wall, but it opens on hinges, and the path inside leads downward. Stairs perhaps."

Conall started away, but she pulled him back. "There's a guard, ye fool."

He nodded, sliding the dirk from its sheath at his waist as he crept forward. At the corner, he pressed back against the wall, leaning his head around to steal a look. Dores was right about the gate. He'd have walked right past the rusty auld thing without giving a second look. The guard was a portly man sitting on an old crate, carving something out of a piece of wood. He'd not be difficult to subdue.

Conall drew back and returned to the others. He needed a plan. He motioned them close, and the three clustered together. "If the tunnel leads underground, I'd wager there are multiple exits through the town."

Davy rubbed beneath his knee where the wooden leg attached. "Goin in, 'twould be like smokin' out a rabbit warren."

Conall nodded. "Sim MacRob and his men would most likely escape, and we don't ken what they'd do with the prisoners. Or, without knowin' our way, we'd likely get trapped inside ourselves. Either way, we've a lesser chance o' findin' Aileen and Jamie."

"An' do ye recommend we do nothin' then?" Dores folded her arms and tapped her foot, obviously frustrated that the men weren't taking action.

Conall pinched his lip, turning over various scenarios in his mind. He shook his head. "Nay, we'll proceed. But we canna rush this. We need information."

Though the time was nearly ten, they still had almost an hour before 'twould be full dark. Should they wait and use the cover of night? He felt an urgency to act and decided against that course. He looked back over his shoulder then at his two cohorts, firming up a plan in his mind. "Davy, find a coach." He pointed with his chin toward a street at the far end of the alley.

Davy nodded and hurried away.

"Come, Mrs. Campbell. I've the perfect task for ye."

After a brief discussion, Conall watched from a dark corner as Dores approached the man. Conall had explained that one unarmed man wasn't intended as a guard but as a sentry. If he felt threatened, all he had to do was call out a warning. Which is where a nonthreatening auld lady came in.

Instead of walking with her usual brisk steps, Dores approached the sentry slowly. She even feigned a very convincing limp. Conall couldn't help but smile at her dedication to the part.

He glanced up as she approached.

"If ye please, young man, I've lost my cat," she said. "Do ye mind helpin' me to search?"

"Away wi' ye," he grumbled.

"But I'm certain she's nay gone far. Perhaps just behind one of yon boxes."

"I said away wi' ye, *cailleach*. I've no time fer the likes o' ye."

Conall saw Dores's spine stiffen. She obviously didn't appreciate being called an auld bag.

She huffed. "Have ye no manners? Wouldna yer mam be ashamed to hear ye speakin' so to yer elders, lad?"

He scowled, looking back down at the wood he was carving.

Conall started to worry that she'd not be able to lure him away from his post. The contingency plan was for Conall to rush the sentry and hopefully silence him before he alerted anyone inside the tunnels.

Dores looked back at Conall, shrugging and shaking her head.

He slid the dirk from its sheath and tensed, ready to charge, but stopped when he saw Dores moving quickly. She snatched the plump sentry's hat from his head and dashed away.

The man leapt to his feet. He cursed and ran after her.

When he rounded the corner, Conall struck him with a board and he toppled over.

"Well done, Mrs. Campbell," he said, giving a salute.

She grinned in return, twirling the cap on her finger. "Tha'll teach him to underestimate a cailleach."

Conall squatted down to grip beneath the man's arms. He glanced toward the road, frowning at the distance. If only they'd caught a smaller sentry, he thought as he grunted and started dragging the man to the coach.

***

An hour later, the sentry with an aching head and no hat sat on a hard chair in Colonel Ravenwood's office. His hands were bound to the chair arms. Conall considered the precaution rather unnecessary since two fully armed red-coated soldiers stood inside the doorway, but he wasna about to criticize.

The colonel hadn't complained at being roused from his bed in the middle of the night. He sat behind his desk, gray hair slicked back, mustache impeccably groomed. In spite of the hour, he looked alert.

Dores occupied the third chair in the room. She held the prisoner's hat. Conall thought she considered it a trophy or perhaps a means to taunt the man, who kept darting looks toward it.

Conall and Davy stood against the wall. The pair had changed from their filthy tavern disguises and looked at least partially respectable. At any rate, they were comfortable. Conall rolled his shoulders, stretching—just because he could. He noticed Davy stood with all of his weight on his good leg. The wooden extension must have caused pain when he'd had narry a chance to rest for days.

"I'll ask you again, sir." The colonel was speaking to the prisoner. He pointed to the town map that spread over his desk. "Where are the other entrances to Sim MacRob's lair?"

The man shook his head, refusing to answer just as he had ever since they'd brought him in. His forehead was drawn low in a scowl, and he looked straight ahead. Colonel Ravenwood blew out an angry breath.

Conall knew that with every moment that passed, their chances of finding Aileen and Jamie grew slimmer. He was tired of being patient. "If I might, Colonel?" He stepped forward, waving toward the prisoner.

"Of course, Sergeant." The colonel scowled at the man bound in the chair then lifted a hand, giving a resigned sigh. "Have at him."

Conall sat on the edge of the colonel's desk, facing the prisoner. He hoped to look relaxed, set the man at ease. "Ye work for a powerful man, sir. And yer loyal. 'Tis admirable."

The man shrugged.

"But is it really loyalty that's tied yer tongue? Or fear of what Sim MacRob would be doin' to ye if he learned ye spoke to the army?"

The man's eyes winced at the name, and Conall knew he'd hit on the truth.

"So he's threatened ye then," he said. "Yer afraid he'll hurt ye." Fear moved over the man's face. "Or he'll hurt someone else."

"I've a daughter," the man said in a voice that was nearly a whisper.

Conall nodded. He understood how men like Sim MacRob worked. They would stoop to any level to protect themselves. The man had likely heard tales of tragedy befalling other henchmen's family members, and the fear for his own daughter was warranted. "What's her name?" He lowered his voice as well, hoping he sounded compassionate.

"Mairi."

Conall nodded. "Ye fear if he finds out ye told us anythin', he'll hurt yer Mairi."

The man watched Conall. "I've *not* told ye anythin'."

"True," Conall said. "But I think ye will."

The man's eyes widened.

"The way I see it, ye've two choices: Ye could remain silent. Ye'd hang o'course. Ye've already confessed to workin' for Sim MacRob."

The man looked confused. "I never—"

But Conall kept speaking. "We raid the tunnels through the entrance ye were guardin', and Sim MacRob escapes through a hidden exit. Mairi loses her father, and Sim MacRob goes free."

The man's face turned pale. He opened his mouth, but no words came out.

Conall held up a hand. "But there's another choice. Ye help us. Give us accurate information—the location of every entrance, a schematic of the tunnel system . . . Ye help us capture Sim MacRob, and *he* goes to the gallows."

The man seemed to be thinking, but the fear remained in his face.

Conall felt time slipping away. His insides were tense, but he held the façade of calm, not wanting to frighten the prisoner into silence. "The man isna loyal to you. In yer place, would he remain silent to protect a simple sentry? He's let men hang to save himself. To him, yer replaceable. But ye're not replaceable to yer daughter." Conall leaned forward until his face was right in front of the prisoner's. He felt pity for the man. "Ye've a chance here, one that none o' his other men have. A chance to return to Mairi. Do it for her."

"If I help ye, I'd go free?"

Conall glanced back at the colonel for permission to make the promise.

"If your information is accurate," Colonel Ravenwood said. "Once we have Sim MacRob in custody, you would be at liberty." The prisoner looked at Conall and then Dores, darting a glance to the soldiers behind him, then he nodded. "Aye, then. I'll tell ye."

***

Conall and Davy stood in a dark alleyway beside a warehouse along with Colonel Ravenwood and a detachment of soldiers. Dores had insisted on accompanying them as well. It seemed none of the soldiers were brave enough to refuse the woman. She even carried a dagger, though Conall had no idea where she'd found it.

The plan was to wait until precisely 4:00 a.m. 'Twould give the other detachments an opportunity to get into position and remove any sentries at the assigned exits. And the colonel was convinced that just before dawn was the best time to raise an attack.

"We've still a bit to wait," Davy said. "I'm going to sit—rest my leg—or I'll be no help to anyone."

Conall nodded. He stood still like the other soldiers, just as he'd been trained, but he didn't feel strong and ready to rush into battle. He'd hardly slept for days; his muscles ached from clenching them in worry. He felt restless, knowing Aileen and Jamie were most likely in distress. Wherever they'd been taken, they were certainly afraid. And he could only pray they'd not been harmed. He fisted his hands, focusing on the mission and not allowing his emotions to intrude. He'd spent years planning and executing raids, often in unfavorable circumstances and with no time for rest. *This should be no different,* he told himself. But he knew the truth: no mission had ever been so personal. If anything had happened to either of them . . .

Dores came to stand beside him. She shivered but did not complain about the chill. "She didna intend to deceive ye," she said.

Conall glanced to the side. He had no answer. His heart and pride had been so injured by the deception that nothing she had to say would change it.

"Jamie isna her son."

Conall froze at the words. He'd expected excuses or attempts at justification—but not that.

Dores gave a small nod. "The three of us fled Glencalvie when Patrick Sellar and the duchess's men burned our homes. Because o' the war, most o' the menfolk were away, ye see— Aileen's da; Sorcha's husband, Balfour." She gave him a pointed look when she said the name. "We'd nowhere to go, no money, no spare clothing or food. We had only each other. 'Twas snowin' something fierce that day, and we fled to the kirkyard, hopin' we'd be safe there, and tha's where Sorcha birthed the child."

In the predawn light, Conall could see tears in the auld woman's eyes. He offered a handkerchief, but she shook her head.

"None o' us knew anythin' aboot birthin', and there was no midwife to assist. Sorcha died within the hour. She begged Aileen to take the boy, pleaded wi' her to keep the child away from Balfour. A bad apple, that one. As ye've seen." She shivered again, pulling Aileen's shawl tight and wrapping her arms around her thin torso, but Conall didna think 'twas the cool wind botherin' her.

"We left Croick, hopin' to travel far enough away tha' none would know us or our families, and we vowed never to speak the truth to anyone." She nodded, her eyes distant at the memory. "Over time, the child became hers, sure as if she'd birthed him from her own body. She loves that Jamie. If 'tweren't for him, I don' ken if she'd have carried on. He gave her a purpose, ye see."

Conall stared at her, feeling an immense surge of compassion for the young woman who'd given her heart so fully to a motherless bairn.

Dores patted his hand in an uncharacteristic show of tenderness. "Like I said, she didna intend to deceive ye. She feared more than anythin' what would happen to the lad if anyone kenned the truth. Perhaps she feared ye'd feel differently aboot Jamie. Perhaps she couldna bring herself to say the words aloud. But ye should know that what she did was out o' love for her child and nothin' else." She gave a nod and moved away to join Davy, leaving Conall with his thoughts.

Aileen, why did ye nay tell me? But he knew the answer. He'd not given her a chance. A wave of shame welled in this throat, nearly choking him. Three days earlier, he'd thought there was nothing she could say that would earn his forgiveness, but now he wondered if there was anything *he* could say to earn hers. *I'm a fool.*

A whispered order jarred him from his thoughts. 'Twas time to move.

As they'd previously decided, Conall and Davy—and o' course Dores—stayed close to the colonel. Conall held the crude map the prisoner—Horace—had drawn, and when they entered the tunnel behind the mass of red-coated soldiers, Conall directed them to Sim MacRob's chambers.

They wove through passageways lit only by torchlight. Conall was amazed such a place existed. It must have been a great undertaking to construct something like this—and in secrecy. From the sounds ahead, the soldiers met with some resistance but not much. Based on the lack of defensive tactics, Sim must have had faith in his ability to escape. Conall hoped they'd effectively quelled that course.

They found the wooden door Horace had described and rushed inside. Conall was stunned by the opulence of the underground chamber. Sim MacRob was certainly not afraid to spend money. He scanned the room. In a matter of seconds, the men inside were detained by the soldiers. Among them, Famhair and his wee companion. None even put up a fight. On the far side, a man in extremely costly clothes was casting a sheaf of papers into a massive fireplace. Sim MacRob.

Conall and Davy rushed over.

Conall pulled Sim away from the fire while Davy used his wooden leg to kick the documents from the flames.

Soldiers took Sim into custody, moving him to join the other prisoners held at gunpoint in a far corner. Conall and Davy stepped on the papers to smother the flames.

Conall could hear Dores scolding the prisoners behind him as he knelt and studied the documents. Some were too charred to read, but he could make out the writing on others if he held them carefully to keep the ash from crumbling.

Colonel Ravenwood had been in conference with his officers at the far side of the room. When he approached, Conall stood.

"None of the other detachments found any prisoners. We have no evidence sufficient to hold any of these men. While barbaric, it is not illegal to inhabit a den below the town." The colonel smoothed his mustache, his lips tight.

Conall handed over the documents. "I think ye'll be findin' plenty o' evidence here. And as for the prisoners, I know where they are." He jabbed his finger at the sheaf of papers. "The *Aurora*. She's to sail at high tide, just after dawn. If you would oblige me, Colonel, I'd be verra grateful for the help o' ye and yer men once again."

Colonel Ravenwood thumbed through the papers, his smile expanding as he began to grasp what they contained. Every transaction had been documented. Names, dates, ships—Sim MacRob kept meticulous records. The colonel looked up and nodded at Conall. "His Majesty's Army is at your service, Color Sergeant Stewart."

Chapter 23

AILEEN HELD JAMIE CLOSE, HARDLY able to believe she'd truly found him. But she had, and he was alive and unharmed, physically, at least. The way he held on to her spoke volumes about the fear the lad had suffered. He'd not said much since she'd been thrust into the dim hold of the ship, only clung to her as if afraid they'd be separated.

Something Aileen vowed would never happen again.

They sat in the only available space, in the middle of the floor. The edges of the narrow cell were already occupied. The spaces where one could lean against the outer bulwark were the most valued and thus occupied by the strongest of the prisoners, followed by the spots along the bars that separated the prisoners from the other goods in the ship's hold. As the smallest of the hold's occupants, Aileen and her son were entitled to the wettest, least comfortable spot available.

Jamie shivered, and Aileen glanced toward the young man wearing her son's coat. His arms were much too long, and the garment would not even come close to fastening around his chest. He leaned back against the bulwark and gave a challenging glare, telling her in no uncertain terms that he wasn't about to return it, no matter how politely she asked. A stocky woman with a bulbous nose wore Jamie's shoes. After just four days, the lad seemed thinner, and Aileen wondered if his food had been taken away by the other prisoners as well.

Aileen didn't want to imagine how it had been for Jamie down here alone. What if she'd not found him? He may not have survived the journey. The thought made tears spring to her eyes, and she wrapped her arms tighter around him, kissing his hair. She'd not allow him to freeze or to go hungry, no matter the cost to herself. She'd make sure they survived and that they stayed together. 'Twas just the two of them now. She was resigned to the fact. Nobody was coming for them.

She felt an overwhelming wave of sorrow, wishing she knew what had happened to Dores—she prayed the men hadn't hurt the auld woman. Aileen's heart hurt at the thought that she'd not see her dear friend again. She'd miss Dores's quick tongue and nosey questions. She smiled thinking of the unwavering loyalty and o' course Dores's interference in Aileen's personal business— namely with Conall.

Though she didna want him to, Conall Stewart took over her thoughts. Conall, the man who had almost become her husband, the man she'd fallen in love with. In spite of his anger toward her, he'd still searched Fort William for Jamie, and for that, she'd always be grateful. But Conall and Davy would never find them now. Even if they did catch a clue of where she'd been taken, the ship was under guard, and according to the whispers of the other passengers, it was destined to sail within a few hours to a place called Charleston.

Jamie still hadn't moved, and his listlessness worried her. Would he become ill on the journey? How could she care for him?

"Mam?" Jamie asked.

"Aye, mo croí?"

"Is Balfour truly my father?"

"I'm afraid he is, dearest."

He remained still, content to be held in her arms, and Aileen brushed his curls. "Who is Sorcha?"

Aileen went cold and felt as if the air had been jerked from her lungs. She had always known the day would come when she'd have to tell Jamie the truth about his parentage, but she felt utterly unprepared. It would change everything—how he saw her, how he saw himself. How could she possibly explain?

She took Jamie by the shoulders, turning him to face her. She knelt on the boards of the deck and held his hands between hers. "Sorcha is yer mother, Jamie." The words acted like a cork, unstopping a torrent of her tears.

Jamie rose on his knees and wiped his palms over her wet cheeks. "Don' cry, Mam."

"I'm sorry, mo croí." Aileen drew in a sobbing breath. She fought to calm herself.

Jamie knelt back down and waited patiently, seeming unbothered by the others surrounding them.

"Sorcha was my friend, my dearest friend," Aileen finally said. "She was beautiful and kind. Ye'd have loved her, Jamie."

"But she died."

"Aye."

"And ye became my mam."

Aileen nodded. "I did. I am. Jamie, ye didna come from my body, but yer my son, and I love ye more than anythin'. Do ye understand?"

Jamie frowned, and a tear slipped onto his cheek. "I'm goin' to ponder on it, all right, Mam?"

"Take all the time ye need."

She shifted back into a sitting position, and Jamie laid down, legs curled into his stomach and cheek resting on Aileen's leg. He stayed quiet for so long that Aileen thought he'd fallen asleep.

"Mam?"

"Aye, Jamie?"

"Will ye tell me aboot Sorcha sometime?"

"Anytime ye like."

His breathing deepened, and she knew he'd fallen asleep. Aileen anticipated more questions in the future, but Jamie hadn't reacted with anger, only sadness for the mother he'd never known. A feeling of pride came over her at the empathetic person Jamie had become. Her worry eased a bit. She didna think she could have asked for a better response.

Hours later, cries and the sounds of pounding feet from the deck above woke the lad. Aileen figured the ship was preparing to launch. She closed her eyes and took a deep breath. She could do this. She could keep them alive.

The hatch in the ceiling opened, but Aileen couldn't make out more than the outline of a man descending in the dim light. Another followed, and the pair moved toward them.

"Conall!" Jamie jumped to his feet.

Aileen grabbed on to his hand. The poor lad was imaginin', settin' himself up to be disappointed. "No, Jamie—"

But Jamie pulled away and bolted to the iron bars.

A key clicked in the lock, and Jamie was swept up into Conall's arms. "I've got ye now, Jamie lad." His voice sounded choked. He pressed his large hand on Jamie's back as the boy held on around his neck, burying his face against the large man.

"I kent ye'd come for us."

"Ye did?" Conall asked, a bit o' humor entering his voice.

"Aye."

"And yer ma?" Conall peered into the gloom. "Is she—?"

"She's here." Jamie twisted. "Mam, Conall's come for us."

Conall's eyes found Aileen among the other prisoners. Their gazes locked, and he strode toward her, limbs and bodies of other prisoners pulling out of his way as he moved into the caged room. He knelt, still holding onto Jamie. "Are ye . . . ?"

"I'm well, Sergeant," she said, rising. "Thank ye." She busied herself with brushing off her skirts, not daring to look at him again. Instead, she glanced around and saw the other occupants all staring at them, questions in their expressions. They no doubt wondered if they'd been rescued as well.

Conall set Jamie on his feet and touched Aileen's arm.

At the sound of a throat clearing, the three of them looked toward the open doorway.

Aileen smiled. "Mr. MacKay, ye came too."

Davy gave a bow, sweeping his hand with a flourish. "Aye, wha' would ye do wi'out me savin' the day?"

"And myself as well." Dores pushed her way into the room. "Ye didna think I'd let the villains take ye away, did ye?"

Dores wrapped the plaid around Aileen's shoulders. She touched Aileen's cheek and embraced her then opened an arm, pulling Jamie into the embrace. "I've my family back," she said in a small voice that Aileen had never heard her use before.

Conall stepped out of the cage and pushed the door until it was fully opened. He turned back, moving his mouth to speak.

A flash of movement drew Aileen's gaze, and she screamed when she saw a man rushing toward Conall, sword raised.

Conall turned just in time and dropped, the man's slash barely missing the top of his head. Conall kicked out, knocking the man to the ground. When Conall came to his feet, his sword was drawn.

The other man charged, but Conall skillfully parried his strikes, finally throwing the man off balance, allowing Conall to drive his shoulder into the attacker and push him to the ground. Conall placed one knee on the man's chest and took the sword from his opponent's hand. Both men were breathing heavily.

"Well, if I'm no' mistaken, 'tis the commander o' this vessel, Captain Gregory. We've been lookin' for ye." Conall handed the captain's sword to Davy then stood, pulling the captain to his feet. He gave the criminal a shove toward the companionway, keeping a grip on his collar.

"Come on, then," Conall called over his shoulder to the prisoners, raising his voice to speak to all of the cell's occupants. "Yer free to go."

The prisoners looked at one another then seemed to realize Conall was in earnest. They started to rise and head for the door.

"Jamie, Davy, see if anyone requires assistance. I'll deliver the captain here to Colonel Ravenwood."

The two nodded and turned to help the others.

"Oh, and whoever's taken my lad's coat and shoes had better be returnin' them before coming on deck," Conall said. "Or I'll no' be so forgivin'."

He took the captain above decks, and Aileen and Dores followed. Aileen's instinct was to bring Jamie, but after his hardship, the boy needed a task, something to make him feel important and rebuild his confidence. Conall seemed to know that. He would have been a fine da to her son. Aileen swallowed her tears at the reminder.

She and Dores climbed the first set of stairs then the next, finally emerging onto the upper deck. The early-morning sun was bright, and she blinked then looked around at the chaos aboard the ship.

Red-coated soldiers had taken over the vessel and stood around the decks, some talking in groups, others guarding the captured sailors, and some guarding the gangway.

Conall had taken Captain Gregory to a group of soldiers that Aileen thought, based on the stripes on their sleeves and the way they appeared to be supervising the operations, must be officers. One man with a gray mustache gave a flick of his hand, and two other soldiers hurried forward to take the captain away.

The mustached man put a hand on Conall's shoulder as they talked and seemed to be congratulating him.

Aileen turned away, walking toward the bulwark rail with Dores, their arms linked together. *'Twould be a good place to wait for Jamie*, she thought. Then they could figure out how to get out of this town and return home to Dunaid.

A soldier stepped in front of them, giving a bow. "If ye don' mind, ladies, Colonel Ravenwood has asked for all the former prisoners to deliver a statement. If ye'll follow me, ye can wait on the constables."

Aileen nodded, and they followed the man toward a shaded spot at the stern, beneath the higher deck.

As the other prisoners emerged from the hold, they were escorted to that space as well. Last of all, Jamie and Davy climbed up the companionway. Davy again wore his coat and shoes. When they spotted Aileen and Dores, they moved toward them. Davy motioned for the woman to sit on the stairs leading to the higher deck.

"Did ye see Conall, Mam? 'Twas jes like Fionn mac Cumhaill fightin' the firebreather o' the Sidhe."

Davy stepped his wooden foot onto the stair. He stuck out his chest and rested his forearm on his knee. "And dinna Finn have a loyal and extremely dashing companion in his heroic exploits?"

"Oh, aye, his wee teacher, Finnegas." Jamie gave a mischevious grin then laughed. The sound was so welcome and such a change from the worry they'd all felt the past four days that they could not help but join him.

Aileen pressed her fingers to her lips. She'd wondered if she'd ever see joy on her child's face again, and the seein' brought a rush of emotion.

Davy leaned forward and ruffled Jamie's hair. "I missed ye, Jamie."

Chapter 24

"FINE WORK, SERGEANT." COLONEL RAVENWOOD slapped Conall on the shoulder. "Well-planned maneuvers, no casualties, few injuries—on our side at least—and you've delivered the ship's commander on a silver platter." He grinned, giving Conall's shoulder a squeeze—very likely thinking about the commendation he'd surely receive. "His Majesty's military has lost a good soldier in you."

"Thank ye, sir."

"Are you certain you're retired? In my experience, I've discovered some men are born soldiers, Sergeant. And you are one of the best. With the conflict in Algiers, I'm certain you'd be a welcome addition to any company."

"I'll keep it in mind, sir."

The colonel nodded and stepped back, sweeping his gaze over the ship and prisoners. "Well, this will take some time to sort out. You'll remain in town to testify before the justice of the peace?"

"Yes, sir." Connal gave a sharp nod.

Colonel Ravenwood nodded back. "Very good, Sergeant."

Conall turned, feeling the same sense of loss as when he'd left the service the first time. He'd been a soldier for so long, 'twas second nature to him. He loved the feeling of camaraderie between men risking their lives together. 'Twould be easy to do just as the colonel suggested and join the conflicts in Africa, but his mind couldn't seem to settle with the idea.

What do I do now? he wondered. *Which path do I take?*

He looked over the ships berthed in the wide loch leading out to the sea. One must certainly be destined for Canada. The impulse to cross the ocean and find his family pulled at him.

Two paths, he thought. And though both met a need within him, neither felt fully right. Neither made him a complete man. Glancing down at his hands, he rubbed thumbs over the calluses created by months of farm work. The satisfaction that came from working the land filled something inside of him that had been empty for too long. But that, still, 'twasn't enough.

His gaze moved to the group clustered on the companionway leading to the quarterdeck. Aileen, Jamie, Dores, and Davy were laughing, no doubt at something the lad had said. The sight made Conall's heart leap and his chest grow warm. Well, if tha' wasna the answer, he didna know what was.

They were what he needed, the people of Dunaid who'd accepted him as one of their own. Aileen and Jamie—his family. The longing to be with them drew him forward like a child's toy attached to a string.

Jamie was saying something to his mother that Conall couldn't hear over the waves hitting the ship's hull.

Conall moved closer, though they still didn't notice him. Aileen's face grew sad as she answered the lad, her voice too soft to make out the words.

"What? Why?" Jamie yelled the words. He jumped to his feet, his face red and pained.

"Mo croí, I am so sorry." Aileen's lip trembled. "Sometimes adults make decisions that are confusin' to a lad."

Jamie shook his head. "No, Mam. Ye love him. I know it. And he loves ye."

Conall's stomach dropped.

Aileen reached for Jamie, but he pulled away from her grasp. He turned and saw Conall.

"Conall, why are ye nay marryin' my mam?"

"Hush, Jamie." Aileen stood and took the lad by the hand.

A boulder had wedged itself in Conall's throat, and he could not have answered if he'd wanted to. What had he done? He'd hurt the two people he loved the most, tha's what.

Jamie sniffed, wiping a dirty fist across his eyes. "Is it because o' me? Because o' Balfour takin' me away?"

"Nay, o' course not . . ." Aileen began. She'd tears o' her own now.

Conall closed the space between them, kneeling to bring his face level with the boy's. "'Tisn't because o' you, Jamie lad."

"Ye tol' me ye loved her." His look was more angry than sad now, his voice accusing. "Ye said marryin' her would make ye happier than anythin' in the world."

"I know," Conall said.

"Then why?" Jamie stuck out a belligerent chin.

Conall glanced up at the others. "Perhaps 'tis a conversation I should be havin' with yer ma."

Dores darted forward and took Jamie's hand, whisking him away before Conall could blink. Davy made an equally quick exit, remarking about having something he forgot to do.

Aileen stood alone looking down at the deck beneath her feet.

He walked closer to face her. "Aileen . . ."

"Ye've blood on yer shirt," she said. "Are ye injured?"

Conall glanced down, for the first time noticing there was indeed blood there. He'd been involved in a few skirmishes while taking over the ship, but he'd not been wounded. "'Tisn't mine." He looked back at her.

Aileen avoided his eyes, choosing instead to study his bloody shirt. She spoke softly. "I ken ye don' want to talk to me, but

I owe ye the truth." She took in a jagged breath. "Jamie isna my—"

He held up his hand, stopping her words. "Don't say it."

"But 'tis the truth," she whispered, her eyes flickering up to meet his then dropping again.

"No. 'Tisn't." He lifted her chin, tipping her face upward.

"But . . ."

"Aileen Leslie, yer that boy's ma as sure as any woman who ever birthed a bairn." He held her gaze, needing her to know that he understood. "I ken why ye didna tell me. 'Tis I who owes ye an apology." He winced. "I abandoned you when ye needed me."

Her eyes shone with unshed tears. "But ye came back. 'Tis the second time ye've rescued me, Conall."

"I'd do it again, every day if I had to." Her tears escaped, and he brushed them off her cheeks with his thumbs. "I'd do anythin' if 'twould mean earnin' back yer trust." He'd hurt her once. And her son. Would she allow him back into her life?

Her cheeks pinked. "Ye don't need to. I'll give it to ye. If ye'll have it."

"I canna think o' anything I want more."

"What aboot Mrs. Ross's haggis?" she teased.

"Nay. It doesna even come close."

He held her cheeks in his palms and kissed her slowly. He poured his heart into the kiss, every bit of him. Promising to her that he was a changed man, the kind of man she deserved. One who would care for her and Jamie as long as he lived, do all within his power to keep them safe from harm. Love her with all he had.

He pulled back and pressed his forehead to hers. "Much better than haggis."

Aileen's bright smile could have melted a block o' ice.

From the corner of his eye, Conall saw Jamie break away from Dores's grasp and run toward them. "Does this mean ye'll marry?"

Conall didna release her. "Does it, Aileen?"

She nodded, her gaze not leaving his. "Aye."

"Well 'tis aboot time the pair o' ye came to yer senses." Dores stood beside Jamie, arms folded. She tried to hold a critical gaze, but her eyebrows would not remain furrowed. She gave an exaggerated sigh. "I suppose Mrs. Ross and I have another weddin' to plan."

"Nay. Not this time," Conall said. He loosed his embrace but held Aileen's hand.

"What do ye mean by that?" Dores asked.

"We'll likely need to tarry in Fort William for a few days while the case is built. The constables may ask Jamie and Aileen to testify before the justice o' the peace." He pointed with his chin toward the town. "I wager we can find a kirk man who'll agree to do the job . . . once we explain the circumstance. The banns were called after all. I don't think 'twill be a problem that 'twas done in another parish. Mr. Graham will understand that we didna want to wait." He squeezed Aileen's hand, hoping he'd not overstepped. Perhaps she wanted to wait and be married in Dunaid. "Do ye agree, Aileen?"

She looked up at him, a small smile forming. "If we canna find a minister, I'm sure some other resident o' the town will witness the vows."

Conall shook his head. "No, we'll do it proper. A kirk weddin'. I'll no' have my wife's memory o' the day involvin' vows said over an anvil. 'Tis too important."

"Oh." Aileen's cheeks turned pink. Her eyes were bright, and he felt a renewed desire to show her she was cherished, that he didna take this weddin' lightly.

"How aboot . . ." He looked at the sun, judging the time. 'Twas near to eight o' clock. "Noon?"

"Today?" Aileen darted her eyes around the group. He was certain she was seein' the five of them—filthy, blood-stained, and sleep deprived—as quite unsuitable for a wedding.

"'Twill give Mrs. Campbell time to help ye find a dress, and Jamie and I have some errands o' our own."

"No, tha' won' do at all," Dores piped up. "A weddin' must happen in the morning. 'Tis bad luck otherwise."

"Could ye be ready by eleven?" Conall asked then stopped, realizing his eagerness was overshadowing his good sense. He shook his head, cutting off any response. "I'll wager none o' us has slept well for the last four days. I don't want any snorin' through the ceremony."

"Hear, hear," Davy said, yawning theatrically.

Conall turned to Aileen. "Are ye stayin' somewhere in town?"

"No, we didna have a chance to find a place before . . ."

"I'll see to the arrangements then. There's a fine inn on the other side o' town. And if I'm not mistaken, 'tis jes' up the street from a quaint kirk."

The women looked at each other. Aileen shrugged, smiling wide. "Tomorrow, 'tis then."

Davy shook her hand, offering congratulations. Aileen knelt and embraced Jamie.

Conall took Dores aside and pressed a few bills into her hand. "I wan' her to feel like the mos' beautiful bride there ever was, ye ken?"

The auld woman touched her fingers to her breastbone, acting insulted, though Conall knew 'twas only in jest. "O' course you dinna think I'd be doin' any less?"

He grinned at her, glad to be on good terms with the woman. She made a better ally than an enemy.

"And what'll I do then?" Davy asked. "I canna replace Mrs. Ross in the weddin' plannin' department, but I'm useful for fetchin' things. Jes' ask Catriona." He winked.

"Ye'll do whatever we need ye to," Dores said.

"Ah, yes. Tha' sounds familiar." He teased. "Jes' like home."

Conall smiled at his friends. His heart felt full as he gazed at the small band. "Then come wi' me," he said to the group, offering his arm to Aileen. "I reckon Colonel Ravenwood would consider weddin' preparations sufficient reason to grant our release from the ship."

Chapter 25

AILEEN TURNED HER HEAD AS Dores finished fastening her dress. It seemed strange, replicating the same actions from her cottage a week earlier. She stood now in an inn above a taproom, which was blessedly silent this early in the morning.

Conall had sent a message the evening of their rescue, telling her something had arisen, and postponing the wedding two more days. Initially, Aileen had been devastated, plagued with thoughts of self-doubt, certain he didna intend to go through with the wedding. But when he'd come to accompany her to the constables to give a statement, he'd not seemed at all withdrawn, as she would have expected if he were having second thoughts. On the contrary, he was every bit as tender as ever, stealing kisses, whispering endearments.

A few times, she'd seen a strange look on his face, a smile that he'd tried to stifle. Rather as if he'd a secret. But when she looked again, his expression was open and pleasant, and she thought she must have been imagining it.

Besides, she'd not complain about the days of rest, shopping in the town with Dores, or the warm baths. She hadn't realized how tired she was until she and Jamie slept an entire day away.

Dores turned her around by the shoulders, just as she'd done before. She gave a smile and a nod. "Verra bonny."

"Thank ye." Aileen smiled. She felt bonny. The dress was a similar color to the one she'd worn a few days earlier, a creamy white, but this gown she'd chosen herself. Instead of silk, the fabric was a light muslin overlaid by a sheer embroidered netting that hung down in light folds from the waist. The sleeves bunched up just below her shoulders, held in place by blue ribbon, and the sheer fabric extended over her arms, just touching the tops of her gloves.

"Now where is tha' Davy wi' the flowers?" Dores muttered, fussing with the flounces on Aileen's shoulders. "He'll make ye late to yer own weddin'."

Dores indicated for her to bend forward. She positioned the veiled bonnet over Aileen's hair and tied it below her chin. "I dinna ken if ye remember Mr. Campbell. He was a fine man as well." She stepped back, scrutinizing Aileen's appearance with a critical eye. "Reminds me o' yer Conall. Broad in the shoulders, full lips, jes' ripe for kiss—"

A knock sounded at the door, and Aileen turned, grateful for the impeccable timing. At her bidding, Davy entered.

"A verra pretty bride, to be sure, Mrs. Leslie," Davy said, grinning broadly. He handed Aileen a bouquet of flowers.

"Thank you, Mr. MacKay." Tingles of anticipation skittered over her skin as she imagined Conall's reaction to seeing her in the gown. She turned to hand the bouquet to Dores, knowing the older woman would want to inspect it to make certain the florist included white heather.

Davy cleared his throat, and when Aileen looked back toward the door, he grinned and stepped aside.

Another man stepped into the room. He was thin, his face weathered and scarred, but his blue eyes were so familiar that Aileen felt the long years drop away until she was a sixteen-year-old girl once more. "Da?"

His eyes filled. "Aye, lass. 'Tis me." He opened his arms, and Aileen fell into his embrace. She felt like her heart was being wrung as tears slid down her cheeks and onto his jacket. She held tightly to her father, fearing if she let go, 'twould all be a dream. "Yer alive." She choked the words through her tight throat.

"That I am. Now stand back and let me look at ye."

He held her at arm's length. "My daughter. Ye've grown so bonny, Aileen."

His voice was so familiar, his face, even the way he smelled— like pipe tobacco and shaving soap. The wrinkles around his eyes and the creases on the sides of his mouth were deeper, but his smile was the same. She wiped at her eyes. "Da, I'm so sorry. I didn't mean to leave wi' no word. I—"

He pulled out a handkerchief and dabbed at her cheeks, just as he used to when she was a child. "Do nay worry yersel', lass. Conall explained everythin' to me. 'Twas quite the tale, and him a born storyteller." He moved to dab her other cheek. "A fine man, yer betrothed. Asked me formally fer yer hand last evenin'."

Aileen flushed, surprised and pleased that Conall had honored the auld tradition.

"And that lad, Jamie. He's a right clever one, isna he?"

"He is at that." She smiled, knowin' her da would be fair taken wi' Jamie. "But how did you find us?"

"I had mysel' a bit o' a wild-goose chase, to be sure. I arrived at Dunaid and learned I'd missed you by a day. A Mrs. Ross helped me to write a letter to Conall here in Fort William, and he sent for me straightaway. Wanted to make sure I arrived in time to see my lassie get married." He folded the handkerchief tidily, just the way she remembered, and returned it to his pocket. "Shall we get on wi' it then? We'll have plenty o' time to become reacquainted, o' that I'm certain." He offered his arm.

Aileen took it and laid her head on her da's shoulder. "We'll have always, da. I'll not lose ye again." She took the bouquet from Dores and drew in a breath.

Davy held open the door. "Yer men are waitin'."

Dores rushed in front of them, holding out her hands as if she were stopping a wild horse. "Wait. Davy, for heaven's sake, please say ye didna forget the horseshoe."

He produced it, and Dores hung it over Aileen's arm then pulled the veil over the bride's face. "Off ye go, lassie."

Aileen made sure to lead with her right foot as she stepped with her father out onto the landing and down the stairs. They left the tavern and walked the short distance to the kirkyard, where Conall and Jamie awaited.

Her breath caught at the sight of them. The two were dressed in matching kilts in the red plaid o' the Royal Stewart tartan. Sashes worn over their jackets were gathered at the shoulder and held in place by a brooch.

Jamie beamed when he saw her, standing tall beside the man he so admired. *His father*, Aileen thought.

Conall's eyes met hers, his smile wide and his eyes soft. She did not believe a person could possibly be as happy as she felt at that moment. Her heart felt nigh to burstin'.

When she reached them, both bent forward in a formal bow.

"At yer service, Mam," Jamie said, his hand over his heart.

Conall straightened and took her hand, kissing her fingers. "Yer lovely, Aileen." The words were low, his voice a trifle unsteady.

Aileen's throat compressed, feeling overwhelmed with love for Conall—for the surprise of bringin' her father and makin' Jamie feel a part the wedding. She curtseyed deep.

Conall greeted her father then offered her his arm.

She kissed her da through the veil then slipped her hand beneath her betrothed's arm.

He clasped her fingers that rested in the crook of his elbow and brushed his thumb over her gloved knuckles in a manner that was somehow both friendly and intimate. Her fingers tingled.

Jamie walked behind with her da followed by Dores and Davy, and the small procession entered the kirk.

Aileen listened to the words of the ceremony, answering the minister at the appropriate times and repeating the vows. Conall slid a silver band embossed with a leaf pattern on her finger, and they knelt to accept the minister's blessing. She'd attended weddings before and always appreciated the beauty of the ceremony—the pledge to be true and care for one another, the prayer for God to bind their hearts, the creation of a new family—but today, she was overcome by the magnitude of it all. She and Conall were a family. Jamie was their son. When they were presented as man and wife to the congregation, she saw the people she loved most in the world smiling back at her.

"Ye may kiss yer bride."

Conall flipped up the veil, pushing it back over her bonnet. A side of his mouth rose in a small smile as he lifted her chin with gentle fingers. At last their lips met, warming her from the inside out. His kiss felt different this time, and Aileen knew 'twas because all her doubts were gone. Conall was her husband, and she had full faith in him, in his love for her and for their son.

Davy stepped forward and handed Conall a sash in the colors of the Stewart tartan. Conall wrapped it from Aileen's waist, up across her chest. He stepped closer to fasten it at her shoulder and spoke the ancient Celtic wedding vow. "Ye are Blood of my Blood, and Bone of my Bone. I give ye my Body, that we Two might be One. I give ye my Spirit, til our Life shall be Done."

Aileen repeated the vow back to him, the Gaelic making the words seem to hold more weight, binding them to their land, their people.

Conall spoke low, for her ears only. "Ye never have to fear anythin' again, Mrs. Aileen Stewart. As long as I've breath in my lungs, I'll keep ye safe."

"I fear ye may have yer work cut out for ye. I seem to require frequent rescuin'."

"'Tis my duty now." His fingers brushed her jawline, making her shiver. "And my pleasure, lass." He kissed her again, the kiss continuing much longer than Aileen considered appropriate for a church wedding.

She heard Davy's laugh and Jamie's complaint but did not let anyone distract her from the business at hand. She returned her husband's kiss, wrapping her arms around his neck and letting the rest of the world fade away.

Epilogue

Ten years later

CONALL LEANED HIS FOREARMS ON the bulwark rail, watching across the water as the port of Halifax, Nova Scotia, grew nearer. He swallowed past a dry throat. So much time had passed.

He and his sister, Elspeth, had exchanged infrequent letters, but once Aileen grew confident with her writing skills, she'd taken over, and the women had corresponded regularly.

In spite of his wife's desire for a visit, Conall had never felt as though the timing was just right. Calving season, harvest, an important meeting with the village council. . . . He worried about Aileen's health if she were to travel while in a family way, then worried again about taking a young child.

Finally, though, his excuses had run out. Their youngest, wee Sorcha, was nearly three years old. Aileen's father could manage the farm during the cold season, and Dunaid would survive without the village's provost for a few months.

Aileen's reassurance that things were fine back home didn't keep him from worrying. Davy and Catriona's baby was close to being born, and he'd have liked to be there for the child's baptism. Mr. MacKenzie and Mr. Ferguson were constantly at odds over whose cattle were allowed to graze on the patch of land between their properties, and the village council still hadn't finished planning the Samhain festival.

"Yer frettin' aboot Dunaid, aren't you?"

Hearing his wife's voice, he turned. He checked to make certain she'd worn a coat out on the chilly deck. Her lungs were still not fully recovered from her latest illness a few months earlier. "I shouldna have left them." He pulled her coat tighter and drew her close.

She nestled beneath his arm, her head resting on his chest. "They'll be fine. This—seein' yer kin—is much more important than worryin' aboot crop rotation or road maintenance. Da will send for Davy if he needs help wi' the farm work, and the bees don't take much tendin' in the winter."

She turned, looking back toward the companionway leading from below. Jamie was bringing the other children on deck. He handed Sorcha to her mother, and the younger boys moved to look out over the rail.

Conall pointed toward the port city, and the children clapped their hands, overjoyed that their journey was nearly at an end.

They watched the crew prepare to dock, and the children asked questions about the grandparents and cousins they'd never met.

Conall heard Aileen make a small noise in her throat that he recognized instantly as the sound she made when she disapproved of something. He glanced over to see what had bothered her.

She was watching Jamie talking and laughing with a man they'd met on the voyage. Nico Fletcher was traveling to New York City to seek his fortune in America. He'd sailed the world with his father, a merchant sea captain, and his tales of adventure and far off places had captivated Jamie.

"He's not a lad any longer," Conall said, "but a man grown."

Aileen made the noise again, huffing as she shifted wee Sorcha to her other hip.

"He'll be off to university soon, and maybe he'll choose to go to America to study."

Aileen fixed him with a flat stare. "An' what could he possibly learn in such a rough land? They've savages and bears, for heaven's sake. The lad should study in Aberdeen or St. Andrew's. Someplace reputable where they don' settle arguments with duels."

"Yer a Highland lass through and through, aren't ye?" Conall said. He understood the lad's wantin' to get away and see the world. He'd done the same at that age. Seein' how it was breakin' Aileen's heart made him ache for the pain he'd caused his parents. He rubbed his eyes.

Aileen gave the baby to one of the boys and slipped her arms around Conall's waist. "Yer nervous." Her voice was soft.

He kissed her. "Aye."

***

Two hours later, they bid farewell to Nico, Jamie already planning to keep up a correspondence with his new friend, in spite of his mother's coolness when he mentioned the idea. The anchor was dropped, luggage organized, and passengers started down the gangway.

Conall's heart was in his throat. The crowded dock was full of people calling to one another, long-lost friends and relatives embracing, porters carrying luggage.

A group in front of him shifted out of his path, and Conall froze.

There they were. After twenty years, he recognized his parents immediately. His da's hair was gray, his face wrinkled. He looked so much older, but he carried himself the same, with the same proud bearing.

Beside him, Conall's ma covered her mouth with her hands. Tears were running down her cheeks.

Conall felt his own tears itching his eyes. He blinked and compressed his mouth. All the things he meant to say, the apologies he'd practiced for two decades floated out of his mind, and he stood still, unsure if his family would ever be able to forgive him.

Aileen's hand slipped into his and squeezed, lending her strength. He squared his shoulders and stepped forward.

His father approached, his face tight, and Conall braced himself for a reprimand.

"My son." The man he'd fought with throughout his teenage years then left behind with a blast of angry words pulled Conall into an embrace and held him close as they both wept. In that moment, all was forgiven, and Conall was finally at peace.

About the Author

JENNIFER MOORE IS A PASSIONATE reader and writer of all things romance due to the need to balance the rest of her world, which includes a perpetually traveling husband and four active sons, who create heaps of laundry that are anything but romantic. Jennifer has a BA in linguistics from the University of Utah and is a Guitar Hero champion. She lives in northern Utah with her family. You can learn more about her at authorjmoore.com.

ENJOY A SNEAK PEEK OF
JENNIFER MOORE'S UPCOMING BOOK,

My Dearest Enemy

"BLAST THE UNITED STATES OF America." Abigail Tidwell spoke in a loud voice, feeling very self-satisfied at the echo the words produced in the empty woodbox. She smiled smugly and almost laughed imagining her father or Isaac's reaction to her vulgarity, but thanks to the blasted United States of America, they were both away. And Abigail was left to manage the house alone. Including the outside chores.

Slamming down the lid, she huffed out a breath, though no one was around to see how inconvenienced she was, then wrapped a cloak around her shoulders and slipped through the door, bracing herself against the onslaught of frigid wind that blew the cold straight through layers of clothing, skin, and muscle, directly into her bones. She'd waited, even after placing the last bit of chopped log onto the fire, hoping the storm would end before going out to the woodshed to replenish the supply by the hearth, but it hadn't let up all day, and if she delayed much longer, the fire would burn out completely, leaving her house cold and dark for the entire night.

She pulled her cloak tighter, noting how, in just a few seconds, the blowing snow had already nearly covered the blue wool in white flakes. Her cheeks stung from the cold. She trudged out toward the woodshed feeling put out. Neither her older brother nor her father would ever have let the woodbox become empty. But there was nothing for it now. If only James Madison hadn't declared war on Great Britain, then she and the rest of Upper Canada would not have to worry about brothers and fathers leaving home, gunships filling the great lakes, and battalions of troops marching through peaceful towns.

The American president was so far away in Washington City, and yet the war seemed so close to Abigail. Close enough that last summer, she'd heard the cannon blasts all the way across the river as the battle raged in Detroit. Luckily the British Army had taken the city and put a stop to the Americans' violence. And even more luckily, His Majesty's soldiers at Fort Detroit and Fort Malden had the services of the very best physician–surgeon in all of the empire: Abigail's father, Dr. William Tidwell.

Another burst of snowy wind nearly bowled her over, and Abigail thought of a few choice phrases she'd learned from Isaac and his military companions. Phrases she knew they would have been aghast to realize a young lady had overheard, but which seemed to perfectly fit as a description for the blue-coated enemy on the other side of the border. If not for the blasted Americans, Isaac—Major Isaac Tidwell, if one was to be particular—would be able to visit his family home on the outskirts of Amherstburg, Ontario more often, instead of being assigned to train soldiers, guard prisoners, plan defenses, and endless matters of war-type business required for a man of his rank.

Abigail hadn't received a letter from Isaac in nearly a month. The true reason for the delay was merely winter. Ships couldn't travel over the frozen Lake Erie, and instead, letters and visiting brothers had to travel slowly and unreliably over the snow-covered land. Though she knew the truth, she found it much more gratifying to blame President Madison and his ridiculous declaration of war for all her inconveniences.

Though it had cost his life, General Brock's well-trained British soldiers had already averted one American attack at Queenston Heights on the Niagara. *It serves those Americans right for trying to invade Upper Canada. With any luck, they won't try again.*

Abigail rounded the corner of the house, pulling her cloak even tighter against the wind. Although the chopped wood was kept in a small shed conveniently located beside the kitchen entrance, she couldn't open the kitchen door without brushing away the heap of snow blocking it. The snow had blown into high drifts against the east side of the house, and so instead of walking close to the outer wall and using it as a protection from the wind, she took a longer path, leaving her more exposed to the elements. And she grumbled the entire time.

The snow was deeper than it had been this morning when she'd gone out to the barn to feed and milk Maggie. She was glad her father and Isaac had patched up loose boards last summer and mended the leaking roof. Maggie's pen would be warm and snug and the feed dry.

Abigail glanced toward the barn, then stopped. She looked more closely, squinting through flurries. But even in the waning daylight, she could see the door was ajar. Surely she'd fastened it this morning. A coldness that had nothing to do with the weather clutched her heart. Had someone gone into the barn?

She turned and hurried back into the house, closing the door behind her and leaning against it. Of course it would be foolish for a young woman to investigate alone. No neighbors lived close enough for her to easily call upon for help, especially not in this storm. The wisest course would be to wait until tomorrow when Mr. Kirby came by to fetch her milk and butter on his way into town. But she could hardly leave Maggie at the mercy of a thief or a wolf, or—she shuddered—a deserter. And what if she had simply forgotten to fasten the latch and raised an alarm for nothing?

Pulling her father's musket from the chimney pegs above the mantle, she opened the small box where he kept the lead balls and powder. Father had insisted she learn to handle the weapon, and Abigail had practiced loading and shooting numerous times. She was proud of her skill with the weapon that many would consider too heavy for her to even lift, but today, her hands were shaking. Would she have to fire it at a person to protect her family's property?

She opened the door and reached for a lantern, hooking it over her arm and carrying it unlit as she stepped outside. She did not wish to give a possible intruder the advantage of remaining hidden in the shadows while illuminating herself.

She hardly noticed the chill or the wind as she approached the barn. Studying the ground outside, she saw no footprints were visible, but if any had existed, the wind would have erased them in any case. Her heart thumped as she clenched the weapon tightly and pushed open the barn door.

Peeking inside, she could see only shadows in the gloom. Maggie lowed from her pen in the far corner, likely displeased with the admittance of cold air. Looking toward the other side of the building, Abigail could see the outline of the wagon and the empty pen where father stabled his horse, Magnus.

She stood still, listening for any other sound, but aside from the wind whistling outside and the whisper of a stray gust blowing straw over the ground, she heard nothing. But something wasn't right. She stood still, studying the inside of the barn as the obscure detail danced on the edge of her thoughts, just out of reach.

After a long moment, she recognized what was amiss. Blood. She smelled blood.

Abigail stepped back outside and lit the lantern, wishing she did not have to set down the musket in order to do so. Her hands were fumbling and she feared someone might approach from behind while she'd set down the musket. What would she find when the interior of the barn was illuminated?

She held the lantern high and still managed to carry the musket—which was much heavier with one hand. Stepping quietly, she moved over the hard-packed dirt floor, and there, in the flickering halo of light she saw him.

Abigail's first impulse was to run and barricade herself inside the house. But she stood frozen, fear stealing her ability to move. While she stared at the figure lying on the ground, two realizations occurred to her at the same time. First of all, the man was not moving, and based on the puddle of blood beneath him and the arrow sticking out of his side, he was injured very badly, if not dead. Secondly—and this realization was a matter of much graver concern—the man in her barn wore an American soldier's uniform.

Terror made her mouth taste like she'd licked a rusty nail. All of Abigail's muscles were clenched tight and her mind first emptied, then filled with a barrage of questions. None of which she knew the answer to. Where had the man come from? Was he alone? Was he a person meaning to do harm? He lay on his side as if he'd collapsed, blood covering his hands and clothes. Was it all his own?

She set the lantern on the ground and prodded his arm with the tip of the musket, but he did not move. Holding the weapon steadily aimed at him, she slid the lantern forward with her foot to get a better look and saw the rise and fall of his chest. He was alive then. But he did not shiver in his wet clothing, which was not a good sign, and blood continued to seep from his side. Though he was yet alive, he wouldn't remain so for long. She poked him again, this time harder, not trusting that he wasn't simply feigning insentience while waiting for her to move closer.

Her poke pushed him over so he rolled onto his back. The man made a noise so soft that it was less a groan than a sigh. The sound did something funny to Abigail's heart. A spot inside her grew warm, melting away some of the fear and opening a space that filled with a swell of compassion. Though he was an enemy, he was still a man—someone's son, or perhaps a father. And Abigail was first and foremost a healer. And besides, she couldn't very well allow a blasted American to die in her barn, could she?

She lifted a coil of rope from a peg on the wall and tied one end around the soldier's wrist, then threaded it through the spokes of a wagon wheel. Continuing along the side of the wagon, she threaded the rope though another wheel and tied it to the man's other wrist, quite proud of herself for the ingenious idea. Now, even if he did wake, he wouldn't be able to grab her while she worked on his wounds. And his hands were separated far enough so he couldn't untie himself, but he could still lie relatively comfortably on the ground.

She rushed back through the dark and returned with blankets, a bucket of water, and her small medical bag. The man still hadn't moved. In the flickering light, she could see he possessed strong cheekbones, and though his face was pale, it was well proportioned with a square jaw. If he wasn't a blasted American, he might be considered handsome. Now that he was bound, he seemed less menacing and the feeling of compassion grew and with it, an urgency.

She removed the shako hat and felt his head. No fever. Well that was good, although his skin was extremely cold. She checked the ends of his fingers, relieved to find no sign of frostbite, then turned her attention to the heavy woolen coat, trying to decide exactly how to remove it. It was wet and wouldn't slide off easily, and she'd already bound his wrists. The arrow had pierced straight through the wool, and she feared fibers would be inside the wound. But she imagined the thick material would have slowed the arrow down, possibly kept it from going too deep into the man's body. She decided she'd have to cut it off. Using scissors, she cut carefully around the arrow, then cut along the length of the sleeves to pull out his arms, and finally drew the coat free, noticing the golden epaulets on the shoulders. She didn't imagine the captain would be pleased when he saw what had become of his uniform, but perhaps she could mend it later.

Next, she cut off his shirt, noticing it was made from soft cotton instead of the thicker homespun she was used to. A fine garment, but decidedly impractical for winter in Upper Canada. The man's chest and arms were muscled, his shoulders broad, and for some reason, this made Abigail blush. She was glad he was unconscious as she pulled away the shirt. She focused on her inspection. Aside from his arrow wound, he'd been cut on his upper arm. The wounds were clean. No swelling or discoloration on the torn flesh.

Abigail wasn't certain whether the soldier had fallen unconscious from the pain of his injuries, or possibly exposure to the elements, or even loss of blood. Perhaps a combination of all three.

She set to work, glad he wasn't awake to feel when she expanded his wound with a scalpel to extract the arrowhead. She moved the lantern close and checked the opening thoroughly to make sure no fibers or dirt had entered with the arrow, then poured water over the wound. When she was satisfied that it was clean, she threaded the curved needle and sutured the lacerations closed. She used a mortar and pestle to crush herbs into a paste, then wrapped thin cotton around the mixture to make a poultice that would hopefully keep away swelling and pain and draw out any infection. Holding the bundle against the wound, she tied bandages around the soldier's middle to keep it in place. Then she repeated the process with the wound on his arm. Luckily it was much shallower.

Abigail worked well into the night, hardly noticing the cold, doing everything in her power to ensure the soldier's survival. Once she was finished, she sat back, pushing away a lock of hair that had fallen over her forehead. So much was still uncertain. Would his body warm up? How much blood had he lost? Would his wounds become inflamed? Would he even awake? She'd done all she could; whether he healed or not was now up to him.